Sweetwater

by Whitney Lynn

Book One
Sweetwater Saga

Little Gray House

Table of Contents

To my children, for being the inspiration to take the leap

Chapter One

The stretch of highway between Reno and the California border wasn't very interesting as the mile markers rushed by. Anna watched them out the passenger side window of her father's RV. She turned her head to watch him as he drove. The years were catching up to the man she loved best in the world. His light brown hair was grayer these days and somehow he'd gotten into the habit of wearing sport socks pulled up his calves with his athletic shoes. She'd draw the line at letting him use a fanny pack. He looked over and smiled.

"How many more miles, navigator?" he asked.

"If we're where I think we are, then we have less than a hundred miles until we get to the turnoff to Sweetwater," she said, looking at the road map again. They'd traveled along State Road 50 after leaving Lake Tahoe, enjoying the mountainous route with all the greenery and blue skies. Even her kids were mildly entertained by the scenery for a while. They'd spent the last few days of this summer road vacation splashing around in the sun and chill waters of Lake Tahoe after staying overnight in Reno. Now the kids were in the back of the RV with their grandmother, Ellen, playing Uno.

Brody, her oldest boy, wore his usual scowl on his face. "Grandma, this is boring. Can I go play my game, please?"

Even though he was only nine years old, he was already starting with the teen attitude. "Let's finish this game first," her mother said to Anna's pouting red-headed oldest son.

"Gramma, is it my turn?" Zoe's small voice piped up.

"Yes, honey," Ellen said. "Do you have anything that matches red or an eight? Or maybe something that has all the colors?"

"If you keep helping her, Grandma, this is going to take forever," Brody grumbled.

"Calm down, Brody," Ellen said. "She's only six. She's still learning."

Zoe's sweet round face with a splash of freckles across her nose scrunched up in concentration as she looked at the cards in her hand and then the discard pile on the table.

"I have a red and another red," she said, quickly putting down the two cards in her hand. "Uno!"

Brody's mouth hung open. "What?"

"I won!" Zoe said, clapping. Her long, auburn curls bounced as she squealed.

"Good job, goober! Give me a high five," Ophelia said as she made her way up to the front. Anna's younger sister grabbed Brody around the neck and tousled his hair. "Come on, Brodster. You can give her one win. You win every other time."

"Ack, stop it!" he said, trying to push his aunt off of him. "Whatever. I'm going to go play my game."

He skulked to the back of the RV. Ophelia and Anna gave each other a look. Anna sighed. Brody had always been a demanding child even as an infant, but as he got older his attitude got worse. It didn't help that he was mature for his age and extremely intelligent. Things he'd inherited from his father. Anna wished he'd inherited more of his father's easy-going friendly nature. Even still, the more likely culprit for Brody's attitude was Darren's death.

Darren. Anna's heart skipped a beat and squeezed so tightly it threatened to bring tears to her eyes. It had been four years since he'd been killed in the auto accident. Four years was a long time to be without the love of your life. Not nearly enough time to forget the gut-jerking agony of getting a phone call from the police one wintery morning and knowing you'll never see that handsome, beloved face again. You'll never again feel him touch you or kiss you. And his children, that you made together, will grow up without knowing how amazing, kind, caring and brilliant he was.

"Hey, Daddy!" Ophelia said, standing between the captain's chairs at the front of the RV.

"Hey, sweet pea," he said.

"How about I take over for a bit?" Ophelia asked. "Anna and I can gossip and you can go take a nap if you want to."

He sighed and tried stretching. "You know that doesn't sound like a half bad idea." He pulled the RV over and they traded places. "Just don't run us off the road, okay?"

Ophelia batted her eyelashes at her father coquettishly. "Why, father, whatever can you mean?"

Art pointed to Ophelia and looking at Anna said, "Watch her."

Anna nodded at her father in what she hoped was some semblance of solemnity while trying to keep her lips from twisting into giggles.

"So, how's life been treating you?" Ophelia said, bouncing in the driver's seat.

"The kids are out of school. We have this vacation. I'll start planning for next school year when we get back and then next year will look the same as the last one," Anna shrugged.

"Dating anyone?"

Anna chuckled. "When would I have time?"

"Right . . ." Ophelia said.

"Whatever."

"Sis, it's been four years since Darren died. Don't you think you deserve to find some happiness?"

"I am happy. I also happen to think my children deserve happiness and stability," Anna said. "You can't have stability when men are coming in and out of their lives all the time."

"I guess that's fair," Ophelia said. "I just don't think you're trying hard enough."

"I'm not trying at all," Anna said.

She took a breath in. She knew Ophelia only worried about her but no man she'd met since Darren's death had held a candle to him. She just didn't feel like wasting her time.

"I'm doing the best I can. My children are happy and I'm content, so why mess that up?"

"Okay, I get it," Ophelia said. "But if you tried hard enough you could find a guy that would offer you happiness and stability for your children as well. They do exist."

"Wow, you don't let up, do you?" Anna said.

"No, I'm serious!"

Anna rolled her eyes. "This Mr. Hypothetical doesn't exist, Phee. Not for me. You should be worried about your own search for happiness, ya dum dum."

"But we're not talking about me," Ophelia said, giving her sister squinty eyes. "Can't find what you're not looking for."

"See all this?" Anna slid her hand down her body. "There's just too much woman here for one Mr. Hypothetical to handle."

"You're planning on more than one? Sister, I'm shocked."

Anna laughed. "You're incorrigible."

"Hey, stop using big words at me," Ophelia complained. "You're just stubborn."

Anna leaned her head back.

"Do you know what it was like in high school?" Anna said. "I would have a crush on a boy but they would look right through me as if I wasn't there. Everyone around me seemed to be getting asked to dances, and I sat at home. Then I go to college, and within six months, I meet Darren. Darren who comes out of nowhere like a knight in shining armor to rescue my spilled papers. He never once saw me as the wheelchair girl. He just saw me as me. I'm not going to find that again."

"Aww, sis," Ophelia said, reaching over and giving her sister's arm a squeeze.

"Darren and I had ten short, wonderful years together. I'm so grateful for them. I'm not going to find anyone like him, so I'm not interested in spinning my wheels, if you know what I mean," Anna sighed. "Now, tell me about you. You've been awfully silent these last couple of weeks about work and Mike."

Ophelia grimaced.

"What?" Anna asked.

"I am no longer employed," Ophelia said.

"What?" Anna exclaimed, though as quietly as possible when Ophelia gave her a look. "When did this happen?"

"The day before we left," Ophelia said. "I . . . I have to tell you something but I don't want you to hate me."

"Phee, I could never hate you," Anna said.

"You could," Ophelia said. "But I swear I didn't know until that day. Mike is married."

Anna was so shocked she could only sit there with her mouth open.

"Anna, I swear I didn't know," Ophelia said. "I never asked. I just assumed if he was coming on to me, he was single. But his wife came into the bakery with his toddler and . . ."

Ophelia's voice sort of drifted off as she swallowed several times. Tears pooled in her eyes.

"Oh, Phee, I'm sorry," Anna said, reaching out and rubbing her sister's arm. "How could you have known if he hadn't told you?"

"I'm standing there staring at this woman and her baby, and I'm feeling so sick. Does she know? She doesn't even look at me so maybe she does. Then when she left, Mike had the nerve to turn around to try and kiss me."

"What did you do?"

"I walked away from him but he followed me and I was so mad that he kept trying to talk to me that I grabbed the first thing I could get my hands on and threw it in his face. Then I followed it up with my apron and told him I quit. I'd rather live alone with my dignity."

"What did you throw at him?"

"Um, a wedding cake he'd been working on for the last two days," Ophelia said with a small giggle.

Anna laughed. "Good for you. Bastard deserved it," she said.

"I mean, I deserve to have true love, right? Something like you and Darren had, or even Mom and Dad. Or maybe I don't deserve that. Seems like every guy I think is okay turns out to be a jerk or loser somehow."

"Of course you deserve happiness, Phee," Anna said. "You have so much to offer someone. Just offer it to the right person next time."

"Yes because it's so simple to just pick out the right guy," Ophelia said. "Please don't be mad at me." Her voice wavered.

"Oh, Phee, I am far from mad at you," Anna said, holding her sister's hand. "I just thought I was the only one in this family who was allowed to have a pathetic love life."

The sisters laughed. Ophelia wiped her tears away with the back of her arm. "Yeah, well, you're my older sister. I have to keep up with you somehow."

"We need to discuss more productive ways of doing that in the future."

"I just really wish for your sake that you could find someone who makes you blissfully happy."

"I had that, Phee," Anna said, giving her sister a sad smile. "I'm not going to find it again."

"You never know what's possible unless you make yourself open to the possibility. That's a famous quote, by the way," Ophelia said. "I think."

"Let me put it to you like this—how likely am I to find someone I love as much as Darren, who's willing to take on a disabled woman and her two children? Not very likely, and you know it's true."

"You tried to say the same thing before you met Darren and you met him and he swept you off your . . . wheelchair seat."

"I just don't want to go through the whole dating thing," Anna said. "I have my teaching job and my kids. I'm happy with how things are."

"Sis," Ophelia said. "I love you so much. But you are stubborn about the silliest things."

"I love you, too, Phee," Anna said. "I know you have good intentions, but I promise I am content with the way things are. I don't need a man to be happy or help me raise my kids. If Brody needs a man to talk to about manly things, Dad can help him with that. I had my once-in-a-lifetime it-never-should-have-happened-in-the-first-place love."

Ophelia rolled her eyes at her sister. "I won't argue with you, but I still think you deserve a hunky stud of a man who will love every inch of you, is willing to be father to your kids, and maybe even give me more adorable nieces and nephews to love on."

Anna pushed her sister playfully. "How about you have some of your own so you don't have to count on me?"

"That would require me finding a man sort of worth keeping long term."

"We need to fix that."

"Good luck," Ophelia said. "I think I'm cursed to pick the idiots. But you know what? You're pretty cool for a girl who sits in a wheelchair all day."

"And you're pretty cool for kicking cheating jerks out of your life. Like a boss, as Brody would say."

The conversation turned to less dangerous topics but Anna couldn't help but think about what Ophelia had said. Anna wasn't totally against the idea of finding love again, but at the same time, she didn't plan on putting in the effort to find it either. What was the point? There hadn't been a better husband or father and she wasn't willing to sift through the chaff just to find a single good kernel, let alone expect him to be of the caliber Darren had been.

Something about the idea of finding love again felt wrong anyway. She had loved Darren so much that she wasn't sure how exactly she'd made it through that first year without him. But she had her children to think of and that kept her going forward when she would have rather just lain in bed. But it didn't stop her from missing everything about him—the way he held and kissed her, the hands-on dad he had been, the optimistic planner of futures, and her calm, steady rock when she needed that extra support. How would it be possible to transition those feelings to someone else? It felt like a betrayal of Darren's love for her, or like she'd forgotten how good he'd been to her. She wasn't going to look for it so it was pointless worrying about it.

Chapter Two

The climb through the mountains of northern California finally leveled off and Art called the grandchildren to the front of the motorhome.

"You see that little teeny tiny square down there?" he said, pointing down into the valley. "That is where we are going. It's got camping, fishing, a chuckwagon dinner and a great big pool!"

Zoe clapped her hands, jumping up and down. "Grandpa, I want to go swimming!"

"Uh, Dad," Ophelia said. "It's in the middle of nowhere."

"Yes, it is," Art said, a broad grin blooming over his face.

"But . . . civilization?" Ophelia said.

"The website says that there's a small town about ten miles from there. There's some civilization for you," Ellen said.

"I'm not sure a backwater town qualifies," Ophelia said, unimpressed.

Anna looked at her sister. "Phee, it has all the modern amenities, like wifi and flushing toilets. We're hardly roughing it."

"You're not helping," Ophelia said, crossing her arms. "Fine, you made me do it. I have just one word for you all—salmonella."

Ellen threw her hands in the air. "They will never let us live that down, Arthur."

"Grandpa," Zoe said, pulling on her grandfather's shirt sleeve. "Where's the pool? I want to go swimming."

"Baby," Anna said, pulling her daughter into a hug. "We have to wait until we check in first. Kind of like at the hotel in Reno except we park the motorhome in our spot."

"It's probably some lame splash pad," Brody's voice sounded from the back.

"You don't know that," Anna said.

"If it's not a splash pad, the first thing I will do is throw you into that pool, clothes, gaming system, and all," Ophelia said. Brody ignored her.

Art pulled into the park after reaching the turnoff. "Everyone stay here. I'll check us in, we'll get settled and then you can run around all you want."

"I hope it's not a splash pad," Zoe said.

Art got a spot close to the lodge, which had blocked the view of the infamous pool when they first came in. Anna was glad because it was also close to the bathrooms and showers. Showering and mid-day potty runs wouldn't be a problem. She looked around the grounds that spread out in front of their pad. It was a large expanse of lawn dotted with trees, and looked to be a perfect place to let the kids run around and play. The pool sat behind the lodge, and tucked behind that was a playground. Along the road that led further back was a large metal pavilion.

It's probably where they have the chuckwagon dinner, Anna thought, trying not to shudder.

Squeals of delight erupted from the motorhome. Zoe and Brody jumped out, already dressed to swim.

"Hey, guys," Anna said. "I like your enthusiasm, but let's get the lay of the land first."

Brody immediately went behind his mother and started pushing her towards the lodge. On closer inspection, she saw that the pool was small but deep enough for the kids to have fun in. Off to the side was a jacuzzi.

Bonus, Anna thought.

They had built the lodge log-cabin style. Once inside, they saw a glass case full of toys and candy. An older woman came up to the counter.

"Most everything in there is twenty-five cents, except for those at the bottom. We also have slushies and ice cream treats for a dollar."

Zoe and Brody immediately started begging for money.

"Okay, one dollar apiece," Anna said, as she handed out the bills.

"Those are some darling children. Are they yours?" the woman said.

"Yes," Anna said.

"I remember when my son was around your boy's age," Marge said. "He and his best friend used to run around crazy like that. He looks to be around ten?"

"Brody is nine and my baby, Zoe, is six."

She couldn't help smiling with pride at her beautiful children.

"I love it when we have children around. So much energy," she said, sighing. "Sorry. My name is Marge. My husband and I run this place."

"Nice to meet you," Anna said, shaking the woman's hand. "I'm Anna."

"Mom, look," Zoe said, almost reverently. "They have a unicorn pencil."

"That's one of the dollar ones," Marge said. "Are you sure you want to spend all your money on that one?"

"Yes, yes! I love the little unicorn eraser!" Zoe said.

Marge looked at Brody. "What'll you have, mister?"

"Can I get a slushie?" he said, holding out his dollar.

"Coming right up, sweet thing."

Anna looked around the rest of the room. Event announcements hung on the wall. Another sign indicated no smoking was allowed except for a bench behind the bathrooms. Stuffed animal heads and mounted antlers adorned the walls. She wheeled closer to a Native American display on a shelf. There were the usual arrowheads and feathers, but what interested her most was a little carving of what looked like two people embracing.

"You found my display," Marge said, coming up behind her.

"This carving is fascinating. Does the figure mean anything?"

"It ties into a local legend," Marge said. "They say if you find love in Sweetwater, then that love will last against all obstacles."

"That's beautiful. Is it true?" Anna asked.

"Well, Hank and I are going on thirty years of marriage. That should count for something because it sure feels like a lifetime."

To the right of the shelf was a large shadow box. Displayed inside was an American flag folded into a triangle, a smaller flag with a yellow star embroidered in the middle, and a picture of a serious-looking man in uniform. Below that, among assorted medals, were a pair of dog tags that read, "Sgt. Scott Teague."

"My boy," Marge said, wiping a bit of dust off the frame. "I lost him in Afghanistan."

"I'm so sorry."

"It was hard, God's honest truth," Marge said. "His friend Phil took it the hardest. They were like brothers."

"I lost my husband four years ago in a car accident, and that was hard," Anna said, breathing out. "But I couldn't imagine losing a child."

"Loss and heartache are a part of life, as much as joy and love," Marge said. "But for a gal as young as you are, life has a funny way of making up for early sorrows."

Anna gave Marge a slight smile. "Maybe."

"Well, you tell your folks that on the fourth of July we have a little celebration with a picnic and fireworks. It's included in your stay. Just something Hank and I like to do for our customers."

"That sounds like a lot of fun. I'll let them know. Thanks!"

Zoe came up to Anna, swishing her unicorn pencil like a wand. "Mommy, can we go swimming now?"

"Not until I get my suit on," Anna said. "Wait for me near the motorhome."

She watched with soft eyes as her kids sped towards the motorhome. She couldn't imagine losing either of them. The thought of it made her sick. She tried to shake off the feeling. Darren always had the knack for living completely in the moment and pushing aside her what-ifs. It was one of the things she loved about him. She needed to do that now.

She sorted through her carry-on as soon as she got back to the motorhome, but it soon became apparent that the swimsuit was not there.

"Mom, do you remember if I put my swimsuit back in my bag at Tahoe?"

"I don't recall."

"I can't find it," Anna said, viciously shoving her clothes back in the bag.

"Check all the outside pockets. You might have stashed it in one of them," Ellen said.

"I am. I'm not seeing it," Anna said, sighing. "I knew it. It figures I would forget it!"

"Does the lodge sell swimsuits?" Ophelia said.

"No. I was just up there," Anna said. "Just basic stuff like toothbrushes, sunscreen, and candy."

"Ooo, candy!" Ophelia said. "Wait. Mom, didn't you say there was a little town not too far down the road?"

"Yes, it looked like it was about ten to fifteen miles."

"These little podunk towns always have a Shop-mart or something," Ophelia said. "Let's go after dinner and see if they have any swimsuits."

"You know, that sounds like a decent plan," Anna said. "We'll go do a night on the town, podunk style."

Chapter Three

The motorhome was cumbersome at best in parking lots, so Anna was glad her dad had brought his old Army jeep. Ophelia unhitched it from the back of the motorhome. They loaded Anna's wheelchair into the back, and the sisters headed into town.

"It's bigger than I thought it would be," Anna said, looking around.

"Yeah, somewhere between Mayberry and Storybrooke," Ophelia said. "And I was right. Behold the Shop-mart!"

They pulled up to the building. It was an older build of the large retail chain. The "M" of the Mart was dim and flickering.

"Yup, we found it," Anna said.

It was a tiny store in comparison to the ones Anna was used to. Despite that, the thought of wheeling all over the store after the long day of traveling was not appealing. Off to the side, Anna saw the motorized seated carts. She smiled as she wheeled up to the cart and transferred herself over.

"What are you doing?" Ophelia demanded.

"Phee, I'm tired and irritated and I'm being lazy, okay?"

"Whatever," Ophelia said. "I hope this thing goes faster than two miles an hour."

Save for a small, persistent squeak of one of the wheels, the thing ran smoothly as they wandered through the store. The produce section left much to be desired but they found some decent looking grapes and a watermelon. Then they headed to the clothing department once the fruit was loaded into the cart.

The rack of bathing suits, when they found it, was minuscule. Large floral prints were the pattern du jour. Anna found a plain black one-piece in her size. She figured it was the best she was going to get with as small a selection as they had. A yellow cover-up caught her attention on another rack. It had slits up the sides to allow the bathing suit to peek through.

"Adorable," Anna said to herself. "Hey, Phee! I'm heading to the fitting rooms to try this suit on."

There was a definite problem when Anna got to the fitting rooms. There was only one stall capable of fitting the monstrous contraption she drove, and it looked iffy. The lady manning the fitting room folded the same pair of panties over and over and didn't look too happy to have someone in her section. Then she saw Anna in the motorized cart. Her eyes widened when she saw Anna eyeing the large stall designated for wheelchairs.

"I'd like to try these on," Anna said when the woman didn't say anything.

"Uh, yeah, just go ahead," the woman said. "Can I help you with . . ."

Anna stared at the interior. "Um, I think I'll be fine."

It's just like driving school, Anna, she thought. It's just like parallel parking.

She drove up a little ahead of the door, turned the steering wheel a sharp left and slowly backed into the stall. The basket barely made clearance and the woman, her face a picture of awe and nervousness, shut the door for her.

Anna managed to get the suit on and it fit nicely. She reached for the cover-up when Ophelia's face appeared under the door. In the background, you could hear the fitting room lady saying, "Uh, miss, someone's already in there."

"What did you find?" Ophelia said, as she crawled under the door. She sat on the overly large bench built into the stall so she had room. "Oh, I like the black. It's got a plunging back to boot. Very sexy."

Anna rolled her eyes at her sister and was halfway to getting the cover-up on when her sister gasped.

"That is so adorable! Where did you find it?"

"On a rack next to it. Doesn't this look great with the suit?"

"Yes," Ophelia said. "I want to try it on."

Ophelia reached over to pull it off Anna.

"Hold on there, bucko," Anna said, pushing her sister's hand away. "The last time I let you try on something I liked, it ended up tearing. Nope, not going to happen."

"Don't be like that," Ophelia said, still trying to angle to get the pullover. "It's knit. You couldn't possibly tear it. And in my defense, I thought we were still the same size when I put that dress on."

"No," Anna said, trying to be serious through her giggles at the ridiculousness of the situation. She leaned back on the far edge of the seat to keep her sister from getting a good grip on the pullover. "I'm officially kicking you out of this fitting room. Go."

Ophelia straightened up and looked like she was about to leave when she suddenly lunged for her sister. In the surprise of the moment, Anna felt herself slipping backward off the side of the seat and landed with a thud, stuck between the wall and the shopping cart. Ophelia's hand flew to her mouth.

"Oh, Ann, I'm so sorry," she said, laughing.

"You are the biggest, stupidest brat," Anna said, attempting to pull herself up from the awkward position. Anna's attempt ended in her falling back into an even more awkward position. "Get over here and help me up!"

Ophelia leaned over the seat and grabbed one of Anna's hands. She pulled as hard as she could but Anna realized that it wasn't just the wedge that made it impossible for her to get up.

"Phee, I think the pullover's hooked on something down here," Anna said. She tried and failed to pull it over her head. It was pulled tightly against her and wouldn't budge in her hapless position.

"We're going to need some help," Ophelia said between giggles. She turned and unlatched the door. The woman working the fitting rooms stood in the doorway, wide-eyed. Her hand flew to her throat and she rushed to her desk and grabbed the phone. The store intercom blared, "Code eleven at the fitting rooms. Code eleven at the fitting rooms."

Blood rushed into Anna's cheeks. Probably the code for a medical emergency. Internally she fumed.

A balding man in a polo shirt and slacks rushed up to the door. His eyes widened at the scene. "Do I need to call an ambulance?"

"No," Anna almost growled. "I just need to get unhooked where this pullover is stuck on the cart."

The man looked at the fitting room lady. "I'm going to get Phil."

Anna sighed. Sure, let's bring the entire store so they can all gawk at the crippled girl.

A few moments later, the store manager returned. Following behind him with a first aid kit and a toolbox was one of the best-looking men Anna had seen in a while. He was tall, with a solidly built frame, light brown hair and a ruggedly handsome face. He reminded her of Hugh Jackman in his Wolverine phase, or a young Mel Gibson. The shirt of his security guard uniform pulled appealingly where his arms and chest stretched the fabric a bit. He grinned when he saw her--a wickedly beautiful half-smile that lit up his face and crinkled the corners of his eyes.

He peeked his head into the stall and looked around trying to assess the situation.

"So, this looks uncomfortable," he said, squatting down on his haunches on the other side of the motorized cart.

"Yup," Anna said, emphasizing the 'P' sound.

"How did you even get in there?" he asked. He actually looked impressed.

"Um, parallel parking?" Anna said. She meant it to be sarcastic but he started to laugh. It was a deep-bellied laugh that made it hard not to smile back at him.

"So, the best I can figure," Phil said, standing up, "we're going to need to take the door and this panel off so I can move the cart out a bit. Then we can figure out how to get you untangled."

Anna nodded and watched in awe as he took charge of the situation despite the store manager standing right there. In less time than she thought possible, the two men had the door and panel off. Phil slid the cart to the side so that she was sitting squarely on the ground. She let out a relieved sigh. Being in the jack-knife position wasn't terribly comfortable and her back let her know in no uncertain terms that it did not appreciate the awkward position. Being able to stretch out felt so good.

Phil knelt beside her and put the side of his head on the ground, looking at the tangle of cloth. His cologne hit her senses like champagne bubbles. She held her breath, not trusting that she wouldn't lean over and sniff him in front of everyone. She could feel even more blood rushing to her cheeks.

"It looks like you are hopelessly tangled," he said, sitting back on his feet.

She looked deeply into his dark brown eyes. She was thinking how beautiful they were until she realized she was staring. She looked away quickly, hoping she didn't just add to her already awkward situation.

"I'm sorry, Bill," Phil said, obviously to the store manager but for some reason he hadn't stopped looking at Anna. "It looks like I'm going to have cut her out of there."

"That's okay," Bill said nervously. "It was going on clearance next week anyway."

"Well. Thank goodness for that," Phil said, his eyes twinkling with amusement.

She giggled in spite of herself. *What am I, sixteen with a crush on the star football player? Geez, Anna, get a grip.*

As Phil was getting a pair of scissors out of his tool kit, Ophelia arrived with Anna's wheelchair. He deftly cut the fabric off of Anna and she was finally able to scoot away from the cart.

"Sorry it took me so long," Ophelia said, out of breath. "Someone had moved your wheelchair and I couldn't find it for a minute."

"That would be me," Phil said to Anna with a sheepish grin on his face. "I saw it sitting near the entrance doors and thought I should move it to a safer place. If you'll allow me, I would be happy to lift you into your wheelchair so you don't have to scoot across the floor anymore."

Anna opened her mouth, but before she could say anything, Ophelia said a little too loudly, "She'd be happy to have you help her!"

Anna shot her sister a nasty glare before Phil looked back at her. "Um, sure. I hope I'm not too heavy for you."

Phil laughed his sexy laugh again. "You can't be any heavier than the rucksacks I've carried on my back."

He took her gently in his arms. She hooked her arm around his neck to take some of her weight off of him which afforded a very good view of those brown eyes. Without even a grunt, he lifted her off the floor and set her down in her chair as if she weighed as much as a pillow. She adjusted her position and smoothed down the swimsuit, suddenly aware that she was wearing almost nothing.

"Can I escort you ladies back to your car?" he asked. "That is if you're finished shopping."

"Definitely, " Ophelia said brightly.

"I think I have to pay for this stuff first," Anna said, poking her sister in the arm with a finger.

"Yes, let me get you to a register, " Bill the manager said. "You won't even have to change out of the suit. Are you sure you don't need any medical attention? I mean, with your situation and all."

"Yes, I'm fine," Anna said. "I'll just pay and we'll be on our way."

Bill fawned on them the whole way to the front registers and rang them up himself. He even pulled a little receipt tape out so he could write his phone number for her to call should any complications arise, he said. It took all of her strength not to roll her eyes at him.

True to his word, Phil followed the sisters out to the jeep. He even put the wheelchair in the backseat for them.

"Thank you, you've been very kind," Anna said.

"My pleasure," he said, giving her his devastating grin. "Drive safe."

"He was so hot!" Ophelia said as they watched him walk back to the store. "And he was so into you!"

"What are you talking about?" Anna said. "He helped me into my wheelchair. That hardly qualifies as being 'into' me."

"Nope, he only had eyes for you," Ophelia said, as she started the jeep. "And you—you looked at him like he was a filet mignon you wanted to take a bite out of."

Anna shoved her sister. "I did not!"

Ophelia just laughed.

"This goes in the sister vault," Anna said. "No telling Mom and Dad. Promise me!"

Ophelia pouted. "Fine. But I get full rights to tease you when they're not around."

"Whatever," Anna said, rolling her eyes. But somehow the smile wouldn't leave her face.

Chapter Four

The two sisters laughed all the way back to the campsite. They were still giggling when they corralled Zoe and Brody into the motorhome for the night.

"Momma, what's so funny?" Zoe said, bottom lip poking out.

"Your Aunt Phee is a silly girl," Anna said.

"We already knew that," Brody said.

"I heard the weatherman says it will be really hot tomorrow," Anna said. "And I got a new bathing suit. How about we spend the morning at the pool?"

"Yes!" Zoe said. "Can you play Gopher with us? Brody cheats and he dunks me all the time."

"I do not!" Brody said. "You're such a baby. That's the point of the game."

"Okay, cool it, guys," Anna said. "I will play Gopher with you, but the minute I hear any arguing we're stopping. Everyone understand?"

The mumbled agreement came from both children. She gave Brody a goodnight kiss before she crawled into bed with Zoe. The little girl yawned big. "Is Aunt Phee going to share the bed too?"

"Yup," Anna said, putting her arms around her daughter. "Then you'll be squished in like a burrito."

"I love you, Momma," Zoe said as her arms wrapped around her mother's neck and promptly fell asleep.

"I love you too, baby," Anna said, stroking her daughter's auburn curls. She felt her heart bursting to explode with love as she cuddled her baby girl in her arms. Tears leaked from her eyes. So many times Darren and she had looked down at their children together and marveled at their beauty—a testament of their love for each other wrapped in a receiving blanket.

Darren had been an excellent father. He loved to hold them and bounce them and talk to them. He was the giver of tickles and wiper of tears. He was not a fan of taking the diaper pail out and dramatically held his scrunched up nose as he dealt with mustard yellow blowouts. Yet, the sweetest image she had of Darren was him bouncing their baby son as he fussed, burning up with an ear infection, so she could get a few precious hours of sleep.

"I miss you so much," Anna whispered. "I don't know why you had to leave me. Sometimes I'm so mad at you, and at God. What made you think I could do this on my own? And these beautiful children are growing up without their father. They need you. Especially Brody. When he's a man, there will be so much he'll need you for." The tears flowed liberally now. Gulping back a sob, Anna held her daughter tighter and fell asleep, like so many nights before, with tears running rivulets down her cheeks and memories of Darren in her dreams.

The sun was just peeking through the motor home's windows when she found herself pounced on by two very exuberant children already in their bathing suits.

"Mom, Mom, Mom, wake up!" Zoe said. "Grandpa says we can't go to the pool until we eat breakfast."

"Mom, I'm starving," Brody said, hunched over in feigned agony.

"Let me get dressed, then I can get you some breakfast," Anna said, sitting up.

She rubbed her tear-encrusted eyes. She grabbed the new bathing suit and threw it on. She looked in the full-length mirror her mother had installed in the motor home. Anna had kept her figure despite the two babies. She sighed, frustrated with her atrophied legs. She wasn't Sports Illustrated material. When Darren was alive, it was a non-issue. He had loved all of her. But Darren wasn't here now. And she had accepted the fact that her body would be as much an issue now, should she decide to date again, as it was in high school. She shook her head, trying to get the negative self-talk out of her mind. She wasn't trying to impress anyone anyway, so it only brought her down.

She got the kids their breakfast of cereal and milk and as soon as they inhaled it, they were out the door.

"Good morning, Anna," Marge said. Marge pushed a large shop broom around the cement walkway to the pool. "It's going to be a hot one today."

"That's what I hear," Anna said. "The kids and I are going to spend some time in the pool this morning."

"Good thinking," Marge said.

Brody and Zoe flew into the pool. Anna parked next to the stair's metal handrail and using her wheelchair's seat for leverage lowered herself down to the top step into the first few inches of water. The pool's temperature felt like bathwater that had just lost its warmth, which was good. Even though the sun had only been up for a couple of hours, a hazy heat had settled over the camping site. Marge wasn't kidding when she said it would be hot, and there was nothing better to be doing when it was hot and dry than take a nice swim in water that wasn't too warm. With a push, Anna swam into the water.

Anna loved swimming. The water never hindered her crippled body and made physical therapy much more fun than it otherwise would have been. When she was little, she would imagine she was a dolphin or selkie, doing lazy figure eights, or splashing up out of the water. She'd gotten so good at swimming she'd even briefly considered trying out for the Paralympics while she was in college, but that quickly took a back seat when she'd met Darren and gotten married instead.

Brody splashed Zoe mercilessly. Anna dove under the water and grabbed Brody's leg and yanked him under. She surfaced and once Brody's head popped up, she yelled, "Gopher!"

"I'm going to get you, Mom!" Brody said, trying to catch his mother. She could easily dunk him again, but she allowed Brody to yank on the back of her swimsuit straps and pull her under. She came up laughing as Brody yelled, "Gopher!" Brody turned to his sister with a sinister grin. Zoe screamed and tried to swim away. Brody was bigger and faster and soon Zoe disappeared under the water, with Brody crowing, "Gopher!"

Anna and the kids took several turns playing Gopher, laughing and half drowning. She swam up to the stairs, winded. Poor Zoe couldn't quite manage to get Brody under the water no matter how hard she tried. Her son was nothing if not a hard-core competitor. She knew, given the choice, he'd never let Zoe catch him.

"Ah, Brody, don't be a spoilsport," she said.

"Fine," he said, the brief distraction giving Zoe an edge. Zoe jumped up behind him, grabbed him around the neck and dragged him under the water.

"Zoe, you jerk," Brody said, sputtering and coughing as he resurfaced. "You're not supposed to choke me."

"I'm sorry," Zoe said, trying to get near her brother, hands extended to hug him.

"Go away," he said, splashing her.

"No!" Zoe said, still attempting to hug him even though he splashed her. "You're my big brother!"

A deep-bellied laugh erupted from behind her. With the kids yelling and splashing, she hadn't noticed anyone join them. A man in American flag swim trunks had settled just behind her on the stairs. To her horror, she realized that it was the security guard from the Shop-mart. The blood rushed to her cheeks as her heart threatened to beat out of her chest. She quickly looked away, wishing there was a hole she could swim into so she wouldn't have to face him.

"I remember when my best friend and I used to do this exact thing," he said. He moved down to the stair she sat on. "I think we ended up inhaling more water than we splashed at each other."

Anna's mind was a blank, trying to think of something clever or witty to say. Nothing. It was bad enough he had been excessively good looking in his security guard uniform, but now he was in nothing more than his swim trunks, and the delectable chest she'd suspected he had was on full display. She debated how she should just introduce herself but worried that her indecision was coming off as rude. In the end, he saved her the trouble.

"Hi, I'm Phillip Laughlin. People call me Phil, mostly." He extended his hand.

She turned to him and took his hand, cheeks blazing. As soon as he got a good look at her face, his eyes widened a bit and he grinned. Anna wondered how all the blood rushing to her face hadn't made her pass out, but she managed to smile back. "I'm Anna Gilbert."

"It's nice to put a name to the face," he said. "I'm assuming those two out there are yours?"

She nodded. "That's my son, Brody, and the little girl is Zoe."

"They look like a lot of fun," he said, turning his head to watch them play. "And a handful."

Anna laughed. His dark brown eyes were more like chocolate than she remembered. She desperately struggled not to gawk at his physique. He didn't look like he worked out—he looked like he worked. With his hands and legs—his whole body. And his tan testified that he was outdoors a lot. Curly brown hair spread across his work-hardened pectorals that led down a trim stomach towards his shorts. As soon as she found herself heading in that direction, she turned away and cleared her throat. "Yes, they are that."

She couldn't think of anything to say, which made the whole thing more ridiculous and confusing. She was a grown woman with an English teaching degree and two children, and she sat floundering for words like she was in junior high. Just his proximity had her pulse racing and her stomach doing flips And worse yet, the longer she was silent the more ridiculous it got. He seemed content to sit near her, but the silence was killing her.

She was about to open her mouth to say something when he did the same. They laughed, but she indicated he should continue. "So, what brings you to Sweetwater? If you don't mind my asking."

"I'm here on vacation with my family," she said.

"Oh," he said. "I guess your husband is off doing something else?"

She almost laughed. Was he seriously checking her single status? "My husband died a few years ago. I'm here with my sister and our parents."

"I'm so sorry," he said, a blush spreading across his cheeks, intensifying the color of his eyes. The way he looked at her, she could see his own pain reflected back at her.

She nodded. "Me, too," she said. "So, it's my turn?" She gave him a small smile.

"Sure," he said.

"Do you live here?"

"If you mean the lodge, no. I have my own place a few miles down the road. But Marge and Hank are like parents to me so I'm always puttering around this place. The Fourth of July barbecue is in a couple of days, and I'm here to help Hank set everything up. Will you be staying for the barbecue?"

"My dad has his own funny timetable for this trip but I doubt he would say no to something he and my kids would enjoy so much."

Phil's smile brightened. "It really is a lot of fun. Hank is a pyromaniac and Independence Day is like Christmas morning to him."

Anna laughed. "Sounds like my dad."

From the corner of her vision, Anna saw a white and pink blur screaming towards them. Ophelia breezed past them and cannonballed into the pool. The resulting tidal wave dunked the kids and splashed Phil and Anna. Anna laughed until she looked over at Phillip. He looked to have a death grip on the stairs and handrail. His eyes were clenched tight and his face pale. He murmured softly to himself. At first, Anna thought he might be upset at Ophelia for splashing them. When his death grip continued, she became concerned. She gave him a moment and then reached a hand over and touched his shoulder.

"Are you okay?" she said.

Phillip startled and opened his eyes. He looked at her with such an intense gaze it took her breath away. He nodded and sat up a little straighter. "I'm fine," he said. He took a deep breath and blew it out slowly.

Ophelia's head popped up from the water in front of them. "Hey, guys!" she said. When she saw Phillip, her smile got positively Cheshire. "Well, hello there, Mr. Security Guard."

"Phillip, this is my sister, Ophelia. I believe you've met," Anna said.

"Yes," Phil said, chuckling weakly. "I remember. Something about an issue with one of the powercarts."

Anna wanted to cover her cheeks with her hands.

"That's right," Ophelia said, looking at her sister. "A very nice Clark Kent kind of guy rescued my sister, and in that suit she's wearing, no less. It's a shame that the cover-up got damaged. But I guess it's lucky she looks amazing in that swimsuit. Doesn't that color accentuate her eyes, Phil?"

"Phee, stop it," Anna growled.

"I thought the same thing a minute ago," Phillip said. He seemed to have recovered somewhat and his grin grew bigger.

Ophelia kept going despite the daggers coming from Anna's eyes.

"So, Phil, what do you do for a living, or is the security guard Clark Kent guy your full-time gig?" Ophelia said.

"It's very part-time," Phillip said. "It gives me something to do. I'm retired military and Marge and Hank keep me busy around here."

"Military, huh?" Ophelia said. "What branch?"

"Army," he said.

"Oh, Dad is going to love you," Ophelia said.

"Phee," Anna said with emphasis.

"Our dad was in the Army, too," Ophelia kept going. "Get him going and he could talk your ear off about the different bases he's been stationed at, and battles and all that stuff."

"Phee!" Anna practically shouted.

"What?" Ophelia said.

"Why don't you go and play Gopher with the kids?" Anna gave her sister a very pointed stare.

"Okay," Ophelia said, still grinning. "You kids have fun talking." She splashed away and immediately pounced on Brody.

"I'm so sorry," Anna said, looking back at Phillip. "She doesn't know when to shut up sometimes."

Phillip smiled. Anna noticed for the first time that his crooked grin tended to dimple his cheek a little when he smiled. "She seems like she is very interested in her family's happiness."

"That's one way you could put it," Anna said, grimacing.

"I was going to swim some laps but I don't want to ruin the kids' fun," he said, standing up. "I'm glad we bumped into each other. See you at the barbecue?"

She nodded. "See you around the lodge."

"I hope so," he said, the side of his mouth ticked up as he walked away.

Chapter Five

"Where did Ophelia get off to?"

Anna had just gotten out of the shower and joined her mom outside where she was laying out lunch. She slid down onto the picnic blanket and claimed a stem of grapes, popping one into her mouth.

"I think she said she was going to take a run along the river," Ellen said. Her mother sighed. "I'm worried about that girl. She can act so silly sometimes, but I can tell she's hurting deep down."

"I agree with you," Anna said as she began scooping food onto plates for her kids, who had run over from playing when they saw her. "I've been worried about her since we started this trip but she's trying hard to seem okay. You never know with her."

"She doesn't fool me," Ellen said, taking a bite of a sandwich. "She's got more going on than just losing her job. She's been seeing someone, hasn't she?"

"Yeah, but they broke up. She doesn't want to talk about it, though."

Ellen nodded. "Well, I guess she'll come to either you or me when she's ready."

"Oh, there's Art!" Ellen said, looking across the lawn. Anna looked up and saw that her father was talking with an older man. She sat up straighter when she saw that he was flanked on the other side by Phillip. They were headed directly for the picnic blanket. Anna's heart and stomach did a flip at the same time. She tried several sitting positions trying to look more relaxed, but she ended up looking like a stunted mermaid. As the men reached the picnic blanket, Phillip smiled at Anna and nodded to her, making heat rise to her cheeks.

"Hank, this is my daughter, Anna." Art said. "These are my two grandmonsters, Brody and Zoe, and my beautiful wife, Ellen." Hank shook everyone's hands cordially.

"And, Ellen, this is Hank's nearly-son, Phillip. He's an Army man," Art said proudly.

Army. Anna's smile faltered as her mind went to Phillip's reaction at the pool. Now it might make sense. Shell-shock, maybe?

"Nice to meet you, ma'am," Phillip said as he shook Ellen's hand. He smiled over at Anna. "And I've already met Anna."

Anna smiled up at him, trying to act natural. She prayed silently that he didn't feel the need to share the adventure at the Shop-mart. Her father was too prone to teasing and she especially didn't want him to have new stories to tell about her.

"It's so nice to meet you all," Ellen said. "I've got plenty here if you boys are hungry."

Art sat down next to the grandkids which left a little room for Phillip right next to Anna.

"Thank you for the invitation. I'd love some food and good company," Phillip said, and glanced over at Anna. "I'm starved."

"We're glad to have you. Go ahead and have a seat," Ellen said. With a bold smile, he squatted down and sat cross-legged next to Anna, his knee just an inch from hers.

Hank remained standing. "I appreciate the offer, folks, but Marge has a honey-do list about a mile long. It only gets longer as the Fourth gets closer. We'll see you tonight at dinner."

"Okay, we'll see you then." Ellen waved him goodbye.

"So, Phillip," Art said. "Where were you last stationed?"

"Fort Bragg, sir," Phillip said, turning away from Anna.

"Ah, yes," Art said. "Did my basic training there. Can't say I miss the deep summer there, though."

"I completely agree," Phillip said, "I'll take dry heat any day."

Anna put a sandwich on a plate for Phillip. She was about to reach for the rest of the food options when he said, "Thank you, but you don't have to serve me." He gently took the plate from her and served himself some grapes and a bag of chips.

Phillip's closeness distracted her despite her best efforts to concentrate on the conversation. His body was warm and electric. The combination of his cologne and his musky, foresty scent was intoxicating. When he leaned back again, he turned and saw her inspecting him. Embarrassed at getting caught, she lowered her eyes and popped another grape in her mouth.

"What did you do in the Army?" Ellen asked, adding a scoop of her potato salad onto his plate.

"Engineering," he said. "I was Special Forces most of the time."

Anna dared to look at him again when she was sure he wasn't looking at her. His jaw muscles flexed as he ate. His whole face lit up when he laughed at one of her dad's corny jokes. She especially liked how the skin around his eyes crinkled when he smiled.

Phillip leaned back, accidentally sweeping his fingertips across hers on the blanket. The small touch sent pleasant tingles up her arm and she tried not to shiver. He looked at her and this time she couldn't look away. She managed a small smile, which he returned.

"Mom, can I go play, please?" Zoe said, breaking the spell of the moment.

"Uh, sure, baby," Anna said, nearly breathless. "Just don't wander where we can't see you."

"Mom, Grandpa said he's going to take me fishing tomorrow," Brody said, excitedly.

"You should come with us, Phil," Art said. "I'm sure neither Brody nor I would mind the company. We're going to Hank's fishing spot."

"That would be so cool," Brody declared. "Can you tell me about the guns you've fired?"

Phillip's smile faltered a bit but he rallied. "I'd love to come." He looked over at Anna. "Will you be going, too?"

"I don't really know how to fish, and it would be difficult to get my chair down such a rocky slope to the shore."

"If you want to come, I wouldn't mind helping you get down there," Phillip said. "I could even teach you to fish."

"I wouldn't want you to go to all that trouble," Anna said.

"It's no trouble," Phillip said, beaming a smile at her. His eyes scanned her face as he spoke. Anna's breath caught when his gaze lingered on her lips for a moment. "I know a shortcut."

"I guess that could be fun," she said. She found herself swooning that Phillip thought to include her. Now she really did feel like that girl who'd just been asked out by the hottest guy in school.

Brody whooped. "Cool! Mom's coming! This is going to be so fun!" he said. His excitement nearly brought tears to her eyes. It had been a long time since she had seen her son excited about anything, except new video games since his father died.

"Yes, I think it will be a lot of fun," Art said looking at his daughter, and then Phillip, with a soft expression on his face. "Seven a.m., Phil?"

"Sounds like a plan," Phillip said.

Ophelia came jogging up and flopped herself onto the blanket. "I am starving. And sweaty."

"Ophelia, this is Phil. He's a family friend of Hank and Marge's," Art said.

"Hello, again, Phil," Ophelia said, then looked back and forth between Phillip and Anna, grinning ear to ear. "We met Phil at the pool this morning. Eating lunch with us?"

"Yes," Anna said. "Until a hot, sweaty mess dropped into the middle of the picnic blanket."

"Aunt Phee, Grandpa's taking me fishing tomorrow! Do you want to come?" Brody said, trying to pull his aunt upright.

"Goober, your Aunt Phee is going to be lounging at the pool all day tomorrow trying to get a sunburn."

"Let's help your grandma clean up and then we'll go find something fun to do," Art said, and the two started gathering paper plates.

"Have a good run?" Anna said, handing her sister some lunch.

"Yes," she said, between bites. "There's nothing like free-running along a beautiful river. Did you know there's a big lake about three miles north of here?"

"Yes," Phillip said. "My best friend and I used to run up there all the time to fish and swim. It's really beautiful this time of year."

"I wished I had taken my phone. I could have gotten some great pictures," Ophelia said, finishing off her sandwich.

"Yeah, it's incredible, especially this time of year. Anna, you'd love it there. When the lake is still, it reflects the sky and the hills and trees. And it's so clear you can see the fish before you cast your line. I'd love to take you out there. Will you go with me?"

Anna froze for a moment. Had she just been asked on a date . . . by this gorgeous, kind man who had somehow made chewing attractive? "I think I'd like that, thanks." I think I'd like to go anywhere with you.

"I need to finish up some stuff Hank needs me to do around here, and then I'll take you," Phillip said standing up.

Chapter Six

Anna approached the lodge and noticed a beat-up pickup parked nearby. The lodge door opened and Phillip came out. Her heart skipped a beat. It'd been a long time since she'd reacted like that to a man and it was pleasant and scary at the same time.

"Hey, you're on time," he said. "Ready to go?"

"Yup. I have sunscreen, an umbrella, and blanket," she said, patting her backpack.

He hesitated for a moment as he looked her wheelchair over. "And do I need to help you in the truck?"

"Probably not," she said, smiling up at him. "Let's see, though. The bigger the lift, the harder it is."

Anna rolled over to the passenger side of the truck and she was happy to see it wasn't that high. As much as she wouldn't mind being near him again, she didn't want him helping her into the truck. She wanted to show him that she was perfectly capable of doing things on her own. She quickly lifted herself in, using the door armrest and the truck seat for leverage.

"Well, damn," Phillip said, rubbing his chin. "I guess you showed me." He grinned at her as she gave him a cheeky grin back. "I'm just going to throw this in the back if you don't mind."

She nodded and once he got the chair in, he drove them towards the lake. He was only on the main roadway for a few minutes before he turned off on a dirt road and they were bouncing along the well-worn path. Anna laughed as the dips and grooves of the road sent them off their seats occasionally, making Anna supremely glad for seatbelts. The ride wouldn't have been nearly as much fun with her head slamming into the roof.

"Just a bit farther," he said, returning the brilliant smile she had on her face. "We're on the Sweetwater Trail which runs along a small dry creek bed. It's how the resort got its name."

The truck crested a ridge when the twinkling sparkles of the small lake could be seen a little way ahead of them. The area around seemed like a small oasis in the middle of the dry country. Trees, scrub oak, and rushes surrounded the northern side, stopping at the line of water-smoothed pebbles that made up its shore.

Phillip pulled right up to the water's edge and got out.

"It's called Yosemite Springs Lake, but I personally don't think it's big enough to be considered a lake. More like a pond. Now, Pine Mountain Lake is a lake but it's too touristy up there. Too busy. Here you can fish in peace and not worry about joyriders on boats scaring the fish away."

He placed her wheelchair next to the door and she got out and looked around.

"It is really beautiful up here," she said. "And I brought my phone."

She took a few pictures of the water and the surrounding area. Phillip had been right about the rockiness being a problem. It was nearly impossible to push her wheelchair where she needed it to go because the wheels sank down into the pebbles with only soft ground underneath.

"Darren would have loved this," she said, almost without thinking. The sudden thought of her husband made water pool a little in her eyes. "He loved being outdoors."

Phillip had been setting up the blanket on the ground but stopped when she mentioned Darren.

"Darren was your husband?" he asked.

She nodded. "He's Brody and Zoe's father." She let out a sigh. Then she realized whose company she was in. "Sorry, it just popped out before I thought about it."

"You don't have to apologize. I've lost people close to me, too. Scott was my best friend since we were kids. He and I loved to come up here any chance we could get. The fishing and swimming were good and our parents didn't seem to mind what we did as long as we were home before dark." He looked out over the lake. "Man, we used to get in so much trouble together."

Anna smirked. "Two boys running wild and free with no supervision, what trouble could you possibly have gotten into?" she asked wryly.

His eyes twinkled as he chuckled. "Plenty, before we both joined the Army. We were the local troublemakers when we were teenagers. I was the obnoxious one getting us into trouble and he was the one that had the ability to talk us out of it."

Anna laughed. "You were quite the pair, it sounds like."

"We were," Phillip said, his face getting serious. "He was there for me and my mother when my father died of a heart attack. The whole family, really—Marge and Hank too. I'm not sure what we would have done without them. And then my mother died of an aneurysm right before I graduated high school. My whole world was gone, but the Teagues took me in and took care of me until I joined the Army."

"That's a lot in a short amount of time and at such a young age, Phillip. I'm so sorry that happened to you."

He kicked some of the pebbles from the shoreline into the water. "Thanks. In a way, it served a purpose. I never really took much of anything seriously growing up. But when I lost my parents, I had to grow up really, really fast. I appreciated things more. I relied more on myself to achieve my goals. I keep myself healthy so that I don't have to leave this earth the way my parents did."

He looked off over the water. Anna was about to say something when he looked back at her.

"You still up for fishing tomorrow? I wasn't kidding when I said I'd be happy to help you at the river. It's about like this as far as rockiness goes."

"Are you sure?" she asked. "I won't just be in the way? I really don't know how to fish."

"It won't be any trouble at all," Phillip said, giving her a soft look. "It'll be fun."

Anna couldn't help blushing and couldn't keep a smile from spreading across her face. It pleased her to know that, despite the wheelchair, he still wanted to be around her. The gesture was sweet, exciting . . . and reminded her so much of the way Darren used to be. He didn't care either about how much more work going places with her could be.

"I know Brody is excited to go."

"Has he ever been fishing before?"

"No, but he's wanted to go," she said. "I wish his dad had gotten a chance to teach him."

"Do you mind if I ask what happened? I remember you said he died a few years ago," Phillip said.

"Car accident. People drive like maniacs on the freeways in Utah, even in the best of conditions," Anna said with a humorless chuckle. "But in the winter, it's worse. Some guy driving an SUV was driving too fast on the snowy roads and tried to stomp on his brakes when traffic stopped. All he did was slide sideways into the car in front of him, which flipped him on top of our car. I doubt Darren even saw it coming." She blinked away some moisture from her eyes.

"Wow," Phillip said. "I'm so very sorry."

"Thank you," Anna said, looking at Phillip. "I am too. He was a good man."

His smile was sad. "It's like they say—only the good die young."

Anna's smile died. She really wanted to say, Well, it shouldn't be that way. It's not fair. But she knew Phillip felt it, too.

"I guess Scott was one of the good ones then," Anna said, adjusting on the blanket. "I saw the picture of him Marge hangs on her wall at the lodge. He looked like a nice, but serious young man."

Phillip laughed. "Yeah, well, those pictures—it's sort of a tradition to not smile in them. You want to look tough and capable. He wasn't just my best friend. We were brothers. We all took his death hard. Sometimes I feel like I took it harder. Scott's tour before his last, it messed him up. But he thought that if he went back out there that somehow he could defeat his demons. I think it just made him more reckless. When Hank called me, I kept asking him if he was sure."

Anna nodded, feeling the familiar tightness in her chest. "I could barely breathe after the hospital called. I kept thinking they had made a mistake or I had heard wrong. I tried to get there as fast as I could. I didn't make it in time to say goodbye." Her voice cracked.

Phillip sat down on the blanket next to her. He squeezed her hand, understanding in his eyes as he looked into hers. Tears slid down the side of her face. His simple but tender touch meant a lot right at that moment. He brought his hand up, hesitated for only a moment before reaching out and wiping away a few of them.

"I'm sorry," she said, her face flushing at the feeling of his hand against her skin.

"You don't have to apologize for loving someone."

"I'm glad you understand, so I'm not making a fool of myself," she said, wiping away the rest of her tears.

"Never," Phillip said.

They sat in silence for a while. Neither one was willing to broach their grief again, but they were content to sit comfortably together enjoying the sound of the water splashing against the shore and the birds singing to each other in the afternoon heat.

Phillip stood up and pulled a cooler out of the back of the truck. "I figured we'd get hungry at some point. Nothing fancy. Just some sandwiches, fruit and bottles of water."

"It's perfect. I'm glad you thought of it ahead of time. It's so nice here. I'm glad we don't have to leave right away."

Phillip pulled out some simple deli sandwiches, orange slices and handed her a bottle of water. It was a perfect light lunch for a hot day. She watched him as they ate. So much pain in one person's life. She thought she'd had it bad—and it had been very bad. But at least she still had her family to help her and love her. Phillip didn't have any family except the Teagues. Her heart went out to him. It was a silly idea but she wished there was something she could do to help him. Then again, he hadn't told her of his heartache because he was asking for help. He probably just wanted to be understood. She understood all too well.

"So you teach high school," Phillip said finally. "That's pretty brave for someone as petite as you."

"Not really," she said, as she took off her shoes and put her feet in the lukewarm water. "I've perfected my schoolmarm death glare. It works about eighty percent of the time."

"Schoolmarm death glare? This I've got to see."

She gave him her best imitation of it and then burst out laughing.

"That gave me chills, seriously," he said, holding up his hands.

She shook her head. "Really, it's not as bad as some people make it out to be. Don't get me wrong, my students can be a handful. But I have to remind myself that teenagers are kids making their first attempts at being adults. They get it right some of the time but they haven't the life experience yet to temper energy with wisdom. So you end up witnessing their little dramas play out from day to day.

"But even though they're young, they have amazingly sharp and insightful minds. You'd be amazed at how you learn from them just as much as they learn from you. When a good conversation gets going, I marvel at how their minds work."

"Sounds like you found your calling," Phillip said. "I thought I had found mine in the Army. But a lot changed that last year and I had to get out. I haven't really done much since."

"A lot changed?" she asked.

He glanced over at her. "My last tour in Afghanistan was rough. We lost a lot of good guys and then I got the news Scott died. I . . ." He went quiet.

She didn't press him further. The conversation had already been so heavy. She really didn't want to talk about her grief anymore either and so she sat silently waiting for him. This was more than shell shock, it was intense trauma. She wished there was a way to help, but she didn't know how. She wasn't a therapist. Just a schoolteacher.

"Phillip," she said after a while. He looked at her, a strange mix of sadness and something else in his eyes. "Thank you for bringing me here. It's so peaceful. And . . . I've enjoyed getting to know you a little better, too."

He gave her a shy smile. "You're welcome. I'm glad you said yes." He paused once again watching his hands. "It's funny. I've only just met you, but there's something about you." He looked to be struggling to find the words. He ran his hand through this hair. "This is going to come out sounding . . . lame, but I feel comfortable talking to you. I've only ever felt the same with the Teagues."

"That doesn't sound lame," she said. "I'm glad I can talk to you, too. It makes me feel better knowing you understand. It's hard to explain to people what it feels like to lose someone you love. Even harder to feel understood."

"Exactly," he said. "I'm glad you feel the same, because otherwise all of that might have made things awkward. It's been nice to hang out. And I'm glad you trusted me enough to come today."

"Same here. I'm glad you weren't worried I'd take advantage of you."

He laughed as he started to gather up the leftovers. "Well, I guess I better get you back to the resort. We'll be getting up early to go fishing."

"Are you suggesting I need my beauty sleep?" she challenged.

He looked at her long and hard. "No, definitely not that."

She smiled but had to look away. Her pulse was skipping beats. For the first time since they'd arrived at the lake, she felt like she needed to get back to her family. The feelings Phillip was creating in her were getting too intense, reminded her too much of how it felt to be with Darren. And even if she could come to some type of acceptance of how he made her feel, they were only going to be at the resort for a couple more days at most. What chance was there of a relationship of any kind? She barely knew him and her entire life was in Utah. She sighed to herself. For her to consider anything between her and Phillip more than a flirtation was basically pointless.

On the drive back to the resort, she snuck glances at Phillip. Even if anything more than flirting was pointless, she knew what he meant about feeling comfortable. It was strange how much she enjoyed being with him, and despite her extreme attraction to him, she felt perfectly comfortable sitting there with him.

Almost like I've known him forever, she thought. And it had been a really long time since she'd felt like that with anyone.

Chapter Seven

The next day Anna sat sandwiched between Phillip and her father in the cab of Phillip's truck as they drove down the dusty back road to the fishing spot. Brody sat in the bed of the truck, a huge smile on his face as he bounced around. She looked back at him for the fiftieth time to make sure he was okay. Visions of them hitting a rock and Brody flying out of the bed danced in her head.

"He'll be fine," Art said, patting her on the knee.

She shook her head. "I just—"

"I've got my eye on him," Phillip said. "Look at him, he's as happy as a frog in a pond."

"I'm glad I'm the only one here worried about his safety," she said, folding her arms.

"I'm driving slow enough he should stay where he's at as long as he doesn't try to stand up or lean over the edge," Phillip said. She glared at him, unconvinced. "It's okay. You're his mother. Your job is to worry."

"Funny," she said, grimacing.

When an amused smile spread across Phillip's face, Anna threw her hands up, exclaiming, "Men!"

Phillip glanced over at her, chuckling. She couldn't help smiling despite herself. His laugh was infectious and genuine. It had quickly become one of her favorite things about him. The sound felt warm and comforting, like hot chocolate on a winter's day. Still, it was annoying that she seemed to be the only one of the three in the cab concerned about her son's safety.

She settled back against the seat, willing herself not to check on Brody again. She was pleasantly distracted by Phillip's proximity. Warmth bled through her soft cotton blouse where his solid bicep touched hers. His touch was electric, and the zaps in her stomach fired off all over her.

Art coughed, redirecting Anna's attention. The electricity sizzled down a bit when she remembered with all the zinging going on her father was sitting right next to her. It was a weird place to be. If her dad found out what was really going on in her head, she'd never hear the end of it. Like the time soon after she and Darren had gotten engaged and had gone to the lake with her family. Her dad couldn't help himself making little comments here and there about wedding nights and make-out sessions. The last thing she wanted was for her father to know, let alone make commentary about whatever it was she and Phillip had. She preferred him to remain blissfully ignorant of the maelstrom of feelings swirling around in her head.

She felt attracted, guilty, and embarrassed by intervals. She was deeply attracted to Phillip. But as good as it felt, something didn't seem right. She knew in her head there was nothing wrong with her friendship with Phillip. Darren's death had been four years ago, but that didn't mean her feelings for him suddenly had an expiration date. This hadn't been a problem before. She didn't date and she'd never found anyone that was even remotely interested in her. Now it was a problem. A short-term problem, but a problem nonetheless.

Phillip slowed the truck down and pointed to a clearing in the scrub oak and sagebrush along the trail. They could see the Merced River peeking out. It flowed serenely in the morning light before them. The riverbank was mostly gravelly rocks with the odd tree branch or flowing grasses. The river itself didn't look too deep, or at least along the riverbanks it wasn't. There was a murky strip of fast-flowing water towards the center. Perfect for fishing. Phillip had brought them to a spot with a lot of shade, for which her white Irish skin was thankful.

The men hopped out of the truck and discussed the best places to set up. Anna scooted to the passenger seat and pulled her legs over to the end of the seat. She looked up and took in a deep breath. The sky was a brilliant blue with wispy clouds trailing along. The air smelled clean and dusty.

"Gorgeous day!" she said when Phillip walked up to her. He leaned on the truck's door frame.

"It'll be hot like it was yesterday."

"Good, I'll have a reason to soak my feet in the water again," she said. She looked over Phillip's handsome face and dark brown eyes. Those eyes—one of the first things she noticed about him after how good he looked in his security guard uniform. They were warm and kind, and she liked the way he looked at her.

Art and Brody strolled up to the pair. "I'd say let's all stick together but since we've got two novices, I think it's better if we split up. Give them a little bit of room. What do you think?"

"I think it sounds like a good idea," Phillip replied. "There's some similar type shade upriver a way if you and Brody want to take up that spot and there's a spot over here where Anna and I can set up."

"Good, then we won't be crossing casts," Art said. "What do you say, Brodster?"

"Let's go!" he exclaimed. "Then Mom can't steal all the fish."

"Smart alec," she said, grabbing her son's arm and pulling him into a hug. "Be good for Grandpa and listen to him, okay?"

Brody squirmed out of his mother's arms but had a huge smile as he came back and quickly gave his mother a kiss on the cheek before running to catch up to his grandfather. With a hitch in her chest, she watched her son scamper off. She loved seeing Brody so happy and carefree. He was too often sullen and pouting. But it seemed this place had a positive effect on him. It was probably because he was out in the sunshine, running around and exploring instead of cooped up indoors on a gaming system.

Phillip pointed to a spot south of the truck. "That over there is my favorite spot. I'll get your chair and then get you over to our spot."

Our spot, huh? Anna thought, with a smirk. She almost said something but Phillip had already pulled her wheelchair out of the back of the truck and was taking it over to the river's edge near some shady trees.

When Phillip returned, he held his arms out to take her out of the truck. With her arm looped around his neck, she tried not to smile at how close her face was to his. Her eyes were drawn to his mouth. The thought came unbidden, *"I wonder how soft his lips are?"* She imagined her unoccupied hand reaching up to run her finger along his cheek, turning his face to hers and softly pressing her mouth to his. Her thoughts were interrupted when she was placed in her chair.

Phillip retrieved the fishing poles and tackle box and set it on the ground next to Anna. Expertly, he added the lures to the lines and then held out the rods to her.

"Pick one," he said. She reached out and grabbed the closest one.

"Now, go slow," she said. "I understand casting, in theory, but I've never actually done it."

"Okay, I'll walk you through it," he said. "Hold the line with your forefinger and flip that wire over so it will release the line. You pull out a bit of line so your lure can swing a bit, pull the rod back, and cast it forward. Like this."

He brought the rod back over his shoulder and flicked the lure forward. The line sailed in a perfect arc over the river and plopped into the water. "Make sure you let go of the line as you cast. Now you try."

Anna drew the rod back and flicked it, but the lure plopped into the shallow water in front of her wheels. "I think I forgot to let the line go."

Phillip chuckled. "Good try!"

"Right," she said dryly. "I need instruction, not humoring."

He shook his head and reeled his line back in. "Okay, watch again. Pull out some line, pull the rod back. As you bring it forward, keep it in line with your forearm, and let go of the line like you're throwing a ball."

"Okay," Anna said. "I can do this. Pull the rod back, throw it forward, annd, crap!" The lure caught on one of her wheel spokes.

Phillip chuckled but this time he put his own rod down. He grabbed a folded blanket and flopped it on the ground next to her wheelchair. Kneeling down, he wrapped an arm around her back. He used his hand to steady her arm and reached around her front to ready the line to cast again. She tried to suppress a smile. She was enjoying his arms around her entirely too much. Her blood rushed through her body, and she resisted the urge to giggle.

Looking deep into her eyes, he said, "Ready?" She nodded. She pulled her arm back. With Phillip's hand guiding the speed and force of her cast, she threw her rod forward. The lure almost landed far enough to fish with. But Phillip's arm had shoved her far enough forward on her seat, that when she cast, the front wheels of her chair sunk into the river bed. The front of her chair pitched downwards and she felt herself sliding off her seat as her weight suddenly shifted forward.

Anna dropped her pole and wrapped her arms around Phillip's neck so she wouldn't fall into the river. His arms caught her and she noticed as her face ended up in his shoulder that he had a pleasant smell, even without the cologne he'd been wearing the other day. She looked up to say something to him and stopped breathing. Their faces were only centimeters apart, so close that the light puffs of air from his mouth caressed her face. So close that all she had to do was shift forward in his arms so slightly and their lips would touch. And for a small moment, she considered doing just that, her curiosity about kissing him burning into a raging inferno.

Phillip cleared his throat and Anna looked up into his eyes, momentarily released from her line of thinking. He smiled and tightened his grip on her waist and under her legs to lift her up.

"That was a close one," he said, supporting her as she adjusted her seat.

"Seriously," she said, her laugh sounding breathy. "I'm just glad you were there to catch me. Thank you. That could have been messy. Could you, um, hand me my pole, and show me one more time?"

Maybe she didn't quite need that one last time but she found she longed for the feeling of his arms around her. After one more instructional cast, he was satisfied that she had a handle on it. They fell into a rhythm of casting and reeling, waiting for a fish to bite.

For Anna, this time was both comfortable and infuriating. She wanted to talk to him, get him talking to her but so far the only thing they'd found they had in common was grief and she didn't want to talk to him about that anymore. They were supposed to be having fun. But at the same time, she knew that if she said nothing that it wouldn't really matter, she liked being around him, liked that there wasn't a pressure to constantly keep up a dialogue. Time passed quickly and soon Art and Brody came to their area for lunch.

They ate their lunch and laughed as Brody demonstrated his new rock-skipping talent.

"You're going to scare away all the fish," Art said. He turned to Phillip and Anna. "He was good for about a couple of hours but he's been antsy for a while. So, I showed him how to skip rocks. Doesn't do much for fishing but it's kept him entertained."

"Brody, you don't want to fish with Grandpa anymore?" Anna asked.

"Yeah, I do!" he said defensively. "I just haven't caught anything and that's boring."

"Just got to be patient," Phillip said.

Brody shrugged, unconvinced.

"All right, mister," Art said, standing up. "Let's go try one more time. If you don't catch anything, I'm sure Phil wouldn't mind driving us back to the campsite."

After her son and father left, she was determined to talk about something. A question had been floating in her mind since they'd talked yesterday about his friend, Scott.

"Phillip?" Anna said, after a while. "Can I ask you a question about Scott?"

He looked over at her. "Sure," he said.

"Why didn't Scott get help?"

"Help?"

"Like counseling or group sessions. I thought that servicemen had stuff like that available to them."

Phillip sat for a long time not saying anything. Anna worried that she had offended him with the question.

"They talk about all this support for vets that come home but they've never been in a VA hospital. They don't pay their doctors and nurses enough, so they don't want to work there. Then the vets have to wait forever for an appointment. If you're having a hard time but not in crisis, you could wait months, or sit hours and hours in the ER, before you get help. It's hard enough as a man, and as a soldier, to admit that you're in pain in the first place. Even if you've managed to convince yourself, or a loved one convinces you, to get help, a lot of guys lose their nerve after waiting so long. It's frustrating."

"I can imagine," Anna said.

"It's one of those things where you wish you could do something to help, something to make a difference."

"What would you do?"

"These guys, they've seen some serious sh— I mean, seriously horrible things, and sometimes it helps to just talk about it. They need someone that's been right there with them and knows. Someone who doesn't look clinical, just a guy who's there to listen."

Anna nodded, a feeling of excitement blooming inside from an idea that was forming. "Have you ever thought about doing something like that?"

"Me?" Phillip said, genuinely shocked. "Like what?"

"Like helping soldiers that are coming home."

"I don't follow."

Anna frowned. "Have you ever thought about getting a degree in something so you can help? Like a social work or psychology degree? Have you used your GI bill yet for anything?"

He shook his head.

"Pick a school and get your degree."

He scoffed. "It's not that easy. Or maybe it was for you, but it's not for me. I never really did well in school."

"I can understand that," Anna said. "College is intimidating. But I heard in your voice such conviction and desire. You want to help, and you can."

He looked off down the river. "They could use more people at the VA."

"Yes, they could."

"Definitely something to think about."

She watched him as this idea took seed. There had been a light in his eyes. All he needed was the encouragement and courage to do it.

An ear-piercing shriek erupted from upriver and both their heads whipped towards it. In the next moment, they saw Art running down the riverbank, Brody limp in his arms. Blood coursed down Brody's head.

"Help!" the old man yelled.

Chapter Eight

A scream ripped out of her. Anna struggled to turn her wheelchair in the gravel and wet sand. Tears of frustration flowed down her cheeks when she realized that she was stuck. Phillip had jumped up when he heard her scream, and raced to Art to help him with a pale and limp Brody. Blood streamed down the boy's head and face.

"What happened?" Phillip said, as he straightened Brody out and started looking him over.

"He was climbing on a boulder. I told him a million times to get down but he wasn't listening. He slipped off and smacked his head against the boulder, then fell onto the rocks below," Art said in a shaky voice.

Anna threw herself to the ground and crawled to get to her son. "Is he breathing?"

Phillip examined Brody with precise and practiced movements. He felt Brody's pulse and listened to his breathing. Phillip's voice was like sharpened granite. "Yes. His pulse is strong and he's breathing. We need to get him out of here."

Phillip pulled his tank top off and wrapped the cloth around the boy's head. He turned to Art and threw his keys to him.

"Art, back the truck up. Anna, I need you to hold his head as still as you can. Just scoot over here and hold his head against your leg. We need to make sure if he has a neck injury that it doesn't get worse."

"Please, baby," Anna said to Brody as she followed Phillip's instructions, kissing the boy's forehead and smoothing his hair. "Wake up for Momma. Please. I love you so much. Just open your eyes for me."

"Anna," Phillip said gently, putting a hand on her back. "Anna, I'm going to put you in front with me and I need you to keep holding Brody's head. Hold it as still as you can and put pressure on the cuts."

Anna did not look up but nodded her head in acknowledgement. "Please, baby, open your eyes."

The truck ground to a halt nearby and Phillip patted her back. "Let's get you in the cab."

Phillip gathered her up to put her in the cab. He put her in and, as gently as handling a newborn baby, picked up Brody and handed him to Anna. She put his head in her lap while Art deposited her wheelchair in the back, and hopped in after it. Phillip jumped into the driver's seat and shoved the truck into first and second, gears protesting loudly. As he urged the truck forward slowly and carefully over the bumpy and rocky terrain as he could, Phillip pulled the rear window open.

"Art, I'm going to drop you off at the entrance to Sweetwater. You can get the girls and meet us at the hospital in Mariposa. I'll have Anna text you the address."

"Sounds like a plan," Art shouted back.

Once Phillip hit paved road, he hit the gas and raced to get back to Sweetwater. When they pulled up to the resort, Phillip put a hand on Anna's arm.

"Are you okay?" Phillip said to Anna.

"No," she said quietly. She caressed Brody's cheek as she looked down at the beautiful but deathly pale face.

I can't do this again, she thought. *Dear God, please. Help my little boy. Make him wake up. He's too young to leave me. I don't have the strength to go through it again.*

She prayed over and over in her head, like a chant. Brody was her beautiful boy with the smattering of freckles across his nose, who loved video games, the playground at recess, and teasing his sister until she screamed. He had been father's shadow, and the snuggler who fell asleep next to her as she cried herself to sleep those months after Darren died. *Not again, please. Please. Not again.*

Brody's eyelids fluttered, then opened all the way. Anna held her breath until he looked right at her.

"Mom," he said weakly. "Where are we?"

Her breath came in sharply. "Phillip!"

Brody's dark blue eyes looked around. "Mom," he said. "I need some medicine. My head hurts so bad."

Laughing and crying she leaned over her son and kissed his face until he tried to push her away. He struggled to sit up but Phillip put a hand on his chest to keep him from rising.

"Hold on there, buddy," Phillip said. "You need to lie still."

"How about you stay up and talk to me? Just until we get to the hospital."

Brody obliged for a while but his eyes fought to keep open as the drive wore on. Anna looked at Phillip.

"How much longer is it going to take to get there?" she asked.

"We're about ten minutes from the hospital now," he said.

"How long does it take to get to the hospital from Sweetwater?" she asked.

"About an hour or so depending on how fast you drive," he said.

Anna nodded, worried and impatient. She leaned into Phillip's side. She felt warm and comforted by him. It was nice to borrow strength from someone again. She felt the necessity of being strong after Darren died, but sometimes it had been exhausting being by herself. Phillip had such a quiet, sure strength about him. When he looked over to make sure she was okay, she could see his strength in his eyes.

"We're here," Phillip said as he finally pulled the truck into a space near the ER entrance. He sprinted for the doors. Shortly afterward he followed some nurses who brought out a gurney.

Anna looked down at Brody. "Baby, you have to lie on the bed and not move, and do what the doctors tell you," she said.

"Mom, I don't want to go!" Brody said, alarmed now as they strapped him down and put a neck collar on him.

"I'll be with you in just a minute. I have to answer some questions and then I'll be right there," Anna said, her heart breaking as she saw the look of panic in Brody's eyes.

The hospital staff rushed him inside. She flew from the cab, as soon as Phillip got out her wheelchair, and raced into the building. She filled out paperwork as quickly as she could, barely able to concentrate. The need to be with her son was so strong.

The nurse escorted her around a corner towards the space sectioned off by curtains where Brody was supposed to be, but turned to Anna before they went in. "Oh, I'm so sorry. Should I go get your husband?"

Anna's cheeks burned. In her hurry to get to Brody, she forgot that Phillip had been standing behind her the whole time. She looked back to see if she could still see him. "I'm . . . Um, he's . . . Yes, please." The color got more intense when he walked around the corner, shirtless, with a big smirk on his face.

"She's right there, hon," the nurse said to Phillip. His lips twitched as if he was trying to stop himself from laughing.

The nurse indicated the chairs in the tiny ER space. Beaming at Anna, the nurse said proudly, "I found your husband. Just let me know if you two need anything. Your son will be back in a minute."

The nurse shut the room door and Anna looked over at Phillip. "Husband, huh?" he leaned over and said to her. His breath on her neck sent chills through her.

"Oh, shush," she said, pushing him. "I figured you'd want to know Brody was okay, and the nurse caught me off guard."

"It's fine," he said, but the smirk remained.

Anna felt like she couldn't sit still. Did it really take this long for x-rays? How could Phillip sit there so calmly? He caught her looking at him and smiled at her.

"It's okay," he said. "He's probably asking the technicians a billion questions."

"Or a huge string of complaints," Anna said.

Finally, Brody was wheeled into the little room. They had replaced the tank top with bandages but he still looked so pale. Anna held his hand as the ER doctor came in.

"Well, he's a fortunate young man," he said, squeezing Brody's arm. "The cuts were deep but mostly superficial. We'll put some stitches in to keep his scalp together. We don't see a skull fracture, but I want to do a CT scan to check for bleeding in his brain, just to be safe. He's asking lots of questions, so his cognitive function looks good. Unless something else alarming shows up, we'll just have you follow standard concussion protocol and you'll be able to take him home later tonight."

"Thank you," Anna said, relief washed over her. She put her face in her hands and cried.

Phillip stood up and went over to Anna, placing his warm hands on her shoulders, rubbing them while he asked the ER doctor a few questions. That gave Anna time to regain her composure by the time the doc excused himself.

"He's asleep," Phillip said softly to Anna. "Want to come back over and take a breather?"

Anna nodded and re-parked her chair next to Phillip's. He pulled her into his side, handing her a tissue to wipe her eyes and nose. His warm hand slowly circled her back and his body melted away the chill that had tightened in her chest when she had seen Brody's limp, prone figure lying on the ground. When she felt like she wanted to sit up a little, Phillip draped his arm along the back of her wheelchair.

"I must look like a mess," she said, self-consciously drying under her eyes.

Phillip smiled at her and shook his head. "You look like a woman who's had the fright of her life."

"Phillip, I feel like all I do is thank you," she said, rubbing her arms. "But I am really thankful for your help today."

"I'm just glad that I was there to be helpful," he said. "Brody's a good kid. And he's got a great mom. I wouldn't want to see anything bad happen to either one."

She looked over at Brody again. They had the comfort of the pulse oximeter to keep track of his breathing and heartbeat. She rolled her shoulders a few times and stretched her arms to relieve the stress she carried there. She leaned back against her backrest and into Phillip's arm he had draped there. He started to rub her bicep. She sighed, feeling the comforting touch release even more of her stress.

Anna surprised herself. She had a very defined sense of personal space. She didn't normally allow people to touch her, much less in such an intimate way. But this felt different. Anna turned her head slightly to examine Phillip. He watched Brody sleep so she took advantage of his distraction to take a very good long look at him.

Good night, America, he was a beautiful man. Everything about him looked good from his sun-browned skin that defined each muscle of his work-hardened chest to the laugh lines on his face that framed his chocolate-colored eyes.

Reality intruded on her pleasant inspection. She may find him exceptionally attractive, and he might flirt with her, even be physically comforting as he was now, but as much as she found herself drawn to Phillip there wasn't a thing to be done about it. Not to mention that flirtation didn't mean anything when it came to true physical attraction. That was never a problem with Darren, even right from the beginning. Darren's physical attraction to her had been as undeniable as his mental attraction, and he made that known without hesitation. But not all men were Darren. And not all men would find her skinny legs or surgery scars on her back and for the c-sections she'd had attractive.

Phillip's eyes met hers and her worries evaporated under the warmth of his gaze. With his free hand, he wiped away a tear she didn't realize was still there. Time slowed down as his fingers lingered on her cheek, sweeping slowly along her jawline, burning a path as they stopped at her chin. Her pulse jumped erratically as his eyes lowered to her lips and then the distance between the faces shrunk. Her breath quickened as she closed her eyes and leaned in, impatient to find out if his lips were truly as soft as they looked. She bit back a gasp as the tips of his lips feathered hers, sending shockwaves through her.

"Okay, kiddo," a nurse said as she slid the curtain open with a snap. "Let's get you some stitches and then we'll take you to get that brain scan."

Anna and Phillip straightened up. She ran her hand through her hair and straightened her shirt, hoping the nurse didn't notice how bright her cheeks were. She wheeled over to the other side of Brody's bed as much to comfort Brody as to get her breathing and heart rate under control. She held his hand as the ER doctor came in and started to stitch Brody's scalp. Brody was so brave enduring the numbing shots and the stitching without so much as a whimper. Anna felt full of pride in her son.

They wheeled Brody out of the room for the CT scan not long after that. It was only then that she found the courage to look at Phillip. He'd been looking at the floor with his forearms resting against his knees, and glanced at Anna after the gurney left. He had a smile on his face like he'd been caught with his hand in the cookie jar.

"Brody did so well," Anna said, returning his grin.

"He did," Philip agreed. "I've seen grown men not do so well as he did."

"I'm, um, glad you're here," Anna said, as she wheeled back over next to him. "You've done so much, and I wanted you to know I really appreciate it."

"Any time, Anna," Phillip said, taking her hand in his. The way he said her name sent pleasant shivers through her.

Anna leaned against him and entwined her fingers with his. He brought her hand up to his lips and kissed it softly. Her heart did strange things at the touch of his mouth on her hand.

Her mind swirled as she sat there with her hand entwined in his larger one. This man that she barely knew, without question or hesitation, had been there for her and Brody. He comforted her and supported her through this nightmare trip to the hospital. She imagined his lips held almost motionless against her. In the four years since Darren died, she had never even remotely wanted someone to kiss her, let alone let them actually try. That nurse couldn't have had worse timing.

Something was happening between them, and it was implausible, frightening and wonderful. She had come to depend on him so instinctually, and now as sat next to him warmed by the easy way their hands melded together, she realized that she cared about him and what happened to him. They had only known each other for a handful of days but that's truly how she felt.

The reality was it couldn't last and that twisted her insides a little. They'd just found each other, but circumstances and time were against them. Too soon, she and her family would be leaving and she would have to go back to being strong all by herself, having tasted what it was like to have such caring support again. It wasn't fair on so many levels. She would not uproot her life and the lives of her children to start over somewhere new, and she would not ask him to do that either. Not on an off-chance of a relationship that statistically shouldn't work out in the first place.

A loud gaggle of talking came from the nurse's station outside the room. Over everything, she could definitely hear Ophelia and her mother's voices. Anna pulled the curtain back and waved her family over. Zoe ran to her mother and jumped up to hug her. At the same time, both Ellen and Ophelia leaned over to give Anna a hug. Phillip stood up and gave Ellen his seat while he went over to talk to Art, who handed him a shirt he'd brought for him.

Ophelia came up to Anna and sat on the floor next to her. She tugged her shirt.

"Hey, so, um, you and Phillip, huh?" Ophelia said quietly.

"What are you talking about?" Anna said.

"Don't be a tease," Ophelia giggled. "I could see you two through the curtains. Cozy as two bugs in a rug."

"We were just sitting together, that's all," Anna said.

"Mm-hmm. I'm letting you off the hook for now, because of Brody," Ophelia said, folding her arms. "But I want full details later!"

Anna was about to say something sassy when the curtain was drawn aside again to reveal Brody eating a Popsicle. He saw the huge party that had arrived just for him and his face broke into a wide, bright smile, eating up all the attention.

She looked over to where her father was speaking to Phillip. She couldn't help feeling a twinge of disappointment now that he was wearing a shirt. But he smiled in amusement as if he knew what she'd been thinking.

Regret and guilt again warred within her. It had been so long since she'd considered herself anything other than Darren's wife and a mom. Phillip had changed all that. He had been so wonderful and she felt really lucky to have him there, and it was nice to have someone else to depend on and be there exclusively for her.

If it were just a matter of them moving on soon maybe the feelings she was developing wouldn't be so bad, but Phillip had her feeling more. Logically, Darren would encourage her to find happiness with someone else. Then why couldn't she convince her heart that he wouldn't feel betrayed by her having feelings for another man? How could she convince herself to feel less conflicted about a relationship?

Relationship. Now her head really hurt. She had jumped from a casual encounter at a Shop-mart to a relationship in less than forty-eight hours? There was no relationship. There couldn't be one. This was insane. And yet she couldn't quite convince herself that her feelings for Phillip were merely platonic. Not when he looked at her, or smiled, or the butterflies popped up in her stomach when he laughed.

The doctor returned a few hours later with the news that the CT scan came back clean. They prepared to take Brody back to Sweetwater. Zoe lay fast asleep on Ellen, for which Anna was grateful. Brody insisted on riding with Phillip and so they loaded him up with Anna right behind him. The entire ride back to Sweetwater, Brody and Phillip talked about the Fourth of July, the fireworks and the party the next day. Anna leaned back into her seat and listened as they talked. A smile played on her lips, hearing how exuberant Brody was despite the fact that he looked like death nearly six hours ago. Soon Brody drifted off to sleep. She pulled him across her lap, grateful he was still with her.

Her smile then was for Phillip. She reached over and took his hand in hers and he squeezed it. They really didn't have to say anything. There was something about him. Something different in his eyes when he smiled at her that looked a lot like promises.

Chapter Nine

Phillip had driven Brody and Anna to Sweetwater and helped get a sleeping Brody inside the motorhome. She followed Phillip out and sat in the doorway. It felt sort of weird to watch him leaving, they'd spent all day together.

"I'm assuming you're going to be at the picnic tomorrow?" she asked him before he left the motorhome. She took in a breath, her insides aflutter as he leaned against the motorhome next to her.

"Yup," Phillip said. "I always help Hank with the barbeque."

"Okay, good. You know you're welcome to join us when you're not busy."

"Do you want me to join you?" he asked. For the first time, he sounded uncertain. He waited for her to answer.

"Yes, I do." She tried to say it as confidently as she could manage with her heartbeat up in her throat.

"Then I'll be there."

The silence extended for a long time. Seemed he didn't want to leave as much as she didn't want him to go.

"I better go," he said. "It's been a long day and you're probably exhausted. So I'll see you tomorrow."

"See you," Anna replied. Before she could talk herself out of it, she reached out and wrapped Phillip up in a hug. She hadn't been quite brave enough to try and kiss him, but it was really hard to hold back a sigh once his arms were around her.

"Thank you again," she said. The warmth bleeding through where their bodies touched sent pleasant tingles through her. Maybe she should have kissed him.

"It really was my pleasure, Anna," Phillip said.

"Mom," Brody's voice carried from inside the RV.

"Coming, Brody," she said, as she let Phillip go reluctantly. "I'll see you tomorrow."

"Right. Tomorrow." Phillip gave her a little wave as he started to walk away but not before he turned back around to give her one last smile before he got halfway through the lawn.

When Phillip was out of sight, she turned to snuggle up to Brody. It was going to be a long night of waking Brody every few hours because of the concussion protocol, and nestling up to her son wasn't quite the same as the comfort and safety she felt just a moment ago with Phillip.

Anna rubbed her face as she got up. She anxiously followed the ER doctor's orders to wake Brody every other hour to make sure he hadn't slipped into a coma. He had woken without trouble every time. Now she felt as much excitement and anticipation as she felt sluggish and sleep-deprived.

Brody had rallied enough that they set him up outside under a tree, wrapped up in a light blanket and gaming system in hand. The intent was to let him watch what was going on for the 4th of July festivities but as usual his nose was in the game and not the other kids running around.

Anna stayed by her son's side, her anxiety not allowing her to leave. She wanted to be there in case of a relapse in his symptoms, but also to keep him from trying to join in on the fun. It was a testament to how rotten he still felt that he didn't fight her much about his boredom.

Ophelia came up to them and before plopping herself to sit down next to Anna, grabbed Brody and hugged him until he weakly started to protest.

"But you're just so cute!" Ophelia declared. "I just had to hug the crap out of you. Just like your mom. She loves hugging too!"

Ophelia had an evil grin on her face as she glanced over to Anna. She leaned over to her sister and in a much lower voice said, "I mean if what I thought I saw last night was what I really saw. Okay, now, spill it. You like him, don't you?"

Anna couldn't help the smile that pulled the corners of her mouth up. "Yes, I like him. I'm not going to deny it."

"Good, it's about freaking time," Ophelia said, leaning back on her elbows as she watched the kids on the lawn running around. The two sisters laughed when they saw Zoe run by with an armful of water balloons.

Zoe was in her element. Hank had placed a large tub in the middle of the lawn and filled it to the brim with water balloons. He threw in some water squirters for good measure before topping the whole thing off with water. The kids at the resort ran around throwing water balloons at each other and getting wet in general.

"But Phee, I can't like him. I shouldn't. We'll be leaving, what, tomorrow? The next day?"

Ophelia let out an exaggerated groan. "Ann, just go with it. Live in the moment. He's got to know you won't be around forever either and that hasn't stopped him."

"You don't think it's leading him on?"

"Come on. This isn't high school. He should know how all this works." Ophelia stared at her sister for a long moment. "You don't have to be afraid. Enjoy yourself, even if it's just for a moment. It's been too long, sis. I love you and so did Darren, and he would want you to be happy."

Anna sighed angrily. The mention of Darren twisted her insides a little. Thinking of Phillip in context to Darren just made the whole thing seem not right, especially when they weren't even going to be here at Sweetwater that much longer. It was so confusing.

"So me making out with some random guy would make Darren happy?"

"You guys made out?" Ophelia sat up. "Where did I miss this? At the lake or the river?"

"Neither," Anna hissed at her. "We haven't made out. I was just saying."

"Don't do that to me!" Ophelia said, pushing her sister. "And yes, you making out with a guy you find attractive, funny, and sexy and one big freaking knight in shining armor would make Darren happy to know you're finally putting yourself out there, if he couldn't be with you."

Anna had to blink back tears this time. Mentions of Darren even after four years still hurt. Ophelia wrapped her arms around Anna.

"He would," Ophelia said. "We all loved him, and he loved you so much he'd have done anything to make you happy. Go be happy."

Anna hugged her sister back. She wanted so much to believe her. Her heart didn't understand it, even if her head said something totally different.

Zoe ran by them screaming as an older boy chased her down with a large water balloon in hand.

"And that is my signal to go even the stakes a little," Ophelia said, getting up from the grass. "Seriously, Ann, Phil is a really good guy. You never know."

Ophelia ran off in the direction of the large tub of water balloons and Anna looked down at her lap. She'd brought out her book, The Princess Bride, to read while she kept watch over Brody. It was going to be part of her curriculum for her students in the upcoming year. But thoughts about Darren, Phillip, and what Ophelia had said distracted her. Why was she thinking about this so hard?

For a while she switched between trying to read her book and watching as Ophelia got into the action. Aunt and niece ambushed a bunch of older boys that had been plaguing Zoe. They held several water balloons a piece, sneaking up to the boys for hits at point-blank range. Ophelia ran over to Brody and handed him a couple of water balloons so that he had the chance to throw some before they were all gone. When the water balloons were gone, the kids resorted to filling up the tub with just water and splashing it around or just running over to the pool to jump in. Everyone looked to be having a good time. Everyone but Anna. Phillip still hadn't shown.

Anna tried looking down at her book again. She got through a few paragraphs before she found herself scanning the lawn and the lodge house. She felt impatient to see Phillip. Maybe he hadn't planned on coming all day, just for the barbeque. Maybe he'd slept in after the day they'd had yesterday. She couldn't help feeling disappointed that he was still absent when Hank and Marge went around announcing the start of the barbecue in the afternoon.

He will come when he comes, she tried telling herself. She looked down at her copy of "The Princess Bride" to read but the words weren't making sense. She made a deal with herself—after she read five paragraphs then she could look up from the book to look for Phillip. She was in the middle of paragraph three when she heard the familiar voice above her that made her stomach flip.

"Hey, buddy," Phillip said. He stood over Brody, but glanced over at Anna with a crooked grin on his face. She gave him a huge grin, relieved he was finally there. "How are you feeling today?"

"I still have a headache," Brody said.

Phillip squatted in front of the boy. "I can believe it. You hit your noggin pretty good." He looked over at Anna. "Is he giving you much trouble?"

"No," she said smiling. "He's being a perfect angel which means he's still feeling a little cruddy."

"I was going through my stuff today, and I found something for you, Brody."

Brody perked up a little.

Phillip handed the boy a box. When he opened it, he pulled out a medal with a purple ribbon. The medal attached was a heart shape, with a relief of George Washington's profile on it.

"Wow," he said, turning it over. "What is it?"

"It's called the Purple Heart. It's given to soldiers who were injured in battle."

"But I wasn't in battle."

"Hey," Phillip said. "Hitting your head was pretty scary, sort of like being in a battle. I watched you when you were getting the stitches in your head. You sat there like any soldier would and didn't squawk a bit. That's bravery, right there."

"So, I can keep this?" Brody asked.

"Yup, keep it safe. Don't lose it," Phillip said. "That proves you were brave that day."

"Thanks, Phil!" Brody put the medal back in the box but protectively held it on his lap.

"Mind if I sit?" Phillip asked, indicating the ground next to Anna.

"Sure," she said, warmth washing through her. "You didn't have to do that."

"I wanted to," he said.

"That was yours?"

"Yup, for Afghanistan," he said, digging a heel into the lawn.

Anna nodded her head. It didn't seem like he wanted to talk about it so she changed the subject.

"Did you get enough beauty sleep?"

"Me?" he said with a grin. "I slept in a little but I've been busy at home doing some things before things really got going."

"I'm glad you made it," she said. That was understatement but she didn't want to look too eager.

"Same," he said. "What's that you got there?" He reached over and took the book out of her hand.

"The Princess Bride."

"Nice. I think I've seen the movie one time, but I've never read the book."

"The book is pretty different from the movie," Anna said. "But I love to use it to start a dialog in my classes about the nature of true love, seeing past outside appearances, and even sexism."

"What? Sexism? Where did I miss that?"

"It's not as strong in the movie as it is in the book but it's always bothered me how the men in Buttercup's life, even her true love, Westly, talk down to her as if she's incapable of thinking for herself. But she proves them wrong. She makes very definitive choices about who and what make her happy, and once she knows she made the right choice, she's not convinced otherwise."

"Do you love the book because she might remind you of yourself?"

Anna's cheeks felt hot.

"Well, sort of. In a different way."

"How do you mean?"

"It has to do with my wheelchair, or my disability, rather. I know how she feels sometimes."

This wasn't a topic she really wanted to talk about. Phillip hadn't done anything to make her think he looked at her as anything other than a person and what if talking about it brought her difference to his attention and made things awkward?

"Have I ever talked down to you?" Phillip asked.

"No!" she said, quickly shaking her head. "Not you. Just people. Some people just have a hard time looking past the wheelchair."

"Huh. That's interesting. I only ever saw you. I mean I can see you're in a wheelchair but that was never something that bothered me."

Anna felt her cheeks heat up even more and she smiled at him. She believed him when he said it. It was refreshing and flattering. "Thanks." She struggled with what to say, and it felt not enough to just thank him. She felt like she was always thanking him.

"You'll probably end up asking anyway so I'll just get it out of the way. When I was a toddler, they found a tumor on my lower spine. They removed it but the surgery took some of the feeling from my legs and weakened the muscles."

Phillip nodded but she saw an amused smile spread across his face.

"What?" she demanded.

"I wasn't even going to ask," he said, chuckling. "I figured you would tell me if it was important but it's good to know."

Anna laughed in spite of her embarrassment. "Wow, I just jumped right into that one."

"I'm sure you get that all the time."

"You have no idea."

Marge jogged up to them. "There you are. I've been trying to get a hold of you for the last half an hour. Are you still going to help Hank or are you busy?" She glanced meaningfully over at Anna with a smile.

"Oh, sorry," Phillip said, standing back up. "I'll be right over." He watched Marge walk off a little before he turned back to Anna. "Before I go, I wanted to thank you for something."

She looked at him surprised. "For what?"

"I've been thinking a lot about what you said about making a difference. It's got me thinking about what I want to do with my life. I don't think I'm content anymore since I got out of the Army. I never would have thought like that if it hadn't been for you."

Anna blinked. "You're welcome," she said. "I hope that whatever you decide to do brings the happiness you deserve in your future."

A frown creased his forehead. "That sounds like a goodbye."

She gave him a sad smile. "It is. I don't know for sure, but my dad had a pretty full schedule for this vacation and we've stayed here a day or two longer than we would have."

"Wow," he said, rubbing the back of his neck. "Time really does fly, doesn't it?"

She nodded.

He sat back down next to her. Leaning in so Brody wouldn't hear him, and so close that his breath misted her face, he said, "Anna, I know this is going to sound crazy and maybe a little creeper-ish, but there's something about you I can't get out of my head. We barely know each other, but I already know I'm going to miss you when you're gone."

His handsome face was so sincere. He was saying exactly what she'd been feeling all day, and she took in a shuddering breath before she could say, "I will too."

"I've got this feeling about you I've never had for anyone before. Things won't be the same because I met you. Am I the only crazy one here?"

She wanted to kiss him so badly, but Brody sat right there and everything was too public where they sat. The idea that they could have such an instant attraction reminded her so much of her and Darren when they'd first met. It scared her to death but she couldn't deny what was going on inside her, the feelings that she felt for Phillip. She settled for leaning in closer so their foreheads were nearly touching. "Heaven help me, Phillip, you are not the only one going crazy."

Relief washed over his face. "Okay, good. This would have been a really awkward conversation if you had said yes."

She giggled nervously. "But what can we do about it? My family and I will be traveling for the next month at least, then I go home to Utah. And you'll stay here in California."

"I don't have to, you know. It's not complicated."

"We both know it's not that simple. I'm not going to ask you to leave everything and everyone you know behind on the off-chance whatever this is works out. I won't uproot my kids or leave my career or family behind."

"I would never ask you to do that. You have too much to lose. I don't."

"Phillip, no," Anna said. Her heart beat so hard against her ribcage it was painful. She looked into this man's eyes, knowing she wanted to say the exact opposite of what she was trying to tell him. She was trying to be sensible, realistic. He was making it really hard for her. She swallowed back emotion creeping up her throat.

Phillip pulled grass up in frustration. "I would do it, you know."

Anna shook her head. "I'm not going to ask you to. It wouldn't be fair."

"Forget fair," he said forcefully, his gaze boring into her. "I would do it for you."

Anna's heart clenched. She believed him.

"We barely know each other," she offered lamely.

"My point exactly," he said, searching her face. "How are we supposed to get to know each other if we're living in different parts of the country?"

"Technology--email, text, phone calls."

He grimaced in irritation. "That's not the point."

"Then I'm not sure what the point is." She was starting to feel irritated too. For every sensible reason, he had a counter.

He reached a hand up and tucked a piece of her hair behind her ear, allowing his fingers to linger on her cheek. "The point is technology is a poor substitute when I want to be close to you."

Anna put her hand against Phillip's. "I don't want to have to leave you here. I don't have any good answers. I want to see if anything is really there between us. That it's as real as it seems now. I want to get to know you better, but the fact is that unless one of us upturns their entire life, it can't happen like either of us would want it to.

"Phillip, I know I couldn't stop you from doing something rash. I just think we need some time to see if there's even a ghost of a chance at a relationship before any major decisions are made."

He paused for a moment and sighed. "I can't argue with that."

The disappointment in his voice killed her.

"Will you be joining us for fireworks later?" she asked.

The intensity of his look shot straight to her heart. "You can count on it."

And with that, he turned and trotted over to where the food was being prepped. She took in some really long, deep breaths as she watched him walk away, fighting the tears that threatened to start.

"I'm going to miss Phil when we leave, Mom," Brody said.

"Me, too, son," she said with a waver in her voice she could not regulate.

Chapter Ten

With the heat of day, even in the shade, Anna had made both her kids go in the RV to take naps. Brody went down without his normal protests and Zoe had run herself to exhaustion so that the instant she hit the pillow, she was out. It took Anna a bit longer to fall asleep herself. When she did, she fell into a dreamless sleep so that by the time she woke up she felt alert and awake. And excited. Dinner would be starting soon and she'd get to see Phillip.

Anna checked the mirror before she left the RV. She looked as well as she could considering she'd been sweating in the heat all day. But the heat had the benefit of putting color in her cheeks and that was only heightened by the little thrill that tickled her belly.

The Mackeys went as a family to the barbeque. Everything a good barbeque would offer lay across the large picnic tables of the pavilion--chips, baked beans, corn on the cob, salads of all kinds and of course as many hot dogs, ribs and hamburgers the whole resort could eat. But despite all the deliciousness, it wasn't what Anna was hungry for.

She finally made contact with the brown eyes and boyish grin she was looking for and returned the smile with just as much enthusiasm.

"Phil, Hank," Art said, reaching out to shake the other men's hands. "This looks amazing. So Hank, are we on for later tonight?"

"Yes, sir," Hank said. "Just stop by the lodge house before dusk and we'll get everything set up."

"What's this?" Anna asked.

"The two of them have a special surprise for this evening," Ellen said. "Involving fireworks. Must have something to do with those big fireworks Arthur bought last year.'"

"Oh, no," Anna said, talking to Phillip. "My dad is a total pyro."

"He's in good company then, because so is Hank," Phillip laughed.

Hank waved his hand at them. "Make fun all you want. Talk to me after the show tonight."

"You're joining us on the lawn, right, Phil?" Ophelia asked.

"That's the plan," he said, winking at Anna.

Anna's smile got so wide it almost hurt.

The family set up on a blanket on the lawn. Anna kept looking back at the pavilion, hoping that dinner had died down enough for Phillip to join them. She was disappointed every time. In between, she tried to concentrate on her kids and the conversations that popped up between her parents and Ophelia.

After what seemed like forever, the sun finally started towards the horizon and darkness started covering the area. Anna sat up when she saw the tall figure headed towards them.

"Welcome," she said to Phillip.

"Hi," he said as he sat down next to her on the blanket they had laid out on the lawn. "Marge has sparklers and glow sticks over at the lodge house for the kids."

"Come on, Zoe, let's go get some," Ophelia said, grabbing the little girl's hand and pulling her towards the large house. Soon they were back with a handful of lit sparklers. Zoe ran around waving the sparklers in the air and even Brody managed enough enthusiasm to wave them around too.

As the adults were distracted by the sparklers, Anna reached her hand out and entwined her fingers with Phillip's. She moved over and sat shoulder to shoulder with him, laughing at Zoe and Ophelia's antics, just savoring being close to him.

"Mama, when are the fireworks going to start?" Zoe asked, coming to sit in her mother's lap.

"Should be any time now," Phillip said. "Hank likes to wait until there's just a tiny bit of light left and then he gets them going, and I'm pretty sure I saw the two old guys go off toward the main road a while ago."

Suddenly a whistling sound came from off the main roadway. A flash popped in the air, silver sparkles twinkling for just a moment. Then another one and the same again.

"Come on, Hank, is this all you got?" Phillip yelled.

Faintly they heard Hank yell back, "Getting there."

Everyone laughed.

As if reacting to the needling, a barrage of aerials went up and sprayed sparkling colors of light into the night sky. Zoe had covered her ears but when she saw the colors bloom, she clapped her little hands in delight.

"Mom, this is lame," Brody said. "When are they getting to the good stuff?"

"Hush," Anna said. "Hank says they're getting there. Just be patient."

"I can't wait until they get to Grandpa's fireworks," Brody said.

A few more little aerials went up to light the sky red for a second. Then the first one hit. BOOM! The sound was so loud you could almost feel the sound wave rush by. Again—BOOM! The sky overhead exploded in silver and red, then moments later canopied in red and blue. Anna clapped with her daughter at the huge blossoms of light streaking the night.

She turned her head to joke with Phillip about her dad's fireworks when she noticed that he was gone. She looked around as another BOOM! went off, to see if she could find him. The darkness made it impossible and the explosive aerials only gave off light for a moment. She asked if anyone had seen Phillip leave, but no one had. They had all been watching the fireworks.

BOOM! Another went off and this time Anna, annoyed, decided she needed to look for him. This was the last night they were going to be able to see each other in person. She had planned on spending the rest of the evening with him and maybe giving him a proper goodbye this time. She got back in her wheelchair and headed to the only logical place she could think of—the bathrooms.

Fireworks lit up the concrete walkway as she made her way towards the lodge house and the bathrooms. She looked around towards the office, but, of course, no one was there. Then she went to the men's room and timidly called his name but no one answered. She was too chicken to go all the way in.

Worry gnawing at her, she was about to turn around when she remembered the smoking-area bench Marge and Hank had set up at the far end of the lodge house. She rolled to that side of the building and there in the dark sat Phillip.

He had his head in his hands, rubbing his face. She wheeled up to him and touched him on his shoulder. He jumped a few inches off his seat and held his hand to his heart until he could breathe properly again.

"I'm sorry I startled you," she said, laying her hand on his arm again. This time she noticed that he was drenched in sweat like he'd been running a mile. "I got worried when I couldn't find you."

"That's nice of you," he said, his labored breathing stuttering his words. "I'm fine."

"You don't look fine, and you don't sound fine."

"Sometimes loud sounds get to me. I just need a second to—"

"Is there something I can do?" she said, trying to hold his hand.

"Just—give me a minute," he said impatiently.

Anna flinched and pulled her hand back. She locked her brakes and stayed near him. She didn't try to talk to him or touch him. She wasn't sure what to do, but she didn't want to leave him like this. He breathed in and out in a steady rhythm and said between breaths, "The bench. The dirt. My shoes. The evening breeze. The sound of fireworks. Anna." His breathing slowed and he leaned back against the building for a long while. He then looked over at her in the darkness.

"Come here," he said, sounding tired. "Please."

She unlocked her brakes and positioned herself in front of him. He grabbed onto the frame and pulled her so that she sat facing him, parked between his legs. He took her hands in his, trembling a bit.

"I'm sorry," he said softly.

"There's nothing to apologize for, Phillip," she said, rubbing the top of his hand with her thumbs.

"Yes, there is," he said. "I shouldn't have used that tone with you." He paused. "I need you to understand something. It's easy to get messed up when you're overseas. You're seeing and experiencing all this stuff that the average person will never see. You face down death every day between the IEDs and being shot at. I caught a lucky break, and somehow I survived.

"When Scott died, it was like a hole had been torn out of my chest. I was so mad at him for being so stupid. He shouldn't have gone out again. I knew he wasn't in a good headspace. He went anyway, and he got himself killed. I was in Afghanistan at the time so there was nothing I could do, not even go to his funeral.

"You can't imagine the guilt. I'm alive and he's dead. Was there something I could have done or said? He was my brother. He would have listened to me, but I wasn't there for him."

Tears dripped from Anna's eyes.

"And you know what the worst thing of all is?" he said, his voice cracking. "I'm still alive to live my life. I watched guys in my unit being blown to bits but I'm the one going home. What about the guy who just found out two days ago that he's a father for the first time? Or the guy whose kid is going to be first in his family to graduate from college? What about those guys? What do they get? Their families get a couple of guys knocking on their door. A folded flag. Why me and not them? They had more at home waiting for them.

"What do I have? The house my parents left me. A couple of old people with a dead son. A crappy job, in a crappy area, and no one waiting for me. And everyone expects me to move on with my life. What life?"

Anna hugged him. She held him as tightly as she could. And he hugged back as if he'd fall apart if he let go.

"I'm sorry," he said. "I sound pathetic." He let go of her, and seemed to draw into himself, distancing himself from her.

Anna couldn't let him believe any of it. He had too many good things about him for him to be thinking like that. And the ache she felt for him propelled her forward. She reached out and pulled his face towards her. She pressed her lips against his, savoring how soft and warm they were, just as she'd imagined. His lips were eager and urgent, deepening the kiss as she wrapped her arms around his neck. He closed any gap between them by grabbing onto her hips and pulling her against him. The blood in her veins sung with a tingling fire releasing any inhibition in the moment.

Anna kissed him harder and deeper, her hands running up the back of his neck and fingers tangling themselves in his hair. She wished so much to take the pain from him, alleviate the loneliness. His hands slid across her back, wrapping his arms around her, holding her tighter against him still. That simple touch brought all the longing she'd tried to deny herself. The longing to be close to someone, to connect on a deep and intimate level. Her heart pounded in her ears and through her chest making her feel faint. She pulled away to breathe.

Phillip pulled her all the way onto his lap, draping her legs over his, holding them secure against him with his hand. She wrapped an arm around his back and tucked her face in his neck. His pulse there galloped at a frenetic pace, perfectly matched in time to hers. She knew this was a goodbye and she didn't want the moment to end. She laid her head on his shoulder.

"I wish you could stay," he said, using his fingers to bring her chin up and kiss her softly.

"Me, too, but I can't," she said, when she reluctantly pulled away again.

"Promise me you'll stay in touch," he said.

"It shouldn't be too hard with all this technology around."

"Technology can't kiss like you do," he said.

 Anna laughed.

"Thank you," she said. "I'll take that compliment. I've been out of practice for a few years."

"No one privileged enough to kiss you would find you wanting," he said. He leaned down and kissed her again. She brought her hand up to hold onto his neck, pulling herself as close as she could get. Her heart ached. There were only a few short hours left before her family would leave.

Only days ago, leaving Sweetwater wasn't something she'd have given no thought to. Just another stop in the Ultimate Mackey Family Vacation. But it mattered now. She was leaving Phillip behind. She wished so deeply as he kissed her that somehow it could work itself out.

Chapter Eleven

The family decided to skip Yosemite, given the extra time they'd spent at Sweetwater. Anna slept away most of the drive down to Anaheim on purpose to make it easier not to think of Phillip. She couldn't shake the feeling she had made the wrong choice and yet there was no other choice to make. The further they got from Sweetwater and from Phillip, the easier it was to think without the raging attraction she felt for him. She started to question her sanity. Phillip was a man she had known for just over seventy-two hours. Who does that? Who falls in love after seventy-two hours? But her heart told her it had happened somehow.

Phillip had been there in the morning they left—to say goodbye to everyone, he said. But the soonest moment he could, he grabbed her hand and pulled her back over to the bench they'd been at the night before. Once there, Phillip stood over Anna, took her face in his hands and kissed her. Her hands clutched his shirt as his lips glided over hers. Her heart ached as she felt the warmth from his hands and face, smelled the masculine scent of him, and got lost in the touch of his mouth against hers.

"I would be out there in a minute," he said, resting his forehead against hers.

"I know," she said, touching his face with her hand. "I can't ask you to do that."

"Anna, those plans I made, that I told you about yesterday—I'm doing it. I'm going back to school. I've already applied," he said, sitting down on the bench, and pulling her into him as he did the night before. "I'm going to prove to you that your faith in me is well founded."

Phillip wrapped his arms around her waist when she sat between the v in his legs.

"I'm glad that you are and I believe you'll do really well. This isn't about that," Anna said, resting her hands on his chest. His arms around her waist were tipping her forward. Not that she minded too much except for the weird angle of her back. She wanted to touch him as much as possible before it wasn't possible anymore. She liked the feeling of his arms around her and being close to him. "This is about us. I want us to make sure we don't do something rash, something one of us might regret later. We need to make sure that what we have is right for both of us."

"And I agree with you. I, too, want to see if this"—he pointed between them—"goes anywhere. "And since we can't be together, for now, I'm willing to do the long-distance thing, if you are."

"I'm willing. I hate it, and I don't want to be stuck dating on the internet, but, for now, nothing makes more sense. Stay here and get your degree. It'll be cheaper here because you're a resident."

"I'm going to prove to you that I'm serious about doing whatever it takes to be the man you and the kids deserve. I'll get my degree, and then we can make solid decisions after that."

She leaned her head forward and rested her head on his chest. She closed her eyes and listened to his heartbeat as his hands slid up her back, smoothing the cloth down. He brought her head up and kissed her slowly and softly.

"It's going to tear me up for you to leave," he said, tucking a piece of hair behind her ear.

She nodded her head, not trusting to use her voice to say the same thing. All she could do was wrap her arms around his neck and hug him.

And then the Mackeys left.

No matter how broken she felt, she owed it to her family and her kids to make the most of this trip. She was determined to enjoy the rest of the vacation. Then after she got back, she'd get ready for the new school year, and try not to think about Phillip too much. Thinking about him, and what might be, was scary, confusing, and depressing. She needed to clear her head. It didn't help that she checked her phone every few minutes to see if he had sent a message.

Art and Ellen, if they had any opinion about Phillip, kept it to themselves. But Ophelia felt no such reserve in making her opinion known about the situation. She cornered Anna the night before they went to Disneyland.

"Now, I'm just going to say this, and then I'm not saying anymore," Ophelia said.

"I'm not holding you to that because I know you won't be able to resist," Anna said, smirking.

"I think you did the right thing," Ophelia said.

Anna sat there with her mouth open wide for a full minute. "Not what I expected from you."

"Seeing you and Phil together was hot," she said, smiling at her sister. "I would really, really, really love to see you with a new hunky hubby giving me more nieces and nephews for me to love on."

"Thank you," Anna said. "But?"

"Anna, I love you so much. It's hard to see you keeping yourself lonely. Not really trying. And then Phillip came and suddenly I realized that you should have hope to find love again. I'd love it if it was Phil but that may not be realistic.'"

"Really?" Anna said.

"Yes," Ophelia said, "Think about it like this. Phil showed you that it is possible to find someone who loves you, wheelchair and all. I don't want to see you close yourself off again."

"If I close myself off again it's because Phillip and I didn't work out and I was tired of trying," Anna said, shaking her head.

"But why? Phil's great, but he's not the only guy out there. Give him a chance but don't give up on finding love for yourself if it doesn't work out. You have so many good things about you. You'd be a great partner to someone who's just as capable at giving you all the things that Darren should have." Ophelia sat down on the bed next to Anna.

"I know, Phee," Anna said, putting her head on her sister's shoulder. "I just can't wrap my head around the unfairness of it all. First, Darren leaves me. I have no choice but to leave Phillip behind. I want so much to believe that everything will work out. But part of me says I'm just setting myself up for heartbreak, that I'm getting my hopes up for something that will ultimately never happen."

"It would be amazing if it worked out. Phil seems like a really cool guy," Ophelia said. "But my point is, if he doesn't, I want you to try with someone else. You don't have to spend the rest of your life alone. I want you to be happy, sis. When you're happy, I'm happy."

The sisters sat in silence for a long time. Anna loved that her sister wanted her to be happy, so she would never admit to Ophelia that being alone was much more appealing than dealing with uncertainty. Uncertainty meant heartbreak. Being alone meant confidence--confidence that things would work out the best way they could. There wouldn't be any wild cards skewing plans, derailing the order in her life.

"Do you think I'm doing the right thing by encouraging him to contact me?"

"How am I supposed to know? I can't even get my own love life straightened out," Ophelia said. "My MO would be to moon over him on the internet and texts, and then Facebook stalk him until something hits me over the head making it painfully obvious that it's over."

"I wish I knew what decisions I could have made to make the situation hurt less. Half of me is tempted to run back there and pick him up and take him with us," Anna said.

"Now there's an idea!" Ophelia said, laughing.

"But on the other hand, those shows you see on Discovery ID keep popping up in my head. The lonely widow finds a guy that treats her like a princess until he steals all her money and kills her when she finds out. Maybe I did myself a favor."

"Okay, stop!" Ophelia said. "Right now. You're just making it ugly."

"What else can I do?" Anna sighed. "Pretend that something so outrageous could actually work? I've almost convinced myself it would just be better for all parties involved if I just cut him off. For both our hearts' sakes."

"You realize how mean and selfish that sounds, right?"

"What?" Anna said, surprised.

"You cutting him off with no other word from you," Ophelia said, actually becoming upset as she spoke. "Not giving him the courtesy of explaining. Or giving up on a chance at happiness just because you don't know how everything's going to turn out. He deserves better than that."

"Hey," Anna said, rubbing her sister's arm. "Settle down. I didn't say I would do it, but it would make the situation easier to deal with."

"For you maybe," Ophelia said.

It *would* make the situation easier to not have to deal with it at all. But as tempting as that sounded, Anna couldn't quite bring herself to actually implement it. There was something inside her that had changed when she looked at Phillip. For the first time in a long time, she felt hope for the future. He lit a fire in her that had burned down to embers for a long time. No one else had done that in the four years since Darren had passed away, and she liked the way it felt.

"Why couldn't he just be the nice security guard at the Shop-mart who helped me get back in my chair and then I never had to see again? Why did he have to be so charming, helpful, gorgeous, and one hell of a kisser?"

Ophelia laughed despite being upset, and Anna, for all her wallowing, joined her.

"I know this will sound silly but I believe that love is the only universal constant. If it's true love then things have a way of working themselves out."

"You're such a romantic, Phee, and I love that about you. But you know what Shakespeare says," Anna said. "'The course of true love never did run smooth.'"

Chapter Twelve

The fall afternoon was crisp and cool. It was perfect weather for Halloween. Anna pulled her van up in front of her parent's house. She opened the side door and Brody and Zoe spilled out, running for the front door. They had rung the doorbell before Anna could get in her wheelchair.

"Trick or treat!" Zoe screamed.

"What adorable children!" Ophelia-witch said as she opened the door. She had ratted her short blonde hair and dyed dark crimson streaks through it. She wore an Elvira-style dress and held a large plastic cauldron full of candy. "I think you guys look good enough to eat!"

"No, we have to go trick or treating first!" Zoe said, jumping up and down.

"Hey!" Ophelia said, hand on her hip, looking at Anna. "Where's your costume?"

"Can't you guess?" Anna said. "I'm a frumpy school teacher who wears an orange spider turtle neck with mom jeans."

"Cheater!" Ophelia said.

Anna shrugged her shoulders and made her way into the house. Ellen was at the stove putting the finishing touches on her chili and cornbread.

"Hi, Mom," Anna said.

"There you are!" Ellen said. "I was afraid you wouldn't make it before dark."

"You know what it's like getting two excited kids ready," Anna said, giving her mother a tired grin. "Add having to keep distracted teenagers on task and, well, it took a little longer than I thought."

"I remember getting the two excited little ones ready," Ellen said. "Your dad's been in the bathroom for the last half hour getting ready himself."

"Anything I can help with?" Anna asked, rolling over to unwrap the Halloween-themed bowls and spoons for dinner.

"I vant to suck your blood!" Art came out doing a terrible Transylvanian accent. He looked like a skinny, old Bella Lugosi. He swept down and gave his oldest daughter a hug. "Are those grandkids ready for some trick-or-treating?"

"Yes, they're out front with Phee," Anna said, laughing. She loved her dad's silly sense of humor. "Waiting for you."

"Arthur, before you leave, make sure I get a picture," Ellen said, as her husband exited the kitchen. "That man. He loves Halloween." She said it with a shake of her head, but she was smiling nonetheless.

Zoe came running into the kitchen and hugged her grandmother.

"Gramma, look at me!" Zoe said. She twirled her pink skirt around.

"Oh, my goodness! You're the loveliest princess I have ever seen!"

"And Gramma, Mom let me wear eye shadow and lipstick," Zoe said.

"The loveliest in the land, my dear," Art said, taking Zoe's hand and leading her to the dining area.

"Ugh," Brody said. "Does she always have to do that?"

"Yes," Anna said. "She does. She's a girl. She likes to be pretty."

"She likes to be annoying," Brody said.

"What are you supposed to be?" Ellen asked Brody.

"I'm Captain Switchblade," Brody said as he bent over and pulled two toy daggers out of his chunky costume boots. He flung his head back to get the multi-colored dreadlocks out of his face and brandished the blades for his grandmother in a dramatic pose.

"Uh, very nice, dear," Ellen said. "Did you make him up on your own?"

"No, he's the coolest character on Beyond Duty," he said.

"Well, you look extremely intimidating," Ellen said.

Brody grinned as he straightened up. "When are we eating? I'm starving!"

"What's Beyond Duty?" Ellen asked when Brody joined his sister and grandfather in the dining room.

"One of his online games," Anna said. "His current favorite."

Anna smiled when her mother gave her an amused but unimpressed smile.

Chili was served, cornbread eaten, picture taken and then Ophelia and Art took the kids out, leaving Ellen and Anna to watch the door.

"How's school?" Ellen said.

"It's fine," Anna said. "Kids are great as usual. Plus, over the summer we lost a few teachers that were causing drama."

"That must have been nice," she said.

"It makes the faculty room quieter, that's for sure," Anna said. She looked out the window and watched as a dad dressed as Sully from Monsters Inc. followed behind his toddler daughter who was dressed as Boo. Anna moved closer.

"Awww, isn't that the sweetest thing?" Anna said, pointing it out to her mom.

"That is adorable," Ellen said. "I miss Zoe being that age."

"Me, too," Anna said, watching the pair as they made their way down the street. "But most likely my two are all I'm going to get so I should just be glad I had it when I did."

"You think so?" Ellen asked. "You don't think there's a future for something else?"

Anna shook her head. "I don't have time for all that. I'm not so lonely I can't bear it and I've heard too many stories about those dating sites to even look at them. Brody and Zoe are my priority as their mother."

"As your mother, my heart aches when I see you raising those kids alone," Ellen said. Anna looked over at her and gave her a sad smile. "You deserve something more."

"Thanks," was all Anna was able to say. For her, it wasn't a matter of deserving. It was a matter of someone being as amazing as Darren. The only one that had come even close to that had been Phillip when she was in California that summer.

"I still think of our vacation to California, and that Phillip at Sweetwater," Ellen said.

The fact that her mother had seemingly plucked the idea out of her head took her completely by surprise. Her chest constricted.

"I wish circumstances had been different," Ellen continued. "How long has it been since you heard from him?"

"It's been a long time," Anna said, keeping her focus on the window. The image of their first kiss rushed to her mind making a flush spread through her. It hurt more than she thought it would. "Two years since his last email. He's just a memory now. A nice memory." She gave her mother a slight smile. "But nothing came of it."

Ellen rubbed her daughter's knee. "One day, something will."

"Knowing me, I'll be too busy to see it," Anna said. "It'd literally have to smack me across the head to get my attention."

Ellen laughed. "You may want to cross your fingers and knock on some wood, then, because the universe has a way of giving you exactly what you ask for."

"That'll be the day," Anna said, smiling. "Maybe I should start asking for a million dollars and a brand new van."

"Guess it couldn't hurt," Ellen said.

Soon the kids were back from trick-or-treating and Art took over candy duty. The women gathered in the kitchen while Brody and Zoe were busy bartering candy.

"So when are you bringing this latest boyfriend of yours around, Phee?" Anna asked.

"When I'm sure I want you to meet him," she said.

"That sounds . . . suspicious," Anna said.

"Only because guys my age end up being losers and it's so much easier to just not go through the bother of bringing them over," Ophelia said. Her cheeks colored a little and she refused to look at Anna. Anna's eyes narrowed at her sister.

"Uh-huh. There's a surefire way to ensure a boyfriend is one you should bring over," Anna said.

"What?"

"Stop dating losers."

"Like that's so easy."

"I guess I shouldn't talk," Anna said. "I haven't been on a real date in . . ." She blushed.

"You girls make it sound like it's hard," Ellen said. "Falling in love with the right person is easy. It's only hard when you give your heart to the wrong person. When I met your dad, it was like a lightning bolt. Didn't hurt that he happened to be in his dress uniform."

"We know—you danced all night long, and then he asked if he could write to you while he was away," Ophelia said.

"Yes," Ellen said. "I said yes without hesitation. I knew I was going to be with him. He was it. The 'one.'"

"You were so trusting, Mom," Ophelia said.

"Only because he never gave me a reason not to be," she said.

Anna leaned her elbows on the table. Phillip had never given her a reason not to trust him. He'd never said or done anything that would have given her pause. She couldn't find one reason in the year they'd corresponded to not like him, not trust him, or not want more. He was like her mother described. Everything had been easy with Phillip. He was easy to talk to, easy to listen to his baritone voice over the line, easy to trust him with her and her son's life that day three years ago. It should have been easy to trust him with her heart. It wasn't, and she had made sure not to give him the chance to break it or run away with it.

"Gramma, look what I got," an excited, pink princess said as she pulled her grandmother towards the haul she'd brought home.

Ophelia came up to Anna and sat down next to her.

"Things must have been different in her day," Ophelia said. "You can't trust that you'll find a guy you can automatically trust. They just don't exist."

"Phillip did," Anna said. It was more of a thought in her head that happened to be spoken aloud before she decided to say it. But her conversation with her mother had her going over the last few years—and the guilt she still carried.

"Yeah, well, Phillip was . . . lovely. Wait, have you heard from him lately?"

"No, Mom and I were just talking about him."

"Oh," Ophelia said. "I guess I hoped there for a second."

Anna smiled at her sister. "Thanks. I haven't heard from him in about two years. Not since right before he was graduating from University of California—Merced. I wonder what he's up to."

"Maybe you could contact him and find out?"

"Phee, would you want to hear from an ex again after two years?"

"I don't know," Ophelia said. "I guess that depends on the reasons."

Anna sighed. Did she really want to let Ophelia know the real reason? The reason that had her crying into her pillow every night until the urgent and somewhat frantic requests to speak to him stopped coming? No, because Ophelia had already made her opinion on the subject quite clear all those years ago.

"Doesn't matter," Anna said. "There are times when I honestly think that Phillip was just a made-up figment of my imagination. Like I idealize him, or think him the perfect man because it sounds nice that someone like that would be interested in me. And then I think I already had that with Darren. He really did love me and showed me every day how much."

"You didn't have a chance to find out if Phillip could have done the same for you."

"How much did I really know about him? How could I trust that he was genuine? You can get to know a person only so much over the phone and text."

Ophelia rolled her eyes. "Anna, I love you so much but you are such dork. Anyone with eyes could see how he looked at you. With you being hot and all, there've been plenty of other guys who have checked you out. Don't shake your head at me—I've noticed, even if you didn't. You've just never noticed until Phillip.

"I know you don't want to, but, if you'd actually listen to me, I would say contact him again. You never know what will happen. The worst he could do is not reply back at all. Then you'd have your answer."

Ophelia's answer made sense somewhat. It was a reasonable suggestion, but it was still one Anna didn't plan on taking. Most of Anna's reasons for cutting Phillip off were still valid to her. She clung to them desperately for justification; they were the driftwood in the whirling maelstrom of her emotions. She couldn't ask him to completely turn his world upside down, couldn't take him away from the only people that were still family to him, nor expect him to abandon everything he knew just for her.

Besides, did he really understand what he would have given all of that up for? For the chance to take on responsibilities that he'd never had to consider? A crippled woman and her two kids. That was a lot for a man—one who'd never been a husband or a father—to shoulder, no matter how much he felt up to the task. He didn't have a frame of reference for the kind of burden that would be.

"I'll think about it," Anna said, giving her sister a small smile.

"Which means no," Ophelia said, grimacing.

"No, it means I'll consider it."

Ophelia shook her head at Anna but smiled anyway. Brody and Zoe had started arguing over the candy trading. Time for the night to end—along with conversations about a certain Special Forces lieutenant.

She hauled her candy-stuffed kids back into her van and drove them home. As she tucked them in, she prayed she didn't have to preside over a worship session at the porcelain god later on. Her dad was a wonderful grandfather but he was pretty indulgent with them too. She was afraid of how much candy he had really let them eat.

She closed the door to her room and got into bed. She pulled out her phone. One of her students had recommended a new YA series. But when she accidentally hit her Gallery button, she found herself scrolling through pictures of that vacation from three years ago. She swiped as she saw her and her sister's smiling faces in Las Vegas. There was a group photo at the Grand Canyon. The obligatory Mackey picture of everyone riding the Teacups at Disneyland and the line to get a pizza. Brody standing next to Flynn Rider with his big purple shiner and his head still swathed in bandages where stitches hid underneath.

The next swipe was a picture that one of her kids must have taken before they left Sweetwater. She hadn't looked through these since they were taken and she was shocked to find that the picture was of her talking to her father and Phillip. She brought the screen closer, then zoomed in. There he was. Not that she'd forgotten what he looked like, but seeing a picture of him brought back a flood of feelings. He looked down at her, intent on what they had been saying. She touched his face on the screen, remembering. He really had been as beautiful as she saw in her head. Taller, though. She closed her eyes and felt those lips on hers. She locked her phone and threw it on her nightstand. She turned over on her side and lay there with the light on. She worried that if she turned the light off now, her dreams would be full of Phillip. Regret was the last feeling she wanted to wake up to in the morning.

Chapter Thirteen

Anna sat at her desk staring bleary-eyed at the stack of test papers that needed grading. No matter how many Diet Cokes she drank, she couldn't seem to concentrate. The electronic tone sounded above, warning her that her first-period class would soon begin. Students with a similar look to hers filed into the room. She appreciated that she wasn't the only one struggling this morning.

The TV screen in her classroom lit up and the students making the morning announcements filled the screen.

"Good morning, Bangerter High! Today's lunch options are—" Anna tuned out the rest. Most of it was announcements for clubs, concerts, and games that she really didn't participate in. Halfway through grading the first paper on the stack, Anna heard, "Last period today is our Veteran's Day assembly. A few members of our community who have been in the Armed Forces have come to talk about their experiences in the military. Let's give them our best Bangerter Boost to make them feel welcome!"

Anna had forgotten there was an assembly. She would never tell her students, but she enjoyed most of the assemblies as much as they did. It broke up the day, especially mid-semester. Anna contemplated her current situation. She didn't necessarily want to go to this one. Other things seemed a bigger priority especially with mid-term and parent-teacher conferences coming up.

The day flew by quicker than she expected considering how restless she felt. The last-period students gathered in her classroom, and they left as a group for the gym. Kids liked being in her class when they had assemblies because they always got to sit in the cushy chairs on the gym floor instead of being jammed on the hard bleachers in the back. She inspected the rows her students were on, giving the fidgety ones the eye.

"Don't make me take the cell phones away, guys," she said. "Put them on silent."

"Mrs. Gilbert, can I go to the bathroom?" a skinny kid named Greg asked.

"You can hold it," she said. "We're almost ready to—"

The band's drumline marched out thumping a beat and the students started clapping and shouting the school fight song as the principal and a line of guests entered from the hallway. Greg stepped over people on his row to get to her, pleading with his eyes. She turned to tell him again to hold it. He had a tendency to use bathroom breaks as an excuse to wander the halls. Out of the corner of her eye, she saw a tall man with brown hair and broad shoulders enter the gym towards the back of the line. Her throat constricted and the air pressure seemed to fade in and out. There, standing at the front of the gym, was Phillip. She must have made a quick movement because in the next second his eyes locked onto hers. The color drained from his face.

"Mrs. Gilbert, I really need to go bad," Greg whined.

"Fine, go, but be quick," she said to Greg without losing eye contact with Phillip. She examined every inch of him. He was just as she remembered. His beard was gone, though, which only brought out his eyes. His handsome face twitched between shock and the ghost of a smile. He was dressed in his blue Special Forces uniform with his beret and looked just as fit and lean as he had three years before. He still reduced her heart to a fluttering mess, she noticed. She was tempted to wave a little to him, but then the guilt hit.

She had been such a coward. The confusion of her emotions about Phillip, about Darren and about her future sent her into a panic the closer Phillip's graduation date got. It was exhausting and, rather than give him a jumbled explanation or admit that she was pretty sure she was in love with him but scared to death of him at the same time, she just stopped everything--the calls, the texts, the emails. Just everything.

But it didn't solve anything like she'd hoped it would. She cried every time she received messages from him, each more frantic than the last, for her to contact him. She told herself that she was protecting him from the inevitable heartache, hoping he would get his degree, find a job, and move on with his life.

Seeing him standing there staring at her made it quite apparent to her that, if nothing else, she had failed miserably to move on from him.

They called his name and he went up to the microphone. He cleared his throat, shaken.

"Hello. My name is Phillip Laughlin. I'm a retired lieutenant in the Army Special Forces. You might know us better by our nickname, the Green Berets. I've seen combat in Iraq and Afghanistan. And now I work up at the VA hospital by the University of Utah providing therapy services and support for soldiers with battle injuries and substance abuse problems."

A general murmur of approval washed over the gym, particularly among the male population of the school. Her hands smoothed down her pencil skirt and the white blouse she had worn that day, praying she didn't look like a frumpy schoolmarm. Phillip continued on with his speech but she heard almost none of it. His voice awakened the longing she had struggled to quell. She could not look away from him, examining in detail every line of this face, his brown eyes, his half-grin as he talked. He, however, did not look at her once during his turn. At the end of his speech, he sat down again and only then did he look over at her briefly before turning away. It ripped her heart out.

Soon enough the assembly was over. She might have tried to say hello to him but he was immediately mobbed by students that wanted to ask him questions and so she quietly took her kids back to her classroom.

The assembly had taken up most of the period, so now it was a matter of waiting for the release bell to ring. She let the kids chat amongst themselves. Her heart still beat like wild horses ran, completely out of control. She sat at her desk pretending she was grading papers when all she really wanted to do was put her head down on her desk and cry. The bell rang and the students hurried out of the building. She gathered her papers to stuff in her backpack, then the phone on her desk rang.

"Anna," the principal's secretary was on the line. "Would you come by the office for a moment? You've got a visitor."

For the second time that day, she felt like she was going to faint. It had to be Phillip. She didn't want to seem too eager to get down to the school office, but she was out the door of her classroom and heading down to the office almost before she'd hung the phone up all the way. Her mind wandered back to Sweetwater, and the frustration and disappointment in his face as they drove away, the feel of his arms around her and his lips against her mouth, and the easy way it had been between them. If he had someone call her down to the office, he obviously wanted to see her again. But what would she say to him? "Sorry, Phillip, I didn't think it would work out. Guess I should have said something." She shook her head.

Fear and excitement tormented her in equal measure. What was he doing in Utah? The last she'd talked to him he'd been preparing to graduate from the University of California Merced. And if he did move to Utah, why didn't he try to get a hold of her? She knew the answer to that—because she'd ditched him all those months before. Why would he try and get a hold of a woman who'd made it perfectly clear she didn't want to talk to him anymore? Then that begged the question, was he married now? Or dating someone? As much as that thought made her sick, she couldn't blame him for moving on with his life like she had wanted him to.

Despite the fear of hearing firsthand that he had moved on from her, she wanted to see him. She needed to find out why he was at her school and if he was disappointed and angry still. One thing she was sure of, Phillip had rocked her world. Without knowing it, he represented the possibility of a future entirely different than the one she had come to expect after Darren died. A future she had barely dared to hope for after her heart had been broken into a million pieces that long-ago winter day.

As soon as she rounded the hall corner, she saw Phillip standing there chatting with the principal's secretary. When Anna opened the door, he looked over at her. In a heartbeat, he was sweeping her up into a hug. They both laughed.

"You know, Mr. Jordan's not going to need his office for a little while. Why don't you go in there and say hello for a minute?" the secretary said, a sly look on her face.

Phillip put her gently back into her wheelchair and, grabbing her hand, pulled her into the office. The second the door was shut he pulled her wheelchair to face him and hugged her again. This time there was nothing she could do to keep the tears escaping the sides of her eyes.

"What are you doing here?" Anna asked. He reached up and wiped the moisture from her cheeks with his thumb.

"Do you know Rob Bishop?" he asked.

"Yes, he's our special education coordinator," she said.

"Rob and I got to be good friends up at the U of U. When he heard that your school was doing a Veteran's Day assembly, he asked me if I wanted to come to talk to the kids." His face turned serious. "I swear, I had no idea this was the school you taught at."

"It's okay," she said. "I'm just so glad to see you. It's been a long time." She wiped an invisible speck of his uniform jacket and looked him up and down. "You look good."

"You are a sight for sore eyes, that is for sure," he said. He looked deeply into her eyes. The tension in the room suddenly increased and she found herself wanting to kiss him, badly. Just the thought of his lips on hers sent shivers down her spine. He chuckled, maybe with a little nervous edge to it? "I know you can't stick around. Can we catch up? Over dinner?"

"Yes," she said. "I would love that. May I have your cell phone?" She put her name and phone number in his cell phone and handed it back. "So you can text me."

"When?"

"The sooner the better."

His face lit up and he wrapped his big arms around her again. She melted into him. She turned her head slightly on his shoulder. She couldn't resist feeling the warmth of his neck against her face, and breathing in the earthy and spice combination of his natural smell mixed with his aftershave. She could have stayed there forever in his arms but she was suddenly overwhelmed with the desire to kiss him. Would he want her to? And even if she dared, would she really want to be caught kissing a man in her boss's office? Before she could really think about what she was doing, she kissed his cheek, too nervous and chicken to go for his lips. He blinked for a minute and then a smile spread across his face.

Reluctantly, he stood up, holding her hands in his large ones. "I'm going to hold you to that."

Chapter Fourteen

I'll meet you at 6.

She looked at the text again to make sure it was for real.

Brody had his shoes on the couch, so she had to switch back to mom mode.

"Brody, feet," she said.

He flung his feet off the couch, sighing harshly. She looked at her son. The teen was strong with this one. He was only twelve but he acted like he was sixteen, and his attitude was getting worse by the day.

"Mom, Zoe's old enough to take care of herself. Why do I have to stick around?" he said, not taking his eyes from his cell phone.

"Because she is not old enough to stay at home alone," she said.

"Why do you have to go anywhere tonight anyway?" he scowled.

"Because—I have some shocking news for you—your mom is an adult, and sometimes she likes to hang out with other adults."

"Boring."

"Exactly, which is why I'm going, and you're not."

"No, it's boring because I have to stay here and take care of someone who can already take care of herself."

Anna shook her head. "I'm not going to argue with you about this. I'll have my cell phone with me and I don't imagine I'll be any later than ten p.m. It is still a school night, so get to bed on time." She kissed her son on his forehead—a kiss which he promptly scrubbed away with his hand. "No friends over."

Anna hurried out the door and got into her van, afraid if she paused at all she'd lose her nerve. Just the thought of being in close proximity to Phillip made her pulse race. The fact that he'd hardly changed since they'd last seen each other didn't help keep her pulse in check either. She remembered back to that kiss on the Fourth of July, where more fireworks were going off than the ones in the sky. She'd drowned in those soft lips that night.

She made her way downtown. Luckily, she made it in one piece so soon after rush hour and the light dusting of snow made driving tricky. Luck was with her again when she found a parking spot under the Joseph Smith Memorial Building. She wouldn't have to deal with scraping off the snow when it was time to go home.

She sat in front of the parking garage's elevators, hesitating for a minute. She rubbed her hands together. She'd been surprised when Phillip had suggested The Garden, the restaurant that she and Darren had come to on their second date. It was strange that she even thought of that. It had been so long since she'd had a constant monologue of "I did this with Darren" or "Darren and I went here." Now she was going to be here with Phillip. She felt equal parts anticipation and nerves. What would they say to each other? What could she say to him if he asked why she had stopped communicating with him? She knew the shivers she felt were not entirely from the cold. She pushed the button.

She rolled into the luxurious and warm colors of the lobby with its imposing columns and the huge crystal chandelier. She looked around as she tried taking her coat off. She struggled to get an arm out when she felt someone grab her jacket from behind and help lift it off. Phillip smiled down on her. He put her coat over one arm, took her hand with the other, and guided her back towards the elevators. She had missed that smile so much.

"Your hands are like ice," he said, grabbing them and rubbing them between his as the elevator took them to the tenth floor. "Don't you believe in wearing gloves in this Antarctic climate?"

"Gloves are slippy," she said. "And they fall apart. If they don't, I usually lose one anyway."

He laughed that deep-bellied laugh, making her smile back at him and her insides quiver. It felt good to hold his hand again.

The rest of the ride was silent. She didn't know what to say, and when she looked at him, she wasn't sure he did either. With the initial excitement of the moment gone yesterday, only reality was left. There were too many questions floating around in her head. There were too many sins to confess to. She hoped she didn't lose her nerve to say what she needed to say before dinner was over.

They were seated next to the floor-to-ceiling windows that looked out over Temple Square. Full darkness blanketed the sky. The temple's lights glowed softly in the snow, like a castle out of a fairy-tale. It was beautiful. Once the waiter had taken their order, Phillip reached over and took Anna's hand again.

"I have so much to say, I'm not sure where to start," he said, smiling shyly.

"I know what you mean," she said, rubbing his warm hand with her thumb. "I have to know how you ended up in Utah," she said.

"That's an easy one. After I finished at UCM, I was looking for a school to do my graduate work. The U of U accepted my application and I liked that the VA hospital was located on campus, or well, close enough to. I almost didn't take it. I knew you lived in the area and after everything . . ." He paused. "I didn't want you to think I was stalking you or something. But, I figured it was a big enough city, so we'd probably never bump into each other." They both grinned at that. "I graduated and because I'd been working with the VA before I graduated, they offered me a permanent position after I became fully licensed."

"Phillip, that is amazing," she said, squeezing his hand. "I'm so proud of you. I knew counseling would be a perfect fit for you, but I'm overwhelmingly happy that it led you to Utah."

He smiled at her, his brown eyes giving her a soft look that took her breath away.

Their server came to get their order. The break in the discussion was somewhat of a relief. Phillip's mere presence had her heart skipping beats, but when he held her hand the heat of it went straight up into her arm and settled in her belly. This influx of feeling was overwhelming to Anna. These feelings she'd tried so hard to repress since they'd left Sweetwater came at her like a tsunami. Phillip was really here. He was sitting next to her, holding her hand and gazing at her in the same way he had before. It was like time had skipped the intervening years and nothing had changed.

"You said yesterday that you specialize in substance abuse?" she asked, once the server left. There was so much she wanted to know about him and she picked the safest topics. She needed to work up to the one she needed answered most of all.

"That's one of the things I do," he said. "I do pretty much any type of mental health counseling, and help the guys get services they need."

"That sounds busy. And rewarding."

"Yeah, it does keep me busy. I like what I do." The smile on his face showed her how much that was true.

"How are Hank and Marge?" she asked.

"They're off on their yearly vacation to Barbados, and enjoying all the warm tropical sun," he said.

"That does sound nice right about now," she said, looking out the window at the snow softly falling.

"How about your family?" he said. "How are your kids? Your parents? Crazy Ophelia?"

"My parents are good. Ophelia has a good job at a bakery downtown. And my kids are good, too. There's really not much to say. We're just living life."

"How's my buddy, Brody?"

Anna frowned. "Being a teenager."

"Wait, how old is he now?"

"Twelve, he'll be thirteen in the spring," she said.

"Wow. They grow up so fast. That or I'm getting old. I probably wouldn't recognize him anymore. What about Zoe? How old is she now?"

"She's just turned nine."

Phillip shook his head from side to side. "Unbelievable."

The server returned and placed Anna's dinner in front of her. She took a deep breath.

Eat. Take a bite before you can't take any, she thought to herself. It was hard to swallow past the lump in her throat.

After taking a couple of bites of his own dinner, he looked up at her, a playful glint in his eye. "So, I'm assuming, since you're out with me tonight, that you don't have a significant other right now?"

Anna's lips ticked up. "No. I don't."

The relief was apparent on his face.

"What about you?" Anna said with a full-on grin now. "Do you have a little missus waiting for you at home?"

"Goodness no," he said. "It's hard to want to date anyone else when a certain someone has set a particularly high standard to compare against."

Anna's heart leapt and she couldn't keep the stupid grin off her face. "I know what you mean."

"And teaching?" he said, taking a bite of his dinner. "Still teaching English?"

"Yes," Anna said. "Different year, same shenanigans."

"I don't know how many grades of mine you saved with your help on some of my early papers," he said.

The conversation lulled. As they ate, her curiosity mixed with her fear of his answers had her feeling almost ill. She couldn't resist any longer. She just opened her mouth and spoke. She couldn't think of any gentler or less awkward way to ask for what she needed to know.

"Anna, I—"

"Phillip—"

"Sorry, you first," he said.

"Phillip, I . . . I missed you," Anna said, covering her cheeks with her hands. "I know I don't have any right to say that. But I did. I want to say I'm sorry, especially if I hurt you."

"Why did you cut me off?" Phillip said. "You never did say. I thought it was because you'd started seeing someone else."

She swallowed back tears that threatened to pool in her eyes. She wanted Phillip but she had to be one-hundred percent honest with him. He had to know the kind of person she was.

"I cut you off because I'm a coward. A coward that didn't have the courtesy to give you an explanation," Anna said, looking at her shaking hands that were now in her lap. "I don't deal with maybes and somedays very well. I didn't trust it would work out. I wasn't like you. You told me we would be together and I didn't believe you. You deserved better than that. Than me. I thought the only way to help you move on was to just go cold turkey."

He sat back, looking incredulous. "You didn't think I would have liked some input on that decision?" he asked.

"I knew you would. I didn't want you to talk me out of it."

He sat silent for a moment. The look on his face killed her. It was a dark mix of anger, confusion and hurt. "I'm sorry, Anna, I still don't understand."

Anna looked at him pleading. "I had myself convinced we were only fooling ourselves. Everything about what we had--it was too good to be true. Real is what I had with Darren. He was in front of my face from the moment we met. I could touch him and feel him close to me; that's not what you and I had, so I couldn't trust it. And as the months went by, everything just seemed to get more and more unlikely. Like we were trying to make up something because it was something we both wanted so badly we were deluding ourselves into thinking it would work. I didn't want that for you or me. I thought if I wasn't a constant distraction, it would be easier for you to move on."

Phillip leaned forward so he was looking directly into her face. Almost close enough she could just bend forward a little and kiss his lips. "I didn't want to move on, Anna. I wanted you. I was willing to wait so things could work out the best they could, not just for me or you but for your kids, too.

"Do you understand what it did to me to have you suddenly stop? I spent night after night wondering what I did wrong that made you stop talking to me. You were so convinced it wasn't going to work, you didn't even give it a chance." He took a deep breath. "Did you move on?"

"From you?" Anna blushed, laughing a bitter laugh. "No, I couldn't. How's that for hypocrisy? I regretted you every time I thought of you. I almost emailed you a hundred times, but I stopped myself. I thought too much time had passed, and that there was no way you could forgive me. Then it seemed pointless because I figured you had probably found someone else."

He shook his head, then looked off to another part of the room. He seemed to be taking in what she had said. Now that he understood what had happened, she steeled herself. She wouldn't blame him if he kindly thanked her for dinner and left her at the table. Looking back on what she had done, it was selfish. She assumed she knew what was best for the both of them and didn't even bring him into the decision. She never would have done that to Darren. She and Darren talked about everything together. They may not have always agreed on what was best, but she never left him out of the loop. She could just see in her mind's eye the look of disappointment on Darren's face if he'd known what she had done to Phillip.

She cast furtive glances at Phillip as he thought. When he finally looked at her again, she held her breath.

"What about now? What do you want now?" he said. He looked hard at her, twisting his napkin in his hands.

Anna was afraid to speak. Could she ask him for a second chance? His brown eyes bored into hers as he waited for her answer. She felt her insides melt under their gaze.

"I do want a second chance, Phillip," she said, almost too softly for him to hear. She trembled, waiting for him to answer. She wanted him to want her. She wanted to finally get the chance to know who the real Phillip was, to explore whatever possibilities existed between them, to spend time with him, laugh with him, be there for him, or sit and do nothing with him. She just hoped he'd be able to forgive her enough to try again.

Phillip's face relaxed into something that looked like gratification. He set his napkin down and moved his chair closer to her. He took her hand and entwined her fingers in his. "You don't know how relieved I am to hear you say that. Can I ask you one thing?" She nodded. "Can you please trust this? Trust these feelings I know we both feel. We don't have to rush to do anything. Let's just get to know each other and see where that takes us." He lifted her hand to his mouth and kissed it softly. "Nothing would make me happier than to try again with you." He leaned over and kissed her softly on the lips. His touch sent waves of warmth through her.

She could barely contain her joy. Her cheek muscles were sore because her smile was so big. Phillip seemed to forgive her and still wanted her. How does that even happen? All the things she hadn't dared hope for after Darren died were sitting right next to her, holding her hand, and telling her there was a chance for happiness.

"Let me take you to your car," he said, gathering their things and paying the ticket.

When they got to her van, he helped her in and put her wheelchair away for her. Then he reopened her door, put hands on both sides of her face, and pulled her toward him in a kiss. This was no peck on the mouth. It was intense and deep. She braced herself by encircling his neck with both arms, holding him captive, losing herself in his kiss.

"I've been wanting to do that since I saw you in the gym."

Anna giggled. "I thought you hated me. You wouldn't even look at me during your presentation."

He laughed his full, bounding laugh. "No, I definitely did not hate you. More like holding myself back from crawling over those kids to get to you."

Neither one moved. Neither one really wanted to.

"When can I see you again?" he asked.

"Can we agree on the weekends?" she said, smiling. "You're too much of a distraction for me to handle when I'm trying to teach."

"Fine. Saturday then? And what about this—bowling with the kids?"

Anna hesitated. Brody definitely remembered Phillip. He had the purple heart medal still hanging on his wall. She wasn't sure Zoe did. And now that she and Phillip were finally heading in the direction of "something more," was it time to re-introduce them? She wasn't sure.

"Maybe not yet," she said. Phillip tipped his head to the side. "Can it just be us for a little while?"

"Am I going to be a secret?" he asked.

"No," Anna said. "I want us to be together for a while. I want to be confident that we're solid as a couple."

Phillip thought about it for a moment. "Okay. I trust that you know what's best for them. But I will say this—if everything goes the way I hope it does, we'll be a family someday. I want you to know that I take that responsibility very seriously. Both for your sake and theirs."

Anna smiled. She reached over and kissed him quickly. "This is the happiest I've been in a long time."

"You and me both," he said as he shut her door, then waved as she drove away.

Chapter Fifteen

Anna's head swirled and her body shook with emotion she could barely contain as she drove home—happiness, abject terror, hope, excitement, dread. He was all and more than she remembered or hoped for. Almost perfect in every respect, as if she had crafted the perfect man in her head and he suddenly appeared right in front of her. She had to talk about it. She whipped out her cell phone and dialed Ophelia's number.

"You realize that I have to be at the bakery at four a.m., right?" Ophelia said by way of answering the call.

"I . . . Phee," Anna found herself stuttering.

"Anna, are you okay?" Ophelia said, sounding concerned.

"No, Phee, the most wonderful thing happened," Anna said, tears leaked from her eyes. "Phillip."

"What?!" Ophelia practically shouted into the phone. "What do you mean, 'Phillip?'"

"I went out with him!" Anna said.

"Wait, I'm so confused," Ophelia said. "How is that even possible? We're talking about Phil from California, right?"

"Yes," Anna said. She told Ophelia about the last couple of days.

"Wow," Ophelia said. "Like major wow. Like trippy wow. Like, this is so amazing! I have no words, sis! Have you told Mom?"

"No, I haven't. I needed to talk to you first," Anna said.

"Awww, I love you too," Ophelia said. "Okay, so are you going out again?"

"Yes, on Saturday afternoon," Anna said.

"He's not wasting any time, is he?" Ophelia said. "Not that I blame him, you are quite the little disabled snack."

"Phee, what am I doing?" Anna said. "Am I insane? Am I doing the right thing?"

"Whoa, there, babe. Take a big, deep breath," Ophelia said. "I'm stealing your big sister card for a second. Get out of your head and let me tell you something. You are doing exactly what you should be doing. You are chasing after happiness. Phillip is going to make you very happy."

"Really?" Anna said, trying to swallow the lump in her throat.

"Yes," Ophelia said. "All you have to do is let him."

"Why are you so sure?" Anna said. "And weren't you the one telling me after we left Sweetwater that I was doing the right thing then?"

"Yes, remember I said only if it didn't work out with Phil. I liked the guy. He was cool," she said. "And I saw the way he looked at you. If you were anywhere in his line of vision, he wasn't looking at anything else. I'm willing to bet that hasn't changed much. Now you have a chance, so take it! Chase real happiness this time!"

Anna laugh-sobbed. "What would I do without you?"

"Probably shrivel up and die," Ophelia said. "Go, be free, be happy, don't let that hunk of a man out of your sight again, or we really will have words. Love you. I really need to go to bed."

"Love you too," Anna said. She wiped some of the tears away from her face. While she wasn't entirely sure she deserved happiness, she thought she knew what Ophelia was trying to say. Phillip represented the possibility of happiness. She hadn't been happy, unguardedly happy, in so long she barely remembered what it felt like. It scared her to death. Being happy in this case meant that her happiness was in large part because of someone else. And the last time she had given over to happiness that completely, she had lost it. Darren took it with him. She had found contentment, acceptance, but not happiness. Her children were her saving grace during those dark months. They were the only things that kept her from succumbing to depression entirely. And she put all her energy and love into them as much for her sake as for theirs. Now there was a twinkling light above the mists of contentment and it mystified and excited her.

I need to trust this, she thought to herself. *I refuse to believe our crossing paths again is coincidental. If he's serious about being in it for the long haul, that should be enough. Darren is gone. He would want me to be happy. He would want someone good helping to raise his children. Right?*

The rest of the week had an uneven feel to it, with stretches of boredom and excitement. And unfortunately, that just made her job harder. After years of teaching them, she knew teenagers were more intuitive than some adults gave them credit for, and, sensing her restlessness, every single period of her classes picked up on that energy. It became a monumental task to get them to focus, participate, and just behave themselves in general. So, when she got a text from Phillip asking her to meet him at the museum that Saturday, she looked forward to that day with mounting enthusiasm. A tour of an art museum seemed like a perfect way to spend an afternoon with an extremely good-looking former Green Beret.

"You're here!" Anna said as she rolled up to the Utah Museum of Fine Art.

"I thought this would be a perfect place for our second date, ," Phillip said.

"I agree," she said. "I love looking at art."

"I can't take total credit for the idea," Phillip said. "A guy I know at work, Justin, suggested it to me."

"Let's see what they have," she said, as she took his hand. He led her inside.

They had been there for a while when she came upon a picture titled "Lunch Time." The scene made her smile. The little boy and girl in the picture reminded her of Brody and Zoe.

"What have you found?" Phillip asked, coming up behind her. "Salmson, Lunch Time. That looks a lot like Brody and Zoe, doesn't it?"

"I know, right?" she said. "I was just thinking the same thing."

"Have you told them yet?" he asked.

"No," she said.

He nodded.

"I thought about what you said. There's no reason to keep it from them, really," she said, looking up at him. "I think the only thing holding me back is the what if? Zoe, I'm sure, will love you immediately. It's Brody I worry about. He's a funny kid and doesn't take to change very well. What if we decide ultimately it's not working? Will they have to deal with the loss of yet another person they care about?"

"I understand," Phillip said. "Too many people suddenly in and out is not good for them."

"I'm glad you understand," Anna said.

"Of course," Phillip said. He sat down on a nearby bench. She rolled her wheelchair over to sit next to him. He reached out and held her hand. "There is something I wanted to ask you."

"Okay," she said, giving him her full attention.

"I'm probably overthinking this. The other day, when I said we felt something for each other—I feel like I may have projected the way I was feeling onto you. I didn't even ask you how you felt, or give you time to think about an honest answer."

"You have graduated with a degree in psychology, haven't you?" Anna said, smiling. "You have nothing to worry about. My feelings for you . . . well, you coming into my life is probably the best thing that's happened to me in a long time."

He beamed. "Okay, good," he said. "I just want us to always be open and honest with each other. Good communication is key in a relationship. I want us to always be comfortable talking about anything. Even the hard stuff."

She nodded. "I think that's a fantastic plan," she said, positioning herself closer to him.

He leaned in to give her a small kiss. She sighed, happy.

"In the spirit of communicating my feelings, I have to be honest about something. This weekend-dates-only thing is going to make the week go by slowly," he said, tucking a piece of hair behind her ear, letting his finger slowly trace the path on her face.

"I think you'll be surprised," she said, a shiver going up her spine. "If what you say is true, then you've got appointments coming out your ears. There will be plenty to distract you."

"I don't really want to be distracted," he said, kissing the side of her face. "Except by you."

"What did I do to deserve you?"

"I could ask the same thing. Maybe Marge is right. She told me a funny story after you left. I had gone over to talk to them about you, to get some advice. She said you had found her little art collection in the lodge house, and she told you about the legend of Sweetwater."

"She did," Anna said. "It was a sweet little story."

"She was so convinced that the spirit of Sweetwater had blessed us that she was devastated when I told her you had stopped contacting me."

"Oh, no!" Anna said. "That makes me sad. I had no idea she felt so strongly about us."

"Oh, yes. She adored your family. She kept saying for a long time after that you've been one of their nicest families to have stayed at Sweetwater," he said. "Thing is, she told me before I moved out here that Sweetwater wasn't done with us yet. I didn't believe her, of course. How could I? But sitting here with you, it occurs to me that maybe Marge wasn't as up in the night as I thought."

"One way or another, I guess we'll find out."

He smiled at her. "Yes, we will. Ready for some lunch?"

She wrapped her arms around him. "Honestly, I am starving."

He chuckled. "Good. I've got the perfect spot."

The Thai restaurant Phillip had brought them to was cheerily busy during its lunch hour. The aroma of spices lingered in the air and Anna breathed it in. Her hand felt warm in Phillip's. The smile had not left her face since he had come into view at the museum. She felt a thrill in her stomach that was both fear and excitement together. She looked up at him and when he looked down at her, she felt warmth spread through her. They could be cleaning up garbage along I-15 and it would be pleasant. All she had to do was be with him.

"Have you ever had Thai food before?" he asked as they were led to their table.

"No," she said. The waitress put long menus in front of both of them and Anna perused the choices. "This menu is huge."

"It's pretty typical to order a few dishes and share them. It'll be a good way to introduce you to several dishes at once. We're definitely going to be bringing home leftovers."

Anna nodded. "I think the only thing that sounds familiar is the yellow curry. It sounds similar to Indian food."

"Okay, let's start with that then," he said. "And I'll get spring rolls, pad thai, and some chicken satay for you to try."

"You're going to have to roll me out of her like Violet Beauregard," Anna said.

"Probably, but you'll roll away happy," Phillip said. The waitress arrived with their water and Phillip gave her his order.

"Can you answer a question for me?" she asked.

"Sure," he said.

"I know you're close with Marge and Hank. Wasn't it hard leaving them behind in California?"

"It was a little, yeah. They'd been so good to me since I'd gotten out of the Army and then afterward when you stopped—well, they were very concerned about both of us. Why do you ask?"

"I was thinking about it after you told me you moved to Utah," she said. "You each were a surrogate for the other; as a mother, I can't imagine what it will be like when I have to say goodbye to my children as they leave to live their own lives. I think it will tear my heart out and make me proud at the same time."

"They have each other," he said. "And I know that they love me and are supporting me. The distance doesn't change that."

The server arrived with their dishes and laid them out in front of them. She watched him eat his lunch and felt her heart swell, reflecting that if it hadn't been for Marge and Hank, he would be entirely alone in the world. Such a sad thing because he had so much to give. He gave so much working at the VA hospital, working with vets in a way someone who wasn't a vet couldn't understand.

He looked up and noticed her watching him. His eyes crinkled as he tried to smile and finish the noodle he'd been eating. They both giggled as he got the noodle down but got sauce all over his chin. She reached over with her napkin and wiped away some of the mess.

"Sometimes I wonder how I haven't scared you off."

"What?" Anna said. "Why would you say that?"

"Oh, all the baggage I've unloaded on you since we met," he said. "I imagine some women would go running for the hills."

"Look, we all have baggage. Some of us more than most. And I can't fault you for your baggage when I've got a trainload myself," Anna said. "Besides, I'm not just any woman."

"I know it," he said. "So, you're not afraid of the adventure I'd take you on?"

"Since day one, that's what it's felt like, Mr. Laughlin."

"And here I thought I was a boring guy."

"No, boring is definitely not the word I would use to describe you."

"Oh?" he said, smiling as he took a sip of water. "Now I'm curious. How would you describe me?"

"Thoughtful. Conscientious, maybe. Dare I say, disarming?"

"Disarming? You mean charming?"

"No, I meant disarming," Anna said. "The first time we met was probably the most awkward and uncomfortable situation imaginable for me. I was so helpless. I'm not used to feeling like that. I've always been very independent, so not being able to help myself was very scary. But you had this way about you—a sweetness and a humor that didn't put me entirely at ease, but at least kept me from wanting to bite your head off."

"I'm glad you decided not to bite my head off," he said. "But honestly, I would have never guessed that's how you were feeling. You seemed so calm and collected at the time."

"I guess I'm a good bluffer," Anna said. "I don't show that side of me very often to people outside my little circle."

"I understand," Phillip said.

"Oh, you'll come to understand," Anna said, putting her napkin away. "Spend any length of time with me and you'll see why I'm so intent on doing it myself. Plus, I'm incredibly stubborn."

Phillip smirked. "I figured that one out a long time ago. Doesn't that one come standard in the redhead's bag of tricks?"

"No," Anna said. "Flash-fire tempers do. You just get a bonus because it's me."

Chapter Sixteen

Anna drove down the freeway letting her mind wander. Having no kids in the car afforded her that luxury. Both Brody and Zoe had begged to play at a friend's house so she had the entire afternoon to herself. She attempted Christmas shopping but nothing the kids had asked for in their Santa letters had been at a reasonable enough price for her to consider it. Frustrated, she drove towards her parents' home for some hot chocolate and talk.

A little stab of guilt hit her gut when she thought about her mom. Phillip and Anna had gone on a few dates already but she hadn't told her parents about it yet. Something held her back. The whole thing felt like a wonderful dream she feared waking from. She certainly didn't want her parents getting their hopes up. Or maybe it was she who didn't want to get her hopes up. Everything had been going too perfectly. She kept waiting for the other shoe to fall so she could snap out of this wonderfully happy phase and come back down to reality. When she finally got to her parents' house, she had worked herself up into a frenzy of nervous emotions.

After greeting her mom, Anna sat at the kitchen table and shuffled through the ads from the newspaper. Her mother excelled at economizing everything, having been a wife of an active-duty soldier for so many years. Anna knew she could count on her to find the best deals at Christmas, but the circulars were barely able to hold her attention.

"I hate Christmas," Anna grumbled, looking at the papers in front of her. Her mother placed the steaming cup of chocolate in front of her.

"No, you don't," Ellen said.

"You're right, I don't," Anna said, sighing. "But it seems like the same amount of money has to cover the kids' increasingly expensive tastes. Especially Brody. At least Santa's going to be good to me this year." She meant to say that under her breath but Anna couldn't help the little smile that spread across her face.

"Okay, what's going on?" Ellen said. "You look like a bear caught with a honey pot."

Talking about Phillip out loud at all made her stomach do flips. "So, Santa may have brought my Christmas present early this year."

"Oh?"

The blush crept up Anna's cheeks. "We had a Veteran's Day assembly at the school. There was this handsome Army Special Forces soldier that spoke to the kids, and well, it turned out to be . . . Phillip."

"Phillip from California?"

"Yes."

Ellen's hand flew to her mouth. "How is that even possible?"

"He completed his degree at University of Utah last year. Now he works at the VA Hospital."

"Prayers can be answered," Ellen said. "So how is Phillip?"

Ellen looked a little too pleased with herself for asking.

"He's fine," Anna said. "He's been out of town actually. He went to spend Thanksgiving with Marge and Hank. We've gone out a few times, but this is his busy time of year. He's so tired that we don't do much else besides text in the evenings before bed."

"I'm glad you're so understanding," Ellen said.

"Not much else I can be," Anna said. "He works so hard. It's quite admirable how dedicated he is to helping other vets."

"Do you think he'd join us for Christmas if we invited him?"

"I think if I asked him, he might," Anna said, smiling.

"I'd love for him to come for dinner at the very least," Ellen said.

Anna paused, looking thoughtfully at her mother. "Mom, can I ask you a question?"

"Sure, honey," she said.

"Do you think I should reintroduce Phillip to the kids?"

"You haven't already?"

"No," Anna said. "I thought if things don't work out then I wouldn't have to explain to them why he's gone again."

"Understandable," Ellen said. "But I wonder if you should reunite them sooner rather than later. It would be good to see how he and the kids are around each other."

"You don't think it could be a problem?"

"No. It's a taste of what's to come if you both decide to make things more official," Ellen said with a little smirk on her face. "And it's not just about how the kids would react to him, but him to them. He's never been a father. I think it would be good to see how he is around the kids. Parenting can be so rewarding, but you know how hard it can be. He's going to go from a single man to a husband and father when he marries you."

"Mom, I love you, but let's not get ahead of ourselves," Anna said, shaking her head.

"It's a lot of responsibility, honey," Ellen said.

"I know you're right," Anna said, "I just don't want to make it seem like I'm making him prove anything. That's not fair to him."

"Don't wait too long," Ellen said. "Now that you're together again, I'm willing to bet, things will move pretty fast."

"Maybe. We've agreed to take it slow for now and get to know each other really well before anything further takes place. And I have to admit, he's everything I imagined he'd be."

"That's wonderful to hear," Ellen said. "Don't be shy about bringing him around here at some point. I'm sure your father would love to see him again."

Anna realized her mother could be right. And she also realized that as much as she wanted to take things slowly, the feeling of things not moving fast enough underlined all the time they'd spent together so far.

"What time is it?" Anna asked. "I better get going. I told Phee that I'd come to have lunch with her at the bakery."

"One more thing," Ellen said. "I want you to know how happy I am for you. Your dad and I loved Phillip. I honestly think it's only a matter of time before he's family."

"We haven't really started talking about marriage yet, so rein your hopes in a little."

As Anna went out the door, the last thing she saw was her mother's knowing grin.

"And so I told Mike that crullers would be the perfect donut for Christmas because they already look like fancy wreaths, and with some green glaze and a few silver sugar pearls dropped over the top, I mean, seriously, perfect!" said Ophelia. Anna took a sip of her soup.

"That's an adorable idea," Anna said.

"Thanks, I thought so, too," Ophelia said. She lowered her voice. "It's just some people's egos here are the size of Australia, and if it's not their idea then they don't want to hear it."

The door opened and the sisters saw Phillip come in. Anna felt her heart soar. "You're back!"

"Phil!" said Ophelia. She stood up and rushed to give him a hug. "I didn't know you were coming. It's so good to see you again!"

"I sent him the address, in case he was able to make it," Anna said, grabbing his hand as he gave her a quick peck on her cheek.

"I meant to be here earlier but you know how the airport is around the holidays. The freeways are a nightmare," Phillip said.

"I'm just glad you could make it, period," Anna said.

"So, how's everything, you two?" Ophelia asked.

Phil grinned at Anna and winked. "Fine," Anna said. "We're going to the lights at Temple Square tonight since Phillip has never been."

"What?" Ophelia said. "How long have you lived in Utah and never went to see them?"

Phillip shrugged. "I was busy and I never had a reason to go. Until now." He smiled at Anna.

"Do you want to go, Phee?" Anna asked.

"With you two? No thanks. Nothing worse than being a third wheel."

"I could take care of that," Phillip said.

Ophelia narrowed her eyes at Phillip. "No."

"What?" Phillip said. "I have a perfect guy in mind."

"No."

"His name is Justin. He's a Physician's Assistant up at the VA clinic and a really nice guy."

"I don't like the military type," Ophelia said.

"Well, that's good because he's never been in the military."

Ophelia rolled her eyes. "Phil, no means no."

"All right. You're missing out," he said.

"I think I'll survive it," Ophelia said. "I need to get back to work. Phil, would you like something for lunch?"

"Sure, I'll take a Reuben."

"Coming right up!"

"Can't blame me for trying," Phillip said as he turned to Anna.

"I don't, and I'm glad. She really needs a different pool of potential interests."

"Can't force it though," Phillip said. "Even if Justin would be a thousand times better. Is she still dating that married guy, Mike? At least Justin can say he's single."

"I'm not sure," Anna said. "She seems to be in Mike-hate mode right now so I don't think so."

"Oh, well," he said.

"How are Marge and Hank doing?" Anna asked.

"They are doing wonderfully. Got back from their vacation just in time for Thanksgiving so they were all tanned and glowing."

Anna giggled. "I'm so glad they had a good time. Seems like they work so hard all summer long."

"They do, but I don't think they'd have it any other way," Phillip said. "Now how is everyone in your world?"

"The kids are fine—asking for the most expensive gifts on the planet," she said. "And my mom and dad are doing well. I actually just came from my parents'. I told my mom about you."

"You just barely told her about us?"

"Yes. I didn't know how to say it before, but I realized I was being silly. My mom is pleased as punch that you're back in the picture. I'm sure my dad would feel the same way."

"That's good to hear," Phillip said. "I liked your parents as well."

"What are your Christmas plans?" Anna asked.

"Wow, I can't believe I forgot about this," Phillip said. "Back in September, some school acquaintances and I booked a fishing trip up in Alaska. I'm so sorry. With everything that's been going on, I completely forgot to mention it."

"Hey, it's okay," Anna said. "You didn't know that we'd reconnect. I'll miss you like crazy but maybe it's for the best. Will you be back for New Years?"

"Yes, so let me make it up to you then," Phillip said, kissing Anna.

"Okay, break it up you two," Ophelia said. She put Phillip's sandwich down. "Will you be joining us for Christmas?"

"No, I had a trip planned before I knew I'd rather be here for the holidays."

"Too bad. Definitely next year, right?"

"Oh, definitely next year," Phillip said, giving Anna a soft look.

Anna heard a knock on her door and found Phillip standing outside, hands behind his back. She invited him in and once inside he handed her a rectangular present. "For you."

"Oh, you didn't have to do that," Anna said, smiling and taking the present. "I haven't wrapped your Christmas present yet."

"It's okay," he said. "I wanted you to have this one tonight."

Anna pulled the wrapping paper off and started to laugh. It was a pair of driving gloves.

"Now your hands won't freeze," he said.

"Thank you," she said. "This is great."

She pulled them out of the box and tried them on. They fit perfectly. The fingers and palm were padded to make pushing her chair easier. Once she got her jacket on, they headed out for Salt Lake City.

The trees wrapped in lights twinkled in the freezing winter air. Phillip pushed Anna through the plaza as they looked at all the trees decked out in their Christmas finery. As they wandered past the Nativity, she saw little families—moms and dads with their little children bundled up in warm coats, hats, and mittens.

She smiled remembering how Darren and she would bring Zoe and Brody here at Christmas time. Darren had loved doing stuff like this, even before the kids. It's probably why she found this event terribly romantic. Darren used to say that it was because the cold was an excuse to stand really, really close to the person you were with. Phillip leaned on the handlebars of her wheelchair allowing him to tower over her. She got the double benefit of his body heat to keep her warm and a nice cloud of Phillip's cologne to breathe in as they wandered.

She looked over and watched some of the other couples walking past. They looked like she felt. She caught the eye of one of the couples as they walked by and she gave them a small smile. But instead of smiling back, they stared at her as if they'd never seen a woman in a wheelchair before. She sighed and tried not to roll her eyes.

"I love this," she said. "We used to come every year and bring the kids."

"This is spectacularly beautiful. I'm glad you brought me," Phillip said. "That white one up by the gate is awesome. It's so huge." He stopped at a giant elm wrapped in thousands of pink lights. "It must have taken forever to wrap these trees like this. Which tree is your favorite?"

He sat down on one of the large granite planter boxes and drew Anna as close as he could. She looked around for a tree that was decked out in her favorite color. Phillip leaned over and kissed the side of her mouth. Anna smiled, about to scold him for distracting her when she noticed an older couple standing nearby. The woman wore a look of sheer disgust. At first, Anna thought she might be looking at someone behind them. She turned her head to peek out of the corner of her eye. There wasn't anyone behind them. The couple had moved on but a sick feeling settled into her stomach. She looked up at Phillip's face.

"So, which one was it?" he asked.

"That one over there," she said, pointing to a large maple strung out in green lights. "It's my favorite color. Reminds me of emeralds."

"You like emeralds?" Phillip asked, and she nodded. "I can see why. They highlight the green in your eyes."

"Phillip, can I ask you a question?" Anna said.

"Sure."

"Why me?"

"Why you?" he said, looking a bit confused. "Does there have to be a specific answer?"

"No, but out of the thousands of single women out there, you're choosing me."

"You say it like . . . Hmm, what's the real question here? There's got to be one or you wouldn't be asking this question out of left field."

Anna's hands fidgeted, and she flinched before she said, "Why choose a disabled lady with kids?"

"You're disabled?" he asked, feigning shock. She punched him and he grinned. "Honestly, love, it never really crosses my mind. Or at least in the places that are important. I love all of you, and I really mean that."

"Thank you," Anna said. "I hate to be insecure but people are going to act weird around us. They may even say things that aren't quite offensive but definitely not nice. And it will be directed at you as much as at me. But the thing is, I'm used to it. I may not like it but I know when to ignore it and when to stand up for myself. I wish I could shield you from it. It was a fact of my life when I was in school, Darren had to put up with it, and if you keep dating me, you'll have to deal with it, too."

"If?" he said, raising an eyebrow. "First, disabuse yourself of the notion that I care a fig about the wheelchair or your disability right now because it doesn't and it won't matter to me. I only see you, and not some metal contraption with wheels. I'm only glad you finally decided to take a chance on me.

"Second, I never have and never will care what people say about me, so they will never have the power to change my opinion of you. But I will never allow people to be cruel to you—not within my earshot."

"I won't make the mistake of underestimating you again," she said, snuggling up to him.

"Better not," he said, smiling. "Gorgeous red-heads in wheelchairs are amazingly hard to find."

Christmas day dawned. As soon as they finished opening their presents, Anna and the kids headed to Ellen and Art's house for a second round. Anna sat back on her parents' couch and enjoyed watching her family open presents. Still, she found herself looking out the window at the snowy backyard. She wished a certain soldier was sitting next to her, enjoying the day with everyone. He sent a picture the day before of him and his buddies posing for a group selfie dressed in their thick sweaters and fishing waders. She hoped he had found the present she had tucked in his duffel bag. Just as she thought it, her phone beeped. Phillip's handsome face brightly smiled as he wore the black and gray trapper earflap hat with faux fur lining and the caption "I found your present. Merry Christmas, beautiful!"

Art approached Anna holding a large gift.

"I was tasked with making sure this present got delivered," he said, handing Anna the package.

Anna looked at the tag. "I only see you—and I love all of you. Love, Phillip." Anna smiled. She opened the box. Inside was a leather-bound, gold-embossed copy of the book The Princess Bride. On top of that was a director's cut copy of the movie. Anna gasped. He remembered. The book was beautiful. She carefully leafed through the heavy cotton print pages and admired the pencil illustrations spread throughout. She held the book to her heart, vowing to give him a deep and passionate thank-you once he got back from his trip.

Chapter Seventeen

Spring in Utah was notorious for being unpredictable. The warm front sitting over the valley had the temperatures reaching into the mid-seventies for the past few days, which made it perfect for concert-going.

Anna held up the light blue cardigan. The cardigan would go well with her spaghetti-strap tank top and jeans. She placed the cardi in her lap and inspected herself in her bathroom mirror.

For being in her mid-thirties, she still looked young. The blessing of the Irish, her mother would say. She put her chin to her shoulder. There was a light sprinkle of freckles on her otherwise creamy white skin. Phillip made her realize how much she missed being desired. When he looked at her with those chocolate brown eyes, she saw the question behind them. She quivered inside with all the possibilities that the question suggested.

Darren had been the only man she'd ever been with and that fact alone made the idea of intimacy with Phillip both exciting and intimidating. Sometimes when she kissed or touched Phillip, the lines blurred a bit and it was Darren's lips she kissed or his hand running down her back. It was an instant buzzkill. Desire warred with guilt. Feeling guilty felt stupid sometimes because she knew in her head Darren would be happy for her. He'd been gone for seven years now, but her stupid brain wouldn't let go. Would Phillip suspect she was comparing him to Darren without meaning to? Especially now when she was losing the desire to put on the brakes physically with Phillip.

Her cell phone rang. She smiled. "Hi."

"Good evening, beautiful," he said. "Nearly ready?"

"Yup, I'm ready," she said. "Come over whenever."

She ended the call and moved to the front room. She draped the cardigan over the arm of her couch and waited. Despite her doubts and fears, every time she heard his voice on the phone or in person, the fears left for a while. His voice comforted her nearly as much as being held in his arms. And it was in those moments when she felt all the doubts were totally unfounded. She reminded herself on more than one occasion that being intimate with Phillip to that extent would be easy. Once a person got to a certain level of passion there wasn't much to consider besides how fast the clothes could come off. She wanted Phillip like that, but she was afraid of disappointing him. Would he be satisfied with the way she looked, or her ability to please him? She hoped so.

Ophelia had volunteered to babysit for her while she and Phillip went to this concert. Ophelia and Phillip had conspired a month ago to give her the best Valentine's Day present that Anna could think of—tickets to see Muse in concert. He'd gotten a very long and enthusiastic kiss for that. They were one of her favorite bands, and she couldn't think of anything better than leaning into Phillip all night listening to "Undisclosed Desires" and "Starlight."

When the doorbell rang, she opened the door and found him with a mischievous look on his face. He held up a single white rose with a red velvet ribbon tied around it. It was so cheesy it was adorable, and she couldn't help but giggle as she turned around to put the rose in a vase.

"Are we leaving right away?" he asked, looking around.

"The kids aren't here," she said. "If that's what you're worried about."

"Good, then they won't be here to see me do this," he said, as he came up to her. With her face in his hands, he kissed her deeply. If her toes could, they would've been curling. The touch of his soft lips made her shiver.

"I'm glad you're here," she said, going over to the couch and patting a cushion. "Want to take a second to get caught up? The parking lot's going to be a nightmare and it'll be hard to hear with all those people."

Phillip sat down next to Anna. He held up her cardigan. "This is nice. Are you wearing this?"

Anna nodded, but she wasn't thinking of the cardigan. She moved up next to him as closely as possible. The rush of adrenaline from his kiss raced through her veins. She wanted more. Her face was nearly on his when he looked at her in amused surprise. She threw her arms around his neck and kissed him deeply. He chuckled but matched the intensity of her kiss. He pulled her onto his lap and wrapped his arms tightly around her.

She couldn't get enough of the tingles his touch excited everywhere in her. Time always seemed to pause as she moved her lips along his and tasted his mouth. Her heart beat erratically as his lips made their way down to her neck. He lingered on the place where her pulse pounded through her skin, making her gasp as electricity sizzled right up to her brain. She sighed as his mouth slid down to her collarbone, marking each half-inch with small kisses. His touch was so hot it was hard to stop, especially when he would look up at her, fire in his eyes and a pleased grin. She rested her forehead against his, trying to slow her breathing down. He reached up and kissed the end of her nose, then went to kiss her mouth. The small gesture wrenched a ragged gasp, jerking her as if the wind had been knocked out of her. She closed her eyes and covered her face with her hands.

"I'm so sorry, Phillip," she said, trying not to cry in her embarrassment.

"Are you okay?" he asked, concerned. He grabbed her hands and pulled them down. His finger turned her chin so she was forced to look at him.

"I—" she coughed. She bit her lip as the tears started to flow out of her eyes. "The kiss on the nose is something Darren used to do. It took me by surprise. I don't mean to be a tease. And I try really hard to make this only about us."

"I'll be honest, Anna. I want you—badly," he said, wiping some of the tears off her face. He let out a long breath. "But I won't do anything you don't want to. I want you to be ready for that. If you're not yet, that's okay."

"I feel bad for starting it."

Phillip grinned. "I'll take it as a good sign that you instigate it sometimes. I might get worried if I was the only one."

"I do want to be with you, Phillip," Anna said. "Sometimes, I feel so ready. But then . . . I don't know what's wrong with me."

"Really. It's okay," he said, giving her a soft kiss and hugging her to him. "You're worth the wait." He said it so sincerely she nearly started crying again. "I believe we have a concert to get to."

"Yes, we should get going," she said, trying to shake off the intense lingering desire she felt for him. "I should warn you. The lead singer, Matt Bellamy, had my heart long before I met you."

Phillip laughed before picking her up and putting her in her wheelchair. He held out her cardigan for her. As he helped her into his truck, she mentally kicked herself. What was she doing? What she was doing was totally unfair to Phillip, that was for sure. It was like a part of her brain shut off when he walked into the room and all she could do was think about the things they could do together—alone. But then when it came right down to it, she lost her nerve or her brain reminded her of Darren. She didn't mean to, and she wished there was a better way she could explain this to Phillip. It was her own issue, and the problem was definitely not him.

Anna predicted correctly that the traffic was a nightmare. The streets outside the amphitheater were worse than the parking lot itself. Only by some miracle were they able to find a disabled-parking spot.

Once settled in her chair, Phillip took her hand to lead her into the concert venue. It became clear pretty quickly that it was easier to get through the crowd if he pushed her wheelchair. She pointed over to an empty spot in one of the wheelchair sections that looked to have a seat spot open. The crowds milled and swirled around like a river of people. She felt Phillip's grip on the back of her wheelchair tighten, his stress level increasing.

"Excuse me," Phillip said loudly. A knot of people was standing around waiting to get down the stairs. His request ignored, Anna could practically feel his teeth gritting. "Really, come on, we're trying to get through."

Anna reached up and tapped the person in front of her on the back of their arm. "Pardon me, can you move over just a bit so we can get through?" The person looked down at her and then before they could fully turn around, she caught them rolling their eyes. They did, however, move a little to the side as well as guide the person they were with to do the same, giving Anna and Phillip just enough room to get by.

By the time they got to the wheelchair section, a woman had her huge beach bag set up on the bench's edge, effectively blocking anyone from sitting there.

"Hi," Anna said, trying to put on a genuine-looking smile. "My date and I would like to sit next to each other. Is there any way you could move your bag so he can sit down?"

The woman looked at each of them. She hesitated for just a moment and then sighed. "Sure, sugar. There should be plenty of room for all of us. My husband's running late and we didn't want to have to sit on the lawn. I didn't realize this was the handicap section."

"It's okay," Anna said.

She turned to Phillip. He looked miserable. She grabbed his hand and rubbed it with her other hand. "You doing okay?"

"Fine," he said, looking around. His eyes darted around to several places, seemingly at once. "I can't believe how crowded it is."

"This was probably a bad idea," Anna said. His hand had a clamminess to it, much like the night on Fourth of July when she'd found him during the fireworks.

"No, no," Phillip said as if coming out of a trance. "Seriously, I'm fine. Let's stay and enjoy the concert. I know you've been waiting to see these guys. It's fine."

"If you're sure," she said softly into his ear, resting her chin on his shoulder. "I don't mind leaving if you're not feeling it."

He turned his head. "No. Let's stay and see how much competition I have in this Matthew guy."

He put his arm around her waist and pulled himself as close as he could get without falling off the bench. Sitting this close to him, she felt every muscle in his body stiff with anxiety. She tried distracting him by telling him about her week but he barely seemed to be paying attention as he scanned the crowds and the entrances. She was about to tell him a funny thing that happened in the faculty room when a man squeezed himself between Phillip and the woman with the bag. The opening act ran onto the stage and started their set.

"Good Lord, Bethany, I told you to make sure there was some room here," the man said, with enough volume to be heard by everyone in a six-yard radius.

"I had to move the bag," she hissed back at him. "That crippled girl needed a place for her boyfriend to sit. This is the handicap section."

"Hey," Phillip said, turning to the couple. "There's plenty of room here for everyone."

The man looked about to say something but his wife grabbed his arm and he shut up. Phillip turned back to Anna, and she gave him a weak smile.

Soon hushed whispers floated over to them. "There'd be plenty of room if whole sections weren't used up for people in wheelchairs. It's bad enough all the good parking spaces are eaten up by their spots."

Phillip tensed. He was about to turn again, when Anna used her hand to turn his face to hers. She kissed him lightly on the mouth. "It's not worth it. I love you so much for trying to defend my honor but it'll just ruin our evening. You wouldn't change his mind with a fist to his face anyway, no matter how badly he deserves it."

"You are an earthbound saint," he said, sighing, teeth gritted. "How do you put up with it?"

"By ignoring it. Most of the time."

"You shouldn't have to, you know."

"I know," she said, turning her body to lean back into his chest, and he wrapped his arms around her waist. "But I've found killing them with kindness works out in my favor more often than not."

He put his face in her hair. She could feel his warm breath on her neck and it gave her shivers. He reached around and pulled her hair out of the way letting the tips of his fingers drag along the sensitive skin. He ghosted his lips there and then gently kissed her right below her ear.

"Stop," she said, shivering again. "We're giving them more of a show than the band is."

"I can't help that I want to be near you," he said, in a low husky voice. She leaned her head back onto his shoulder making it impossible for him to play with her neck.

"How was your day at work?" Anna asked.

"Busy," Phillip said.

"You always say that," she said. "I know you can't tell me specifics, but was there anything unique that happened today?"

He sat and thought a minute. "You know it's not so much unique as it is awe-inspiring. Sometimes I feel like I have a treadmill in my office. But I just have to remind myself that these guys are looking for help, and I can offer help, even if I sometimes feel like it doesn't do much good."

"You know as well as I do your help means a lot to those guys," Anna said.

He ran his hand through his hair. "Yeah," he said. "Big help."

Anna opened her mouth to ask why he acted so defeated, but the lights on the stage in the amphitheater went out and the opening act ran off the stage. A pulsing bass started to play and flashing lights shot out in all directions. She sat up to see if the band had run out on stage yet but the stage remained empty. Anna turned to Phillip.

"In just a few minutes, you'll see your rival for my affections," she said, leaning in close so her cheek was touching his. Phillip managed a wan smile. Suddenly, a shout went up from the crowd as the band ran on stage to start their set. The people around them leapt to their feet to welcome the band.

"Are you serious?" Phillip said. A wall of bodies effectively blocked the view of the stage. She stopped him from reaching out to tell the people in front of them to sit down.

"But you can't see anything!" he said. She nodded and pulled him down next to her again.

"I'm not in high school anymore," she said in his ear, "and I'd much rather look at you than Matt what's-his-name, anyway."

He looked at her smiling and shaking his head. "Sweet talker."

"Not at all, soldier," she said. "You're definitely easy on the eyes."

He surprised her with a blush and a shy smile. "I am a lucky man." He repositioned his arms around her waist, and she leaned into his chest again. They sat like that together, listening to the band sing,

Anna's nerves were hyper-aware of Phillip's closeness. It had been a long time since she'd felt this attracted to anyone. She had loved and desired Darren, and their connection had been powerful. So powerful that she wasn't sure how she survived that first year without him. Sitting cradled in Phillip's arms, she felt that same powerful force, familiar, and yet, new.

She loved him, but despite that, doubts crept their way in. He traced lazy circles in her arm where his hand rested. She loved the person he was. He was funny and self-effacing. He was kind and patient. There were so many adjectives she could use to describe him that all added up to her idea of the perfect man and good life companion. His caring for her inspired her to re-examine whether she wanted to be alone anymore. But he deserved better than the titles of caregiver and insta-daddy. Being with her meant taking care of her physically more than the average able-bodied woman. And as she got older that need would only grow. Why would he want to saddle himself with a wife that couldn't walk, and her kids? She still couldn't understand even though he'd reassured her enough times that he was walking into her mess with eyes wide open.

Stop it, she thought to herself. *Like Phee always says, I'll talk myself out of it. Then that might talk him out of it, and then my heart would break all over again if he left.*

Things were ramping up for her and Phillip, Anna could feel it. It was a possibility that excited her, and yes, scared the living crap out of her. It was going to involve the kids. As she laid her head on his shoulder, she thought of Brody and Zoe. She hadn't been exactly evasive about Phillip. She talked to him on the phone in front of them. She never said who it was she was talking to, and they never really asked. She just never had Phillip around when the kids were there. It wasn't that she didn't trust Phillip, but she worried that her dating would needlessly worry or confuse them. In the beginning, she worried the thing they had felt in Sweetwater was just two lonely people making eyes at each other, or that it was merely a sexual attraction with not enough substance to sustain a long-term relationship. The attraction was far more than sexual. She wondered how she could live without him if she had to, and it was getting harder and harder to send him home to his apartment at the end of their evenings together.

On the drive back home, Anna made a decision. "Phillip, do you want to come hang out with the kids and me some time?"

Phillip looked over at her. "Really? You're sure?"

"Yes," she smiled. "I think things have been going pretty well between us, and I don't see why they can't get to know you before we make any big decisions about our future."

Phillip put his eyes back on the road but a surprised smile spread across his face. "When?"

"How about Sunday? Maybe we'll do a picnic in the park."

"I really hate to be that guy and state the obvious," he said. "But that sounded an awful lot like you're ready to take things to the next level between us."

"I've been ready, but I've been holding back for my kids. Now I don't see why they can't know how wonderful you are, too. Kind of selfish of me, don't you think?" she asked, reaching out and holding his hand.

"Sometimes I wonder how I got so lucky—twice."

"I don't believe it was luck. Couldn't possibly be if we found each other twice."

He nodded. "Call it serendipity, destiny, or divine intervention, then. I still feel like a lucky man."

Chapter Eighteen

Anna's insides roiled with anxiety. Brody's nose was in his cell phone as usual, while Zoe ran around on the grass in the park just like she had on that Fourth of July a few years ago. She scanned the parking lot for Phillip's truck. Nothing.

Anna looked over at her son. This was the moment of truth. Brody was a smart kid. Too smart for his own good sometimes. She hoped he would at least give Phillip a chance. That was the funny thing about him. He wasn't impressed easily, and even less so now that he was moving into teenager-hood. She might as well address the elephant in the room Brody didn't know was there. "Do you know why we're here?"

"No," he said without looking up. "One of Zoe's stupid friends' birthdays?"

"No," Anna said. "We're here because I want you to meet someone."

"I knew it!" Brody said, looking at her. "I knew you were dating somebody."

"You make it sound like it's a bad thing," she said.

Brody shrugged. "It's whatever, I guess."

"Aren't you curious to know who it is?"

"If you're dating one of the teachers at my school, that would be so cringy."

"It's not, but you do know him."

"Then who is it, if I know him?" Brody said. "Or her, Mom, I'm not here to judge."

"Funny. His name is Phillip."

Brody slowly looked up from his phone, shock in his eyes. "Phil from California?"

"Yes."

"What the hell?" he said. "Since when does he live in Utah?"

"Since a couple of years ago," Anna said.

Brody paused for a moment. "So what's his deal now?"

"He's working up at the VA hospital as a social worker."

"How did you find him?"

"He came to my school for a Veteran's Day assembly. He was one of the speakers."

"Nice." Brody looked back down at his phone but Anna could see his mind working furiously. "So, what? Are you guys getting married or something?"

"We haven't talked about that yet."

"Why not?" he challenged, looking her in the eye.

"Because our getting married is a lot bigger than just him and me. It includes you guys as well."

"You want my permission or something?"

"Not exactly," Anna said. "But I do want you and Zoe to get to know Phillip again."

Brody shrugged. He occupied himself in his phone again, the conversation apparently over for him. She took it as a small triumph.

She looked up to scan the lawn and saw Phillip casually approaching them. He sat down on the blanket next to Anna. He looked as nervous as she felt.

"Sorry I'm late," he said, giving her a quick kiss on the cheek.

"Brody, you remember Phillip," Anna said.

Brody looked Phillip up and down, and then tipped his head back quickly. "Hey." He went back to his phone.

Anna waved Zoe over. "Zoe, this is my friend Phillip." Zoe's head cocked to one side. "Do you remember the camper trip we took with Grandma and Grandpa? Phillip was with us in the park on that Fourth of July." Zoe managed a shy wave and a small "Hi." She did not remember him. It was probably just as well considering Brody's reaction.

"He would like to get to know us better, so we're going to hang out and—"

"Zoe, he's Mom's boyfriend," Brody said. "They want to get married."

Zoe sharply took in some air and then clapped her hands and squealed. Anna looked over to check Phillip's reaction and found his lips twitching in barely contained amusement.

"Now hold on, guys," Anna said. "We're not to the marriage part yet. Let's just enjoy Phillip's company and see what happens, okay?"

Zoe had stars in her eyes for Phillip. "If you guys get married, can you please give me a baby sister?"

Phillip started laughing outright and Anna honestly couldn't help a smile herself. Brody, however, scowled.

"We'll see what we can do, sweetheart," Phillip said. Anna shoved his shoulder and gave him a look that said Don't encourage her. It's not that the idea of having a child with Phillip didn't secretly thrill her, but for her own sanity's sake things needed to go in their proper sequence and pace.

She pulled out the sandwiches and sides she had made for everyone. As she was setting it out, Zoe walked over and sat right next to Phillip. Her innocent eyes looked up at him and Anna's heart expanded when Phillip looked down at her daughter with a gentle look.

"Phillip," Zoe said. "I'm in the school program at my school. Do you want to come with my mom to see it?"

Phillip smiled. "Sure. When is it so I'll make sure to get off work in time?"

Bless her sweet little heart, Anna thought. Her daughter had the uncanny ability to get people to love her in an instant. It looked like Phillip was not immune to her charms as he asked her about her part in the program.

"So, Brody, what grade are you in now?" Phillip asked, looking over at her son.

"Seventh," Brody said.

"Any class you like in particular?"

"No."

Anna looked from her son to Phillip. Brody certainly wasn't making it easy for Phillip. It was something she expected would happen. She had hoped that Brody would remember Phillip and be interested in picking up where they left off back in Sweetwater. Phillip's charm seemed to have dimmed for her son.

"Can I ask a question?" Brody said.

"Sure," Phillip said.

"What are your intentions with my mom?"

"Well, she and I plan to get to know each other better, we'll go on dates, and that's good enough for now."

"Right," Brody said. "Do you want to marry her?"

Phillip looked over at Anna. "Yes, I would like to, but it's not something we've decided for sure yet."

Anna looked in her lap, hoping that her cheeks weren't blazing red.

"Why do you want to marry her?"

"Brody!" Anna chided.

Phillip put a hand on her arm. "It's okay. It's a fair question. The first time I laid eyes on your mom, I knew she was someone special. She's smart. She's caring and encouraging. And most of all I want to marry her because I love her."

Anna's heart beat in her chest at a million miles an hour. It's one thing to think about how someone feels about you and their expectations. But it was something else to actually hear it out loud. She braved a look at Phillip. He was still looking at Brody who sat there looking like he was at a loss for words. Phillip turned to Anna and smiled, and her heart melted.

"Do you have a plate for me?" Phillip asked.

"Yes, of course," Anna said, shaking herself out of her enthrallment of Phillip and loading up his plate. She then hurried and got the other plates ready.

Brody's phone was in his face again, with his plate sitting on his lap untouched.

"How about putting that away while we eat?" she warned. For a beat, Brody looked to be considering ignoring her. Instead, he rolled his eyes and put his phone down. Phillip adjusted his seat. He looked shocked and a muscle in his jaw tightened, but he concentrated on his food.

As they ate, she watched Brody watching Phillip. Her son's face was unfathomable. Phillip seemed completely unaware of the scrutiny and chatted with Zoe.

Brody's phone pinged. He shoved the rest of his sandwich in his mouth and picked up his cell phone.

"Hey, Brody," Phillip said. "I'm pretty sure your mom asked you to put that away while we're eating."

"I did eat," Brody said, holding up his empty plate, his mouth still half full.

"Brody," Anna cautioned.

"What? I did what you asked me to," he said.

Phillip glared at the boy. "Excuse me?" Phillip started to say.

Anna reached over and put her hand on Phillip's arm.

"Drop the attitude or you'll lose the phone, son," she said.

Making a disgusted noise, Brody shoved the phone into the pocket of his hoodie, then scrunched further down the tree he was sitting against and folded his arms. He refused to look at anyone.

Anna felt the muscles in Phillip's arm relax, but he still maintained his disapproving stare at Brody. For a moment, she thought he might say something else, but he didn't. He just leaned back and kept silent. The conversation was less lively than it had been before, and before long, they all headed to Anna's house.

Phillip sat on the couch with Anna in her front room. She had sent the kids to bed soon after they had gotten home. Brody, being Brody, had tried to challenge Phillip to a game of Beyond Duty. It was an obvious delay tactic on Brody's part. Phillip, whether sincere or calculating, exclaimed his ignorance of the game. Brody had no other choice but to go to bed like he'd been asked.

"Well, that was interesting," he said.

"The day didn't go quite the way I hoped, but it wasn't too bad, was it?" Anna asked.

"No, not too bad," he said, pulling her legs onto his lap. He looked deep in thought. "Do you let him sass you like that all the time?"

"Brody?"

Phillip nodded.

"Um, not all the time, I don't think," Anna said.

"I'm going to be honest here," he said. "Growing up, if I had ever been caught talking to my mother the way Brody was talking to you, my dad would have strung me up faster than I could say 'back-mouth.' It's not right."

"You have to understand," she said. "I have to pick my battles with him. He's a good kid, but very headstrong."

"I understand," Phillip said. "It still doesn't give him the right to sass you when he's upset."

"I don't let him get away with sassing me, Phillip. Didn't you catch my threat to take away his phone?"

"But do you really think that's enough to nip that kind of attitude in the bud?"

"I'm so glad you're here to give me expert parenting advice."

"There's no need to get sarcastic," he said. "Anna, I'm on your side. He shouldn't be able to talk to you any old way he feels like it. He should respect you as his mother, whether he's upset with you or not."

"And as his mother, I feel like I know best how to handle him when he is disrespectful," Anna said, folding her arms.

"I agree," he said, putting his hand on her arms. "I'm just worried that as he gets older, little episodes of disrespect will turn into something you can't handle."

"Really?" she said. The heat rising to her cheeks this time was not passion. It was annoyance. She transferred from the couch to her wheelchair. "Your confidence in me is overwhelming."

He tried to grab her hand, but she pulled back and folded her arms.

"I'm not criticizing your parenting skills."

"It sure sounds like it."

"What I mean is I'm offering a united front. I wanted to let you know I have your back. Brody is going into an age where he's going to try and push boundaries. And when he does I'll be there to help push back."

"I don't want any pushing at all," Anna said. "Thank you. I appreciate knowing you'll be there for me. I just don't believe in physical punishment, or even loud verbal punishment, when it comes to my children. I know you just want to help but I've managed fine without you for nine years so far, I think I can handle the next nine just fine."

Phillip hung his head. "This is coming out all wrong," Phillip said, running a hand through his hair. "You do what you think is best. That's not for me to say."

"For now, I think it's best if I'm the one who parents. We can re-evaluate that if or when our status changes, but for right now, I don't want to blur the lines between boyfriend and co-parent. It's just easier that way."

"Fine. But don't be surprised if I forget our little agreement occasionally when he sasses and I see red. I'll let it be. I don't like it, but I'll do my best to stay out of it."

"Thank you," she said with a hard set to her jaw. "It's getting late. We both have work tomorrow. You should probably go."

He blinked. "Okay, if that's what you want." He got up and kissed her. "I'll call you tomorrow."

She nodded but didn't say anything. He left the house, and she took herself to her room, resisting the urge to slam the door.

What Phillip said had stung. As if she couldn't handle her own son without his help. She worked with teenagers for a living, it wasn't like she didn't know how it worked. Most especially, she did not believe in "spare the rod, spoil the child." There were better ways to deal with discipline than intimidation. The whole conversation bothered her, and she found it impossible to be still, let alone sleep.

Her phone pinged. She picked up. It was a text from Phillip. She was still angry and was tempted to put the phone on silent and in her side-table drawer. She had promised Phillip to be honest about her feelings. Well, he wanted feelings? He was gonna get some.

Are you okay?

I'm not sure I should talk about it right now

Are you sure? You seemed pretty upset with me

That's because I am

Tell me what's going on. I'm not sure I understand

There were some things I did just fine before you entered the picture

I believe that

So I will still be able to do those things by myself even if you are there

I don't doubt that

She shook her head. What, is he being purposely obtuse? she thought.

I don't need you to rescue me from my own son

There was a pause in Phillip's response.

You feel I overstepped a line

Yes

I'm sorry. I was only trying to help
Sleep well

She had probably made him upset as well. A part of her felt like saying, "Well, too bad." They were her kids and being around them for short periods of time hardly made him an expert in their personalities and challenges, especially since he wasn't a father himself.

There was another part of her that felt a little guilty. It was this part that understood that he was just trying to stand up for her, but if she didn't establish those boundaries now, then it could cause problems in their relationship later.

She got into bed and pulled up the covers. Things were getting complicated. It had never been this complicated with Darren. Of course, she and Darren had gotten together before kids were thrown into the mix. She needed to decide now what she wanted out of Phillip. It wouldn't be fair to anyone to rush into a marriage and just hope everything worked out the way it was supposed to. But the idea of Phillip stepping forward to dispense discipline just didn't sit well with her. She had no idea how he was raised. She and Darren just grew into discipline as the kids grew so they basically had similar ideas of how it was supposed to go. But this was so much different. It was something she and Phillip needed to talk about.

She sighed. Wasn't love supposed to be like old-time musicals where the only problems were before you got together, then after the I love yous, you got your happily ever after? If that were the case, Darren wouldn't have died and they would've ridden the carousel of life together until they were old and gray. But Darren wasn't here, and Phillip was.

Darren, if you're watching over me and the kids like I think you are, find some way to let me know I'm doing the right thing, she thought, as she closed her eyes to go to sleep.

Chapter Nineteen

Anna hadn't the nerve to start a *discussion* about parenting. She still smarted from what she felt was undue criticism from an unqualified source. She had no idea how Phillip felt about it other than he agreed to stick by her wishes to let her head up the parenting. She didn't want to fight so she let it lie, though it drove her mad that she didn't know what Phillip was thinking.

In addition to these dubious feelings, Brody had been acting out. It corresponded perfectly with the time Phillip had been in their lives. She'd been getting calls from his school and emails from his teachers—he acted defiant, rude and uncooperative. When she talked to him about it, he just said school sucked and shrugged his shoulders.

If that were true, then why is he still getting straight As, she thought. It would have been a lot easier if his grades had slipped because then she would have a standard by which he needed to measure himself. As it was, his punishments, she knew, were hardly punishments. He had started leaving Zoe alone at home. He would get home, throw his stuff in his room and then leave the house, going who knows where. There were a few times Zoe and she had to get in the van and search for him. The most frustrating part of it all was there was nothing she could do about it. He got out of school at least an hour or so before she could get home and he took it as permission to do what he wanted. She couldn't stop him.

She was getting ready for her last class of the day when her cell phone rang with an unknown number. She answered it.

"Mrs. Gilbert?"

"Yes."

"This is Sargent Miller of the Sandy police department," the voice said.

Her hand flew to her mouth, tears forming in her eyes. "Is there something wrong?" she managed to get out.

"Yes, ma'am," he said. "I have your son Brody here at the station. He was picked up for shoplifting earlier today and I need to know what you'd like me to do with him."

"Shoplifting?!" she nearly screeched.

"It was the little corner shop off of Thirteenth East. The owners don't necessarily want to press charges, but we brought him here so we could talk to him. Would you like to come get him?"

"Yes, uh, wait. The school day isn't over. I can't get over there." She wracked her brain. "Would it be okay if I sent my parents over to get him?"

"That should be fine. Just give me their names and they'll have to provide a photo ID."

"Yes, they can do that," she turned herself away from the class so they didn't see the tears starting to stream down her face. She gave the officer the information he asked for. "Thank you so much for calling me, officer."

She ended the call and held the phone to her chest, taking in deep breaths. She wiped her tears away and then turned to the class.

"You guys'll be okay if I just make a quick call in the hallway?"

They looked disinterested and she took that as a yes. Escaping to the hallway, she dialed Phillip's phone number.

"Hey, beautiful," he said. He sounded tired.

"Phillip, I need to ask a favor," she said.

"What is it?"

"Can you go pick up Brody from my parents' house in about an hour?"

"What? What's he doing over there?"

"Oh, Phillip, it's terrible. I just got a call from Sandy police. Brody was picked up for shoplifting."

A sigh came from the other end. "I can do that. Are you sure you want me to?"

"Do you mean you can't?"

"No. It's going to be really hard for me not to say anything to him before you get a hold of him."

"I'm taking my chances," she said. "I'm asking for back-up just this once. Please?"

"Okay," he said. "If that's what you want. I'll be there."

She closed her eyes, praying she was doing the right thing. She quickly called her parents and then did her best to get through the last class of the day. A dark pit formed in her stomach. She dreaded what she would find as she got closer to her house. Phillip's truck was parked outside. Tears ran down her cheeks again. At least Phillip is here, she kept saying to herself.

When she got in the house, it was very quiet. Brody sat in the armchair, arms folded, glaring at Phillip who sat on the couch across from him, glaring right back. Zoe sat on the other end of the couch, tensely watching the two. When Anna came all the way in, Brody looked over scowling, but as soon as he saw her, a kaleidoscope of emotion passed over his face—guilt, anger, defiance, sadness, fear.

"Well?" she said very quietly. "What do you have to say for yourself?"

"It was Chad's idea," Brody said. "He said he does it all the time and never gets caught."

"Which is exactly why you shouldn't do it," she said. "You'll always get caught."

"This is so stupid," he said under his breath.

"I'm not sure you appreciate how much trouble you're in, young man."

"You're going to take my phone away? Big deal."

"That's definitely the start," she said. "You're not allowed to hang out with friends, no TV, no gaming system, and you're going to work off the money you stole from the store and the amount it took for the police to have to pick you up."

"What?" he said, jumping to his feet. "That's so unfair."

"Fair?" she said, tears gone, fire burning. "How about you ask the people you tried to steal from how fair it was to them?"

"But the police?" he said. "That's stupid. How am I supposed to know how much that is?"

"You're a smart kid," she said. "You can figure it out. But until you do, you better not so much as sneeze out of place, or your punishment will get much worse."

"This is stupid!" Brody said, hopping to his feet. "Screw this."

Brody made to walk past Anna when, as fast as a flash, Phillip jumped out of his seat and stepped in front of Brody, blocking his path out of the room. "I don't think your mom was done talking to you."

"Well, I am," Brody said, trying to walk around Phillip. But he underestimated Phillip's size and Phillip merely blocked the hallway with his body.

"Get out of the way!" Brody growled. "You're not my dad!" Brody's hands bunched into fists and for a moment Anna worried he might try to physically harm Phillip.

Phillip didn't move. He didn't even blink. "I wish I was your dad," he said. "Then maybe I could make you understand how much you hurt your mom with a stunt like this." His tone was soft, even sad. Brody stared at Phillip, shocked. For a long time, they stood there just staring at one another. But then finally Phillip moved out of the way and Brody skulked past him and slammed the door. Zoe rushed from the couch and held her mother, her tears dampening her sleeve.

Anna stroked her daughter's hair. "It's okay," Anna said. She had Zoe look her in the eyes, wiping the tears from her cheeks. "Brody just needs to cool off in his room for a bit."

Zoe nodded and then went over to Phillip and hugged him. Philip looked up at Anna, a small smile on his face.

"Honey, I need to talk to Phillip, okay?" The little girl nodded and ran to her room. Anna transferred over to the couch, and put her head in her hands. The shaking she thought she had under control came back full force.

"Do you think I did the right thing?" she asked, searching his face.

"With Brody's punishment?" he said, a smirk appearing at his lips. "It was brilliant."

Phillip joined her on the couch and pulled her into his arms. She shook her head against his chest.

"Sluffing school and shoplifting," she said. "What was he thinking?"

"I don't know," he said. "Kids his age can be interesting. They need guidance but they don't want it from Mom and Dad."

"So what you're saying is that whatever I do, it's not going to be enough."

"No, that's not what I'm saying," Phillip said. "He still needs you. You are the one that establishes and enforces those boundaries and he'll test those boundaries to see how far you'll let him go. You passed today's test, I'm pretty sure. I think I'm a little scared of you."

"Whatever," she said. "Dealing with Brody is so different from my teens at school. They already see me as an authority figure. I don't need to establish my leadership with them. With Brody, I'm just Mom. I have a feeling it's going to be two steps forward, and one step back."

"And I'll always back you up, if you need it."

She brought her lips to his. "Thank you. I'm not sure why you're trying to sign up for this zoo, but I'm glad you are."

"I kinda like the zookeeper. She's hot," he said. She slapped him on his chest. He hugged her tighter.

"Did you mean what you said to Brody?"

"About being Brody's dad?" Phillip asked. "Every syllable. I can't ask you to love me if I can't love the most important people in your life. That wouldn't be fair to you. For you, I'm willing to help you with that responsibility. Besides, there are just some things guys understand about other guys. Brody needs a guy."

"I could make all kinds of comments about sexism—"

"It's not about sexism. He needs his dad. Brody knows I'm not his dad. I know I'm not either. And even though I'm not looking to replace Darren, he needs someone he can go to for the stuff he'd never go to his mom for. If he'll let me, I want to be that for him. I care about Brody, and I'll help him if he asks for it."

The comment shot straight through her. He really wanted that responsibility. He hadn't even hesitated when he said it. But it's easy to want something when you don't know what you're asking for.

"I'm just worried that's exactly what Brody is thinking—that'd you try and replace his dad."

"Well, it is what he's thinking," he said. "And he's going to test me on it until he becomes a man himself and realizes that I'm not his dad's competitor. I'm just the guy that loves both his mom and him, and wants to take care of the both of you."

Saturday morning dawned and Anna was in the kitchen doing her bills. Brody was lying on the couch reading a book when the doorbell rang.

"I wonder who's here so early," Anna said, going to answer it.

"Not one of my friends, that's for sure," Brody said sullenly.

Anna opened the door and found Phillip standing there.

"Well, isn't this a nice surprise?" Anna said, giving Phillip a quick kiss and rolling aside to let him in. He held a large gift bag in his hand. When he saw Brody lying on the couch, he threw the bag at him.

"What the—?"

"Open it," Phillip said.

Brody opened the bag and pulled out a tank top, running shorts, a water bottle and then a box containing a pair of running shoes.

"What is all this?" Brody asked.

"I'll make you a deal," Phillip said. "You come running with me Saturday mornings, and you can get your gaming privileges back long enough to teach me how to play Beyond Duty, if it's ok with your mom."

"Serious?" Brody said, looking back at Anna.

Anna smirked at Phillip. "I guess that's an acceptable compromise."

"Go get dressed, Brody, and I'll meet you outside."

Brody hurried to pick up all the gear Phillip had gotten him and ran to his room.

"Running?" Anna said, parking her chair near to where Phillip sat on the arm of the couch.

"It's exercise, which his couch potato generation needs more of. It will help him release some of that aggression he's got balled up inside, and he gets dude time. And I get a running buddy, and leet skills playing Beyond Duty."

Anna smiled. "You really are fantastic, you know."

Phillip shrugged. "I have a good idea here and there."

Anna grabbed the front of Phillip's tank top and pulled him down for another kiss.

"Ugh, really?" Brody said, covering his eyes with his hand. "Do you guys have to do that out in public?"

"It's not public, it's my house, thank you very much," Anna said.

"Gross," Brody said. "Can we go now?"

"Yup, let's go get warmed up and then we'll head out," Phillip said. "Hmm, let's say an hour to an hour and half. Just for starters anyway."

"Have fun!" Anna waved them out of the house.

Chapter Twenty

Anna sat in her van outside the VA. Tonight was date night, her favorite part of the week. Phillip had surprised her with tickets to the Utah Symphony. Not only that but a program of Mozart's piano concertos. She sighed. Phillip's ability to sniff out the most romantic things for them to do continued to amaze her. Well, there were a lot of things Phillip did that made her wonder why she had gotten so lucky.

Now that she had reintroduced the kids to Phillip, he'd been spending more time at the house. And it wasn't just when he and Brody went running on Saturday mornings. He liked to just be there, talking with them and being useful around the house. He helped Zoe with homework or watched her favorite pony cartoons with her. Sometimes even Brody sought Phillip out when he needed help with a project or just to have someone to talk to. She knew Brody was starting to trust that Phillip was going to stick around. Brody was a kid of few words. He usually only ever came to her to complain or to ask for something. Lately, he'd been coming into her room right before bedtime to talk to her about Phillip. Their time together running had created a bond between them, and Brody's moods had improved as well.

She looked at the time on her watch. They still had a couple of hours before the concert, but she was eager to see Phillip, so she decided to head into the building anyway. Alice, the department's secretary, was such a nice person and she was fun to talk to so why not wait inside?

"Hi, Anna," Alice said. "Don't you look nice!"

"Thank you," Anna said. "Phillip's taking me to the symphony tonight."

"Oh, that will be extra nice," she said. "He's still in with a patient but if you want to hang out here you can wait for him."

Anna parked herself against a row of chairs in the waiting room. "Phillip's been really busy lately, hasn't he?"

"We all have, believe me," Alice said. "He's such a hard worker. You must be proud of him."

"I am," Anna smiled.

From down the hallway she heard men's voices talking and laughing. Phillip escorted a man in fatigues. Phillip's face brightened when he saw Anna sitting there.

"Oh, good, you're here," he said, as he bent over to give her a quick kiss. In a low voice, he said, "You look beautiful and you smell even better." He tucked a piece of her hair behind her ear.

"James, if you don't mind, I'd like to introduce you to my girlfriend, Anna."

"Phil, when you said she was beautiful, I didn't think you had such a talent for understatement. How are you, Anna?"

Anna blushed. "I'm doing well, thank you. Just waiting for this guy to get done."

"I won't keep you but it was really nice to finally put a face to a name. Phil talks about you all the time."

He clapped Phillip on the back and walked out the door.

"Good night, Alice," Anna said, as Phillip took her hand and ushered her out the door.

"Another day done," Phillip said. "Shall we go hear some piano music?"

"Sounds good to me," Anna said. "James seems like a good guy."

"Yeah, he is," Phillip said, as he helped her in the truck. Phillip got in himself and they headed for the concert hall. "I mean I can't really talk about specifics, because of client privilege but it's really nice to have a guy like James to work with. Sometimes I don't feel like we're in a session. It's like we're just two buddies having a chat. He has a long way to go but I can already see the strides he's made from when we first started."

Her heart warmed to see him so excited about his job. She knew that helping people was something Phillip loved doing, and as much stress as he'd been under lately, it made her glad that there was an occasional bright spot.

"I was thinking when we were talking earlier that he reminds me a lot of Scott," he said. "He's got the same sense of humor, and determination."

Anna smiled. As busy as he was, he had little time to develop friendships outside her family group. Anna thought having more male companionship, with someone close to his age, would be good for him.

"What about Justin?"

"I don't get to see him as much as I'd like. We work in different buildings." A sly smirk spread across his face. "But every time I run into him, I keep thinking he'd be perfect for Ophelia. You know, laid back and friendly to her crazy friendly? We should set them up sometime."

"Phee would murder you first and then come after me," Anna laughed. "Even if Justin would be a much better alternative."

"I'll come up with something. Don't you worry your pretty little head," Phillip said. "She won't know what hit her."

Anna shook her head. She wasn't exaggerating when she said Ophelia would go savage on them both if they tried to set her up with someone she didn't know. It might be a good idea anyway. Ophelia had been vague, even evasive, lately when Anna would ask about the man she was dating. That worried Anna a little considering her sister, in Anna's opinion, had the worst taste in men. She either mixed herself up with total narcissists or ones that merely saw her as a good time.

"So tomorrow, are you up for a little shopping trip for Easter?"

"Yes," Phillip said. "It sounds like a lot of fun."

"Are you sure you want to?" Anna asked.

"Yes, why is it even a question?" Phillip asked, glancing over at her.

"I don't know," Anna said. "I just don't want you to feel obligated I guess."

Phillip's face read stupefied. "Obligated? Love, at some point in the future, we are going to be a family and you're telling me that shopping for Easter is somehow a burden of obligation?"

"Look, I've never done this before—the whole working a boyfriend into the family thing," she said. "I know you care for me and my kids, and I want you to be included in all of it. I just worry that you're trying to bite off more than you can chew."

"Shouldn't I be the one to determine that?"

She bit her lip. "Yes," she said, slowly dragging out the S.

Phillip chuckled. "Seriously, I think I can handle it. But if you don't have faith that I can do it . . ."

"It's not that," she said. "I wish I had the right words."

"You're worried that I am jumping into the daddy role too quickly," he said.

"Yes, sort of," she said. "I never want to take for granted your willingness to help out, or take advantage of you."

"Rest assured, I am fine," he said.

The heavy traffic around them on the highway slowed to a snail's pace, closing them in.

"Oh, boy," Anna said. "I forgot about Friday night rush hour. I wonder if there's a game."

"Son of a—" Phillip said, leaning forward on the steering wheel, brake lights painting his face red.

"I hope it clears up before we go to dinner after the concert," Anna said, looking out the window.

"Come on!" Phillip said. "Did you see that? He shoved his nose in there and just about caused an accident."

Anna watched Phillip, his face screwed up into a scowl.

"Let me in! I've had my turn signal on for a year!" Phillip said, trying to maneuver his lane change.

"Breathe, Phillip," Anna said. "It's okay."

"Just let me handle this, okay?" he said, looking over his shoulder to see if the person had made room for him.

Anna held her hands up. "Fine."

Phillip gripped the wheel tighter. "I swear to—" He laid on his horn. Anna folded her arms and watched Phillip mumble under his breath. If he wasn't so intense, the whole thing would be hilarious. As it was, she didn't find it amusing.

"What are we waiting for—an invitation?" he said.

"Phillip," Anna said.

"You must be blind! I'm right here!"

"I was thinking we can just go to my parents' house on Sunday for din—," Anna said.

"It's a freaking turn lane, just go!"

"Phillip!"

"What?!" Phillip said, then took in a breath. "I'm sorry. Traffic puts me on edge."

"I understand. I've been trying to distract you," Anna said.

"I appreciate it, but I would rather just get there so we don't have to worry about all these crazies out here for a while."

"I would appreciate it," she said, "if you stop verbally assaulting every driver who does something you don't like."

"You mean I'm not allowed to express my frustrations?"

"Do you have to do it so loudly?"

"Isn't that implied in the definition of frustration?"

He wasn't wrong. They did manage to make it to the concert hall without further verbal assaults but it took Phillip a little while to shake off the annoyed, grudging aura. As the music started to swirl around them, she could feel the tension in Phillip ease and then she felt like she could relax. Phillip looked over at her, kissing the top of her hand. She forgave him for his outburst. It's not like she was perfect.

The thoughts of kids and marriage had been running around in her head all day. She looked at Phillip and she couldn't imagine her life without him anymore. Yet bringing him fully into the dynamic of her little family was unfamiliar territory and that scared her a little. How would Phillip ultimately fit in with them? She had these nightmare scenarios in her head that he'd make that commitment and come to resent her for overwhelming him with it. It didn't matter what he said; he didn't know what he was talking about. He didn't realize the kind of commitment he was making when he ultimately took responsibility for her and the kids. She loved him so much. She wished there was a way he could fully understand the scope of that responsibility so that she could reassure herself he'd stick around forever.

"I was wondering if we could talk about something?" she said, as soon as they were seated for dinner after the concert.

"Okay," he said. "Am I in trouble?"

"Oh. No," Anna said. "Am I that bad?"

"No, no!" he said quickly. "It just sounded like one of those talks."

"Maybe it is, but that doesn't mean you're in trouble."

"That's good then," he said, sounding somewhat unconvinced. "Sometimes these talks come out of left field. What did you want to talk about?"

"You know how sometimes things you understand in theory are, in reality, not what you expected?"

"Like what?"

"Well, like having sex for the first time."

"We're having a sex talk right here in the restaurant?"

"No," she said, laughing. "Sorry, bad example. I was just trying to find an example you could relate to. But what I'm talking about is marriage and parenting."

"Mmhmm," he said. "And I'm pretty sure we've talked about this before."

"I know. I just want to be sure. It's been good that you've been coming over as much as you have," she said. "Not just good for me, because I love it, but good so that you can see what it will be like if you ended up living with us full time at some point."

"You're still worried I may not be able to handle it?"

"Not that. I think you'll do just fine mostly," she said. "Kids are awesome and funny and all sorts of other good adjectives. But they can also be argumentative, noisy, messy, and just all-around annoying at times."

He nodded and waited for her to continue.

"So, I guess what I'm trying to say is that I hope you know that besides being supportive and fun and present, being a parent also requires patience and quite a bit of biting your tongue. It means sitting down and talking when you feel like screaming your head off, or putting yourself in time out when all you want to do is put them in time out.

"And before you accuse me of being critical, I'm not saying that you aren't capable of any of that. I'm saying that's how I hope you'll be when it comes time to co-parent with me. I want to make sure you're given fair warning that we're in for a roller coaster as Brody moves further into his teen years."

Phillip arched an eyebrow. "Okay. I know I'm not going to be perfect at it. But that's why it's helpful to care about the kids so that I have an investment in their happiness, too. Anna, I'm not sure what's got you so spooked. Are you worried that I'm going to try and dominate you and the kids?"

"No, not that, really," she said, folding her hands together. "I just worry that our individual versions of parenting will clash."

"Ah, I see," he said. "This is about the other week with Brody. So, we agree to work that out before we make anything official."

"For what it's worth," Anna said, holding his hand. "I have every confidence that you will be an excellent parent when the time comes."

He smiled back at her. "It's really nice to hear that from you. I sometimes wonder if you think I'll have what it takes."

"If I ever gave you that impression, I'm sorry," Anna said. "I guess I can be overprotective of my kids sometimes."

"Yes."

"You don't have to agree with me so fast."

He smiled. "Well, it's true. That doesn't mean it's a bad thing—necessarily."

"Necessarily?"

"Mama Bear is great for when you need to advocate for your kids, like at school," he said. "But sometimes it can be directed at people that are just trying to help."

Was she like that? She didn't think so but she remembered the disagreement they'd had after the park. She felt fully within her rights to determine how her kids were disciplined and by whom. But that was going to change eventually. It was a complication she wasn't sure how to handle. She didn't know how to respond to his accusation, so she didn't.

It had become a bit of a tradition at the end of the night for them to hang out in her van for a little while before they parted ways. Mostly, it gave them a chance to get physical without having to sneak around the kids. She loved having the chance to kiss Phillip unrestrained, feeling him touch her and just being close. She felt safe sitting here in his arms—safe and totally at peace. It also kept them out of trouble, though lately she had started to wonder what she was waiting for any more. When Phillip kissed her, she felt her entire body come alive with fire, and she could never get enough of him. She by lengths had taken their make-out sessions further and further, encouraged by the way he excited her, made her feel beautiful, until she knew they'd have to find a place to be alone besides a van.

She had her head on his shoulder, while he softly caressed the back of her arm.

"Phillip, you know I haven't really said it, even though I feel it every day, but I wanted you to know how much I love you," she said.

He smiled, and looked down at her. "I love you too. There's no place I'd rather be. There's no one else I'd rather be with."

"Can I ask you something?" she said, kissing his neck.

"Sure."

"Did you want children?"

There was a pause. "Why do you ask?"

"Because I think you'd make a wonderful dad," she said, teasing his earlobe with the tip of her nose.

"Did you want more?" he said, trying to clear his throat.

"I wouldn't mind," she said. "I'm not the biggest fan of pregnancy but there's something special about making a new life out of the love you share with someone."

She sat up so she could look him directly in the eyes. His eyes burned with an intense heat. He looked like he was trying to say something but the words weren't coming out.

"It's okay," she said, kissing him softly on the lips. "It's not a decision we have to make tonight. I just wanted to know how you felt about it."

"It is something I want," he said finally. "And I want it with you. But there should be a ring on that finger before we get there."

"I agree," she said. Her stomach did flip-flops at the idea of holding that little bundle with his daddy's good looks and her red hair, and watching Phillip cherish every moment with his own child. She wanted that for him.

His finger lifted her chin up and he kissed her so gently that the flip-flops went up into her throat. She sighed as his hands reached up to twine in her hair. She could feel him smile against her lips.

"I better get you home so we don't make that baby before we're ready for it," he said.

Anna giggled. "Too bad. I somehow can't get enough of your kisses."

He grinned. "The feeling's mutual."

Anna sat in bed after she'd gotten home looking through a scrapbook she had made when she and Darren were first married. It was full of pictures of their dating antics and their engagement and wedding pictures. She had made it all the way to Brody's birth before giving up on it. She looked over at the jewelry box sitting on her dresser. She had taken her wedding set off just before that fateful vacation. She looked down at her hand and the indentation where her rings had been all those years. She rubbed that finger with her thumb. She thought she should feel guilty, or at least a little bad, that Darren's things and memories were slowly being mingled with Phillip's. She was head-over-heels in love with Phillip. But it didn't diminish the way she felt about Darren. That was the surprising part. Darren was the father of her two children. He had given her his love freely, and truly cherished her. An idea slammed into her like a hit to the gut—cherished her much like Phillip did. Tears formed in her eyes. Was this the sign from Darren she'd been waiting for? She put her face in her hands and sobbed. Her heart was too full. She reached over and grabbed her cell phone off the nightstand.

I love you

A few minutes later her phone beeped.

I love you too, beautiful

Chapter Twenty-One

Anna was in her room boxing a few things she intended to put in the basement. It was Saturday and she was hurrying to get everything taped up before Phillip got there so he and Brody could store them for her. Brody had had a late-over with a friend the night before and no matter how many times she went to his room, he still hadn't gotten out of bed. The doorbell rang. She hurried to answer it. Phillip stood on her doorstep, looking annoyed.

"Hi," she said, allowing him to come in.

He looked down at his watch instead of answering her.

"Is everything okay?" she said, trying to go down the hallway to her bedroom without losing sight of him.

"Where are those boxes you needed me to take care of?" he asked in a flat voice.

"In here," she said, trying to keep her tone cheerful. She didn't want to press her luck if this grouchy Phillip wouldn't even answer her. It would be good for him to take that run to shake off whatever was eating up his craw.

He picked up the first box and headed for the basement stairs. "Where's Brody?" he asked.

"As far as I know he's still in bed," she said.

"Of all the— He knew I was going to be coming this morning," he said as he walked down the stairs.

Anna turned and went to Brody's room. He had finally sat up in bed and was scratching his head when she opened the door. "Is Phillip here?"

"Yes, I think it would be a good idea—"

"Hey!" Phillip said over the top of Anna. "Daylight's burning. Get up and at 'em." Phillip turned and picked up another box out of her room before looking over Anna's shoulder to make sure Brody had indeed gotten out of bed. When he got back from the basement he stood by the front door, impatiently tapping his foot.

Brody gave his mom a What gives? face.

"Just hurry up and get dressed," Anna said.

"May I talk to you for just a second, please, Mr. Laughlin?" Anna said, directing Phillip into the kitchen. "What is your problem?"

"My problem is I get here, like I've gotten here several weeks in a row, and find that he hasn't even gotten out of bed yet. I don't have to do this, so I don't appreciate being made to wait," he said, his arms folded across his chest.

"You got here sixty seconds ago, I hardly think that qualifies as waiting," Anna said.

"You don't understand—that's not the point. He needs to learn respect," Phillip said. "And when you respect people, you don't keep them waiting."

"I concede that he should have known to be ready by now," Anna said. "But he's thirteen years old. You honestly expect him to do everything perfectly all the time?"

"I expect that he would be held to a higher standard considering his attitude and the shoplifting," Phillip said.

Anna narrowed her eyes at Phillip. "Seriously? Are you trying to pick a fight with me?"

"I don't have time to pick fights with you," Phillip said.

"Oh? Where's this all-important place you have to be on a Saturday morning?"

"Now who's picking fights?" He peeked his head around the hallway wall. "Brody! Aren't you done yet?"

Brody came around the corner to the kitchen. The cautious look on his face told Anna he'd been listening in on their argument.

"You know what? I don't think Brody needs to go today," Anna said. "I don't think he needs to be subjected to someone yelling at him for something as dumb as being five minutes late."

Phillip glowered at her. "Fine. You all have a nice morning, doing whatever." His jaw flexed as he turned around and walked out the door.

"Mom, I wanted to go," Brody said.

"You did?" Anna said. "After the way he was acting?"

"Well, we don't talk very much when we're running so I don't think it's going to be a big deal."

Anna sighed. "I'm leaving it up to you. But if he starts being a bully you come straight back home."

Anna shook her head as she watched Brody follow after Phillip down the road. *What the hell was all that?* Anna thought. *Last night he's all lovey-dovey and kissy and stuff, and all of a sudden this morning he's biting my head off.*

What ran out that door was like a Mr. Hyde to Phillip's normally sweet Dr. Jekyll. It was so unlike him. Or at least, unlike the Phillip that she'd known so far. She couldn't have seen it during her week at Sweetwater, nor in their email and phone conversations after that. It would be easy to hide the negative parts of yourself with that much distance. His outburst in traffic the other day came to mind. She couldn't have him stomping around the house raging at any minor thing she and the kids did. Especially the kids because kids tended to do stuff that was annoying. It was part and parcel of having kids. Brody might be able to stand up to it, but she was afraid Zoe would internalize that bad behavior or think it was acceptable for the men in her life to treat her like that. Heaven knows she certainly didn't like being treated like that. She spent the majority of the time Brody and Phillip were gone trying to think of ways to approach Phillip about his outburst.

It was a wasted effort. Brody came in by himself and Phillip had already driven off. That hurt. He normally stayed around a bit to shower, hang out with the family, and just be present. She consoled herself with the notion that if he was going to be a grade-A jerk, then he was better off going back to his own apartment to sulk.

She waited a while before she pulled out her cell phone.

How was your run

Fine

Are you feeling better

I have no idea what you're talking about

Really?

Yes

You bit off a piece of my hide this morning and not in a good way

Sorry you felt that way

I did and I wasn't the only one

I don't know what you want me to say

I would like to understand why

Do we really have to talk about this right now?

Excuse me? You're the LCSW and you don't want to talk about it?

Can't a guy have a bad morning without being harassed

The corners of Anna's vision turned red. How dare he suggest that she was nagging him! She put her phone down, and took some deep, shaky breaths. Phillip may have lost his temper before, but he seemed to get it under control pretty quickly. Never in all the time they had known each other had he done anything to make her feel disrespected. This was the man that she had wanted to spend the rest of her life with, and now she wasn't sure. Not with him acting like this.

The rest of the day passed by as Saturdays usually did, except Phillip wasn't there. She hadn't texted him back because she wasn't in the mood to fight, and anything she had to say would surely start one. She was still angry with him for his insinuation that she was a nag.

She wandered the aisles of their local Shop-mart doing a supply run. Brody balked at the idea of coming so she left him home with Zoe. Truth be told, wandering the aisles without being begged for treats or listening to the kids bicker was nice. She had a million things to remember, but all she could think of was Phillip.

She found herself looking through the racks in the men's clothing section, noting what would look good on Phillip, before she realized what she was doing. She turned away, but when she looked up, the baby clothes department was right in front of her. No amount of blinking could keep the tears from forming at the corners of her eyes. She hurried to the front to check out.

She was still fighting tears when she pulled up to the house and saw Phillip's truck parked out front. When she got inside, Phillip was on the couch with Brody and Zoe. The two boys were playing Beyond Duty, and Zoe was there cheering them on.

"What?" Brody yelled. "You could have made that shot so easy!"

"Hey, get over here," Phillip said. "I'm being ganged up on."

"Nope, you're on your own, noob," Brody said. The two started laughing at something that happened in the game and they slapped each other's hand.

On the kitchen counter was a very large bouquet of white roses tied with a scarlet ribbon. When she looked back at the TV room, she saw Phillip looking at her. She looked away, not trusting herself to keep her composure at that moment. He made a show of giving up and handed his controller to Zoe, then stood and crossed to Anna.

"Come out and sit with me on the patio?" he asked.

She nodded, opened the sliding glass door to her patio, and rolled her chair through. Phillip came out and shut the door behind him. He stood behind Anna and started to massage her shoulders a little before he sat down in a patio chair and pulled her closer. He tucked some hair behind her ear. "I came to apologize. I was out of line. I was—what did Brody call it?— a royal asshat."

Anna managed a small smile, even though her tears still threatened to fall.

"I hate doing stuff that I realize I have to apologize for later," he said.

"Is everything okay?" Anna said. "Lately it seems like you're too stressed. Is work getting to you? Or is it our relationship?"

"I'm fine, really," he said. "It's nothing I can't handle. I promise."

"I care about you," she said. "You can always talk to me about anything. You should talk to me, because you're not on your own anymore. You have me. If we plan on getting married at some point, then you should trust me enough to tell me when you're hurting as much as when you're happy."

"I had no idea you felt like that," he said.

"You would if you'd talk to me," she said. "All I get lately is 'I'm fine' or 'It's not a big deal.'" She sighed and folded her arms across her chest.

Phillip reached over and rubbed her arms. "I'd say I'm sorry, but I think you already get the idea. I promise I'll try and do better."

She looked at him. "That's all I'm asking."

He leaned forward and kissed her. "For you, I'd do anything."

The hollow spot in Anna's heart declared that she only wished she believed him.

Chapter Twenty-Two

Phillip and Anna drove down the freeway with the windows down, their hands entwined together. Phillip was in a particularly good mood. Earlier, Anna'd had to banish him to a separate room a couple of times just to keep his hands off of her. Now they were headed to the brewpub in Sugarhouse Phillip had heard about. The summer weather was perfect for sitting outside enjoying good conversation. She smiled over at Phillip. She loved getting lost in those chocolate brown eyes of his. It had been a few days since his angry outburst. True to his word he'd been on his best behavior and she was starting to trust his moods again.

When Phillip pulled up into a nearby parking spot he started to laugh. "What do you know? James is here."

He pointed out a couple coming out of the building. She was greeted by James's broad grin and standing next to him was a petite brunette who gave Anna a shy wave.

Phillip grabbed James's hand after they'd gotten out of the truck.

"Phil, this is my wife, Amanda," James said, introducing the woman next to him. "Amanda, this is Phil's girlfriend, Anna."

"It's so nice to meet you," Anna said, shaking the woman's hand. This close up Anna noticed that the smile on Amanda's face seemed strained and the smile didn't quite extend to her eyes.

Phillip and James bantered about how the food at the restaurant compared to the mess hall at Fort Leonard Wood. "All of it was better than the MREs, though," Phillip said. "Except the ones with the tiny bottles of Tabasco--"

"Tabasco--" James said at the same time. The men started chortling in laughter. Anna turned to Amanda to make a comment but she looked over in time to see her disappear into the restaurant.

"Well, it was good running into you," Phillip said. "I have a dinner date with this gorgeous lady."

"Yeah, good to run into you as well," James said. "We were just on our way out. Don't want to have to pay the babysitter any more than have to. See you next Wed--" He glanced all around, pivoting and craning his neck. "Have you seen Amanda?"

"She went into the restaurant. Maybe she had to use the restroom. Do you want me to check?" Anna asked.

"Yeah, you check the restaurant and I'll make sure she hasn't snuck back up to the bar," James said, his smile faltering just a bit.

Anna passed into the restaurant after Phillip opened the door for her, and looked around. She didn't see anyone in the dining area that looked like Amanda, so she made her way to the bathrooms.

Anna immediately heard the sound of sniffling coming from the handicap stall as soon as she entered.

"Amanda?" Anna said as gently as she could. She knocked on the door of the stall. "Are you okay?"

Anna sat for a moment without speaking. Amanda didn't know her from Adam. Would she want to show Anna how upset she was? Anna hated crying in front of strangers, but she couldn't just leave Amanda there. She hoped Amanda would allow her to be of use to her somehow, but Anna couldn't think of any way to make that suggestion without making the situation awkward. Amanda's face would be a mess after crying like she had been. Anna went to the sink and got some paper towels dampened with cold water.

Anna softly knocked on the door again. "Can I come in?"

The door opened and she found Amanda sitting on the toilet, eyes red, face puffy from crying.

"Are you okay?" Anna said, holding out the towels and rubbing Amanda's arm.

"I . . . no," Amanda hiccuped. "I'm so worried about James. He's been . . . different, and I don't know what to do. We were fighting before you showed up, and then, with Phil, he acted like everything was fine. I couldn't stand it."

"Did you want me to speak to Phillip?"

Amanda touched the towels to her face. "I guess you could. I don't know what good it would do."

"I wish I could do something."

Amanda stood up from the toilet taking in a few deep breaths. "Thank you. I wish I knew what I could ask for that might actually help. If nothing else, it's nice to know someone was interested in listening."

"Anytime," Anna said. "James is looking for you in the dining area."

Amanda gave Anna a weak smile and nodded. She floated out of the bathroom like a ghost, pale and hopeless.

When they returned to the waiting area Phillip was standing with an anxious-looking James. They said brief goodbyes before being seated at their table.

"What was that all about?" Phillip asked.

Anna gave him a summary of their conversation in the bathroom. Phillip's face was troubled.

"I wish she'd been more specific," Phillip said, fiddling with his straw.

"She seemed really hopeless, like even if she told me, it wouldn't matter. Do you think there's something going on with him he's not telling you about?"

Phillip grimaced. "Maybe. But I can only help him with the things he tells me about."

"Okay" Anna said. "I'm just worried."

"Can you just trust that I know how to do my job? I'll take care of it."

Anna sat back, surprised a little at the terseness of his tone. The troubled look hadn't left his face, so she let it go. If she had a student she was worried about, being told how to do her job, or even things that implied criticism, would have made her very upset.

They spent the rest of dinner in silence and when he would normally park and take advantage of the solitude to kiss her, he didn't. He hopped out and got her wheelchair out of the back of the truck. The best she got was a chaste peck on the mouth as she went into her house. Her disappointment was acute, and she sat in the doorway watching Phillip drive away.

He had gotten so touchy. She hadn't meant to hurt his feelings. Men could be so sensitive about their competency whether in life or work. Even Darren was like that sometimes. But it was something that Darren was usually able to shake off after a while. She wondered how long it would take Phillip.

She got ready for bed. She wished she had told him that she admired his work, and felt proud of him. Maybe he needed to hear it. Maybe it was something he wasn't getting enough of at work. She understood what it was like to have to deal with the same challenges year after year within the same restrictive rule set. But at least with teaching, she saw the fruits of her labor blossom in front of her—the light bulb of understanding flashing on, like a writing assignment where a struggling child writes beautifully for the first time. But was it like that for Phillip? In his sessions with his patients, did he get to see the mind coming out of the fog of depression or the confusion of anxiety? Did he get to see the warrior truly come home from the war?

As she got into bed, she promised herself she would tell Phillip how proud she was of him. If nothing else, and despite the hardships he endured in his professional life, she had to be sure he knew she saw the good he did, and admired him for it. That, to her, he was still a hero.

Chapter Twenty-Three

Anna stirred the tomato sauce and added a bit more pepper to it. She turned and looked at Ophelia. Ophelia sat at the breakfast bar coloring with Zoe.

"It's my birthday. I can throw a birthday party for myself if I want," Ophelia said. "I'm not ten anymore."

"Hey, I'm going to be ten soon!" Zoe said, looking up at her aunt.

"Really? Already? Weren't you just born last week?"

"No!" Zoe scrunched up her nose at Ophelia. "Can I come to your party?"

"That would be like the coolest thing ever," Ophelia said. "But I think this time, I'm just inviting adults."

"Oh," Zoe said deflated.

"Hey," Ophelia said, poking her with a crayon. "How about we do something fun for your birthday? How about getting a mani-pedi and cupcakes?"

"That sounds like a lot of fun!" Zoe said, looking back down at her coloring book.

Anna smiled at her daughter and then her sister.

"So anyway, I was thinking of an adult-ish kind of party," Ophelia said. "Nothing fancy, just music, food, drink, standing around talking. You could bring Phil."

"That sounds like fun," Anna said. "Is you-know-who coming?"

Ophelia scowled at her sister. "No. He was officially uninvited this weekend when he thought he could lie to me."

Anna sighed. "I really wish I could find you someone who's worth your time and effort."

"The heart wants what the heart wants," Ophelia said, though as much as she tried to make it light-hearted, her heart wasn't in it.

"Would you consider someone Phillip works with?" Anna asked.

"Um, if either of you set me up on a date with someone," Ophelia said, "then we're going to have some words. Those are fighting words."

"Come on," Anna said. "Guys know about other guys and at least this way Phillip can sort of screen out any potential losers."

"Hmmm, I'll maybe think about it. But only because it's Phil," Ophelia said, giving her sister a suspicious eye.

"Fine. Who else are you inviting?"

"I totally forgot to tell you—Byrant is in town!"

"Like Aunt Debbie's Calvin-Klein-underwear-modeling son?"

"The very one," Ophelia said. "I bet he'd come too."

"What is he doing out here? He was in Paris the last time I looked at Facebook."

"Not sure," Ophelia said. "Mom only said he was out visiting Debbie and he was probably going to be here through Christmas."

"Awesome!" Anna said, covering the saucepan to simmer. "It'll be good to catch up. Is he still dating what's-his-name?"

"Garrett?" Ophelia asked. "Yes, but he's been suspiciously absent from Bryant's Facebook posts lately."

"Too bad," Anna said. "He never seems to catch a break, similar to a sister of mine."

Ophelia rolled her eyes. "Ugh, must we keep bringing it up?"

"No, we can talk about something else," Anna said, looking at the clock on the wall. "Are you staying for dinner? Phillip should be over any minute."

"No, I should get going," Ophelia said. "Come here, munchkin. Love you lots." She hugged Zoe and waved to her sister.

Brody walked into the kitchen. "I'm hungry. When are we eating?"

"Just as soon as Phillip gets here," she said, pulling some dishes out of the dishwasher and handing them to Zoe. "Let's get the table set so we can eat as soon as he does."

Brody sighed. He put his book on the table and got up and started getting some drink glasses.

"What are you reading?" she asked.

"Um, the Count of Monte Cristo," he said.

"How is it?"

Brody shrugged. "It's okay. That Fernand guy is a jerk."

Anna nodded, smiling. "Yup, he's pretty slimy."

"I mean isn't it bad enough that he got his best friend thrown in jail, then married his best friend's girlfriend, but he treats his son like crap. No wonder it was so easy for Dantes to kidnap Albert—the kid's dad ignores him."

Anna looked at her son for a moment. She was about to say something when she heard knocking. Zoe ran for the door. "Phillip!" she squealed. He came around the corner carrying Zoe on his back. Anna smiled and was about to ask for a kiss when she noticed the dark circles under his eyes. He put Zoe down at the table, and then bent over to kiss Anna. Without saying a word, he went into the kitchen.

Anna turned around. Phillip sampled the sauce off the lid and nodded. "Tastes good."

"Thanks," Anna said. "Do you want to take it to the table for me?"

He brought the saucepan over and went back for the noodles.

"Do you want to take your jacket off?" Anna said. "I'll go put it over on the couch."

"No, I'm fine."

Anna grimaced but didn't say anything. She looked over to her children and they, too, watched Phillip. Usually, he was talkative and interested in how their day went, but he seemed to want to sit and eat in silence.

"So, um, Ophelia's birthday is coming up," Anna said. "She's thinking of having a party at her duplex and wants to invite us."

Phillip continued to stare at his plate but nodded. "Sure, we can go, if you want."

"I mean, we don't have to go, if you don't want to," Anna said.

"We can go," he said harshly. "If that's what you want, we'll do it."

Anna blinked. She turned to her kids. "So, what do you guys want to do tonight? Is everyone's homework done?"

"I'd rather just read in my room," Brody said, eyeing Phillip warily.

"Mom, can we watch the new princess movie?" Zoe asked. "I want to sit next to Phillip."

"Phillip?" Anna asked.

He nodded, exhaustion etching his face.

They ate dinner in silence. Every once in a while, Anna would look up to watch Phillip. He pushed his food around more than he ate it. This silence was almost scarier than his outburst the other week. It was just so unlike him.

Dinner finished without incident but also in almost complete silence. Brody got up and took his book into his room. Phillip and Zoe went over to the couch and Anna put the movie on. He rested his arm against the armrest on the couch and held his head with this hand. Zoe tucked herself in next to him and he watched the movie impassively with her. Anna grabbed her grading stack and sat down on the other end of the couch. She watched Phillip instead of the movie. She really wished he would look over so she could smile at him or anything to help this funk he found himself in. Soon the credits started to roll, and when she looked up again, she found that both Zoe and Phillip had fallen asleep.

Anna bit her lip. He looked tired beyond words. Was the overwhelming workload catching up to him? Maybe he was having a problem that he hadn't told her about? His hand slipped and his head jerked up. He looked around and then saw Anna, giving her the first hint of a smile. He looked down and noticed Zoe asleep on him.

"How about I put her to bed and then we can talk?" he said, sliding out from under the sleeping girl.

Anna's heart skipped a few times as she watched him gather Zoe gently into his arms and walk her down the hallway to her room. There was seriously nothing sexier than a man taking care of a child. He came back and sat down on the couch next to her and gathered her up in his arms. He kissed her hair.

"Everything okay?" Anna asked.

"Oh, if you mean about earlier, I'm sorry. I didn't mean for it to come out so rudely," he said.

"I know. We all have bad days. I'm just concerned at how tired you look," she said. "Are you not sleeping? Is everything okay at work?"

"What is there to say?" he said, shifting. "The load at work is rough. I deal with it the best I can, and I spend time with you."

"There's got to be more to it than that," she said, looking up at him.

"I'm telling you, I'm fine. Just a bit tired from the workload." He sighed. "I should probably go."

"No, stay please," she said.

He looked into her eyes. "Okay, for a little while."

She held her hands to his chest and pressed her lips to his. He brought a hand to her face and kissed back. She pulled herself closer, caught up in the scent of him and his soft lips as they glided against hers. She wished that there was a kind of kiss that would make all the hard parts of life go away. She tried deepening the kiss but he pulled away and he leaned his head against her shoulder. She ran her fingers through the hair on the back of his head.

"You are so beautiful," he said.

"You're not so bad yourself," she said, trying to smile.

"I should honestly get going. I'm going to fall asleep before I get back to the apartment."

Disappointment pitted in her gut. "Phillip, please. Talk to me."

"What do you want me to say?" he said, irritated. He got up from the couch. "That I have a stack of case files two feet high on my desk. Every time I turn around there's someone there needing something from me that I don't have the authority or ability to help them with. There's not enough help to go around. I fight for these guys every day, but at least as a soldier, I knew who the enemy was. There is no enemy now. At least not an enemy you can see."

Anna sat silent, not sure what to say to that.

"They stretch you thin, and then ask how much more you can take," he said, running his hand through his hair. He'd worked himself up into a sort of frenzy of emotion she'd never seen from him and it worried her. "Do you know how many vet suicides there were last month?"

Anna shook her head.

"We lost six guys. Six! That's twice the number I lost in my unit over two years! Six guys who probably thought it was pointless to come into the VA to get help. And were they right?"

"Phillip, don't you think you're shouldering too much of the responsibility?"

"Who else is going to?"

"What I'm trying to say is, maybe you should talk to someone yourself," she said carefully. "Get a fresh perspective."

He looked at her in shock. "That's insulting. Really."

"What are you talking about?" Anna said.

"You should just come out and say it—a counselor who needs counseling. How ineffectual do you think I am?"

"Don't put words in my mouth, Phillip," Anna said, fully upset. "You know that I think you're one of the kindest and most thoughtful men in the world, and you're the last person in the world I would call ineffectual. But I think you're shouldering too much of the responsibility of this job. You're only one person."

"Damn it," he said. "You really don't get it, do you?"

"I guess not," she said with a tight jaw.

He walked towards the front door. "I'm going to go before I say something really stupid."

It's a little late for that, she thought, as she watched him go through the door. She sat back on the couch, suddenly in need of something to smash with a baseball bat.

Chapter Twenty-Four

Anna heard the music before she even got out of her van. People spilled out of the duplex onto its little lawn where Ophelia had set out some Adirondack chairs with tiki torches of citronella. Anna checked her cell phone. Phillip promised he'd come tonight. The run he'd taken with Brody in the morning had seemed to take the edge off his wild emotions, but he still didn't look like he was sleeping. She had encouraged him to take some relaxation time at his apartment but now she wondered if that was a mistake. She debated on whether to go to his apartment to pick him up but she stopped herself. He said he was going to be at the party. She had to allow him to take care of himself and keep his promises.

Ophelia talked to some people but the minute she saw her sister pull up, she ran to help out with Anna's wheelchair and then envelope her in a big hug.

"Bryant! Garrett!" Ophelia yelled. Two beautiful men came down off the porch and each gave Anna a hug.

"Oh my gosh, Bryant! It has been forever since we saw each other last!" Anna said. "I thought you were in Paris."

"I was," he said. "But my mom has been begging me forever to come home, so I told her as long as Garrett was invited, I'd come back."

"Garrett," Anna hugged the other man standing next to Bryant. "It's nice to finally meet you. We hear about you all the time on social media."

"It's great to meet you too," he said. "I've never been to Utah before, and Bryant said I had to come."

"I hope you like hiking," Anna said.

"I love hiking," he said. "We've been up around the . . . Alpine Loop? Right?" Anna nodded. "And Sundance. The mountains around here are amazing."

"Anna!" Bryant said. "Where is this gorgeous boyfriend of yours Phee's been telling us about?"

"He got stuck at work and told me to come ahead," she said. "And hands off, he's mine."

"No worries," Bryant said. "Not into the military type. Looks great in shirtless fatigues but that's about it."

"Speak for yourself," Garrett said.

Ophelia hugged both men around their waists. "Shall we get Anna inside?"

They were about to head to the stairs leading into the house when a young man came walking up. He was tall with sandy blonde hair, glasses, and a simple outfit of khakis and a polo. He had striking light blue eyes, and a pink gift bag in his hand. Both Bryant and Garrett reacted with brilliant smiles but the blonde looked completely out of his depth.

"Hi!" Ophelia said. "Are you here for my party?"

"Yes," he said, a blush blooming across his face. "You must be Ophelia. You look just like the picture Phillip showed me."

"Oh, you must be Justin!" Anna said. "Glad you could make it. Phillip wasn't sure if you could or not."

"Come along," Ophelia said, grabbing his hand. "These other two are going to help Anna in the house, and then you can show me what you brought."

Like Anna was nothing more than a bag of leaves, they lifted her, wheelchair and all, into the duplex. She made her way into the sitting room where Ophelia was talking to Justin. "Bryant and Garrett both have worked for Calvin Klein and a bunch of other designers but I can never keep track of them all. So, is this for me?"

Justin handed the bag over to Ophelia. She took the tissue out and pulled out a smaller dark brown bag. "Wow, Justin," she said, a blush spreading across her cheeks.

"What is it?" Anna said.

"It's a hundred-dollar three-kilogram bag of Vlahrona chocolate," Ophelia said, looking wide-eyed at the package. "That's amazing. And too much." She looked up at Justin.

He pointed to the bag. "There's something else."

She reached in and pulled out a jar. She laughed. "Edible gold leaf. I love it!"

"Phillip told me you're a pastry chef so I went to Orson Gygi. The sales people there were very helpful."

Ophelia jumped up and hugged Justin. "Thank you. It's really too much but I still love it anyway. No one's gotten me expensive pastry-making stuff before."

Justin smiled down at her, hugging her back. "You're welcome."

"Come here. I need to show this to someone and I want you to come with me," she said, stuffing the gifts back in the bag, taking Justin's hand, and dragging him across the room.

Bryant laughed. "Totally twitterpated."

"Which one?" Anna asked.

"Definitely Justin," he said. "He looks like he was just presented with a huge pink and blonde fluffy snack."

"I don't know," Anna said with a grin. "I think he made quite the impression on Phee, as well. He's good looking enough for her."

"I guess we'll see," Bryant said, happily as he sat down on the couch in Ophelia's front room. Garrett sat down on the arm next to his boyfriend.

"We just need to make sure Mike's hooks stay out of her first, then Justin stands a very good chance."

"Is she seriously still dating him?"

"Hard to tell these days," Anna said. "She keeps saying, 'This time it's over.' And then it's not and then it is."

Bryant shook his head. "Married hooks are bad hooks. And speaking of *married*, Ophelia says it's pretty serious between you and this guy Phillip."

Anna blushed. "You might say that it is. He's a wonderful man, and I'd be lucky to have him."

"But?" Bryant said.

"He's been acting off lately," Anna said. Both Bryant and Garrett's eyes widened. "He's been working a lot and doesn't give himself time to really turn it off. It's getting to him. At first, it just made him sulky and now . . . he just flies off the handle sometimes."

"He better not have—" Garrett said, face darkening.

"No, no," Anna said. "He's never ever laid a hand on me, or my kids. And I don't think he ever would . . . but the raging is getting old."

"Yeah, definitely something to resolve before you make anything official. Better to be alone than with an abusive man in your lives. The hurt from someone like that will stay with them forever," Garrett said.

"Babe, you seem to know something about this," Bryant said.

"Oh, you know," he said. "Our family was the typical movie of the week story—single mom with a bunch of kids falls in love with who she thought was a good guy, only to find out later that he really adhered to 'spare the rod, spoil the child' way of parenting."

Anna's breath caught in her throat, and for a minute she felt a little sick.

"Babe, you never told me about any of this," Bryant said.

"I don't like to talk about it or him," Garrett said. "They were only married for six months officially but it was the worst two years of my life. I was glad when she sent that one packing."

Anna put a hand on Garrett's shoulder. "I'm sorry you had to deal with that. I'm glad your mom was brave enough to break it off with him instead of making everyone suffer for years and years."

"Just be careful," Garrett said, his eyes a little misty. "I mean I barely know you but you and Ophelia seem to be really awesome people. I would hate for wonderful people to suffer like we did when I knew I could have at least warned you."

Anna nodded. "I appreciate it. I love Phillip and he really is a good man. But my children come first and I have to take care of them the best way I know how, whether he agrees with me or not."

Bryant grabbed her hand. "Well, cuz, if Phillip is the kind of man you think he is, then he's a super lucky man. I'm sad we don't get to spend more time with each other, otherwise I'd say he'd have to go through me first before you're allowed to marry him."

Anna laughed. "Get in line behind Uncle Arthur."

Garrett leaned over and whispered something in Bryant's ear. "Are you serious?" Bryant laughed. "I am not asking her. You do it. You're so crazy."

Garrett looked sheepishly at Anna. "Would it be okay if I tried out your wheelchair?" Bryant clicked his teeth but still kept the amused smile on his face.

"What?" Garrett protested. "I've always wanted to try one that wasn't one of those clunky hospital ones."

Anna laughed. "I don't mind if it's just for a minute. Knowing Ophelia's friends, there would be a line out the door of people wanting to try it."

Bryant came over and picked Anna up from her chair and settled on the couch with her next to him. She took the opportunity to give Bryant one more squeeze as they both giggled at Garrett's attempts at popping a wheelie.

"Be careful!" Anna said. "It's harder than it looks and you could find yourself on your back staring at the ceiling."

Garrett tried again and nearly succeeded in landing on his back. Anna and Bryant laughed themselves breathless. She took air into her lungs and was about to scold Garrett for trying to break her wheelchair when she looked up and saw Phillip standing in the doorway. She raised her hand to wave at him but stopped when she saw his face. His brows were like storm clouds gathering over the Great Salt Lake, but his face looked like he was going to be sick.

"Hey, isn't that your . . . ?" Bryant stopped when he saw her face.

"Please put me back in my chair, Bryant," she said.

Garrett immediately hopped out and held it while Bryant put her back in the chair. She shoved people out of the way to get to Phillip, but he had turned around and left the house.

"Phillip!" she called. He kept going as if he didn't hear her. She yelled his name again and only when he was in his truck and put his seatbelt on did he look up at her. She motioned for him to come back. Instead, he put his truck in gear and peeled down the road disappearing around the corner.

"What the hell?" Anna ripped her cell phone out of her pocket and pressed his number. It went straight to voicemail. "Damn it, Phillip!" She put her head in her hands. Ophelia came running up to her with Justin in tow.

"What happened?" Ophelia said, looking up at Bryant and Garrett.

"If that was Phillip that just left, then he might have gotten the wrong impression," Bryant said.

"He came in when Bryant had Anna sitting on his lap," Garrett said.

"He just drove off, Phee," Anna said, holding tears back, angrier than she'd ever been in her life. "He just left and didn't let me explain anything. And he turned his damn phone off!"

"What do you want to do?" Ophelia said. "Do you need me to do anything?"

"I've got to find him," Anna said.

"Where would he go?" Ophelia said.

"Where else would a bear who's hurt go?" Anna said. "Back to his cave."

Garrett and Bryant helped her back out of the house. She sped down the road once she was back in her van and headed straight for Phillip's apartment. The sun was setting as she pulled into the closest parking stall and noted his truck nearby. She approached his apartment door and slammed her fist against it several times.

"Open this door right now, Phillip." There was no sound of movement on the other side. "If you don't want me to get any louder, then open the damn door." For a moment, she really thought he might not open the door. She was about to start the pounding again when the door opened into his dark apartment. Phillip stood in the doorway, his eyes red-rimmed and face drawn. She didn't wait for him to invite her in. She pushed the door the rest of the way open and pulled herself in, slamming it behind her.

"Shouldn't you be at the party with your boyfriend?" he growled. "I saw him all over you."

Anna clenched her fists, really tempted to smack him.

"He was good looking," he said. "He should make you very happy."

She folded her arms and looked up at him.

"So, you're not going to say anything? Or are you here to break up with me, or just rub it in?"

"Are you done yet?" she said. He looked away from her. "He's my cousin. And he's gay."

Phillip staggered backward against his couch and sat down hard.

"I can't believe you thought I would even—" she said.

"What was I supposed to think?" Phillip asked, voiced raised. "You never mentioned him before and you were in his lap, hanging on him!"

"Because his *boyfriend* was trying out my wheelchair!" Anna snapped. "He's my cousin, so why not sit on his lap? I hadn't seen him in years. And you—you honestly thought I would betray your trust like that! The man that says he loves me. Did you forget that I've been married before? I know how it works. I know what's appropriate and what's not. Darren had no complaints about me before he died. If you're so easily convinced that I'd do something so grotesque as that, then why are we even together?"

Anna shook with fury. A lump formed in her throat she tried unsuccessfully to swallow. She didn't even want to be in the same room with him. Teeth gritted, she pulled her keys out of her purse.

"You know what? Why did I even come here? As if I needed to explain myself! I need to get out of here. Pull it together, Laughlin, and then call me." She reached for the front door, the tears already falling to her lap.

"Wait, Anna."

Before she could get a hold of the doorknob, a force pulled her backward and whipped her around.

Tears floated in Philip's eyes. "I don't want you to go. Please."

Anna grabbed his face with her hands. She kissed him so hard she was sure she had bruised her lips and his.

Phillip's chest hitched as if he held back sobs. She forced him to look at her. "I love you. Only you. I only want you. No one else," she said softly as she watched a single tear escape his eyes. She reached over to wrap her arms around his neck and kissed the tear away.

Phillip pulled her to him to straddle his lap. His trembling hands stroked her back as his lips burned her with their intensity. Her breaths came raggedly as the heady combination of her tears and the taste of his mouth hit her like a drug. Her anger and fear melted away as Phillip's touch became more insistent. Her heartbeat galloped out of control. Phillip was doing that to her and his heat only spurred her to want more.

Phillip wrapped his arms tighter around her, and nuzzled his face in her neck as she softly ran her fingers through his hair. "I need you," he whispered into her ear, sending warm electricity zooming down her spine. She needed him too. She needed every part of him. For whatever reason, the fire burning between them now had melted away any doubt or fear of being physical with him. Having him whisper his need to her only emboldened her to grab his shirt and whip it up over his head and onto the floor. Now she could touch that chest in the way she'd always wanted to but had never allowed herself to.

He pulled her shirt up over her head as well. The roughness of his hands against her skin made her shudder in pleasure, whipping the fire of her passion into an inferno. His lips sought hers again and her insides liquified as she hugged herself to him. She yearned for him to be closer. She craved to feel his skin against hers, feel the racing of his heart, the urgency in his kiss.

"I love you so much. I'm sorry," he whispered in her ear. His mouth blazed a path down to the galloping beat of the pulse of her neck. His lips lightly feathered the skin there, his soft, hot breath causing goosebumps to sprout. She lost herself to it as he moved down towards her chest.

He was making it impossible to think straight. But she had to so she could make him understand that how he had been acting lately wasn't okay, but that she wasn't abandoning him. He'd become a part of her life she wasn't sure she could live without now.

But before she could say anything he tightened his grip on her thighs and stood up. She wrapped her arms tightly around his neck clinging to him as he lifted her. She kissed his neck, burying her face in it. All she could do for now was breathe in the soft scent of him, feel the bristles of his facial hair against her cheek.

Once they reached his bedroom, he placed her on this bed and crawled over the top of her, kissing her skin until he reached her mouth again. She put her hands against his chest.

"Phillip, you once asked me to trust what we have," she said, looking into his eyes. "I'm asking for the same thing. Trust me. Trust my love for you. I'm not going anywhere. I don't want to be anywhere else. I just want you."

"I know," he said. "I don't know what I was doing, why I was thinking you would-- Doesn't matter. I know you would never. You're the best thing that's ever happened to me, Anna. And I almost screwed that up."

Hard or easy, deeply in love or fighting, he was everything to her. She caressed the muscles of his upper arms and slid her hands up his toned back. She wouldn't let him get away that easily. Not without a fight. Not without him knowing the depths of the love she felt for him, the admiration for him that swelled her chest, and the good man he was, even if he wasn't entirely convinced of that himself. She pulled on his hips as she kissed him. Things were going too slowly now.

He drew his head back and blinked at her. "I don't know what to do," he said, looking sheepish and concerned. "With you."

She smiled at him, running her hand down his chest. "Nothing special. It all pretty much works the same."

"What if I do something wrong?" His panting breaths sent goosebumps over her skin.

"You won't," she said. "Just take your time and I'll help you figure out the rest."

He leaned down to kiss her again, falling into her arms.

She woke later in the night expecting to feel his warm body next to her. He was standing next to a window with a single slat open.

"Phillip?" she said. He turned his head around.

"I thought you were asleep," he said, coming back to the bed and sitting down.

"I was, but I guess I got a chill," she said, rubbing her hand on his arm.

"I have something for you," he said. He went over to his dresser and pulled a box out of a bag and brought it over. "This is going a little differently than I planned. I'd rather you know how much I love you right now—now that we're alone—than a big show to say the same thing."

He turned a lamp on and handed her the box. It was black velvet. She looked up at him, smiling. She opened it and inside was the most beautiful emerald and diamond ring she'd ever seen. A huge lump caught in her throat and tears spilled from her eyes. She buried her face in Phillip's shoulder. He took the box from her and pulled the ring out. He took her hand.

"I know things have been hard lately. But I never want you to doubt my love for you. You came into my life and you were everything I didn't know I wanted, needed. Now I don't think I can live without you. Life would just feel wrong. I knew you were special the first time I looked into your blue eyes, and now I want to show you how special you are to me. Would you agree to be mine? Would you marry me, Anna Gilbert?"

She was gulping with full-fledged sobs now and barely managed to breathe out the word between hiccups, "Yes."

He put the ring on her finger, where it glinted in the soft light of his lamp. She sat up and grabbed him and kissed his lips. She pulled him back into bed, back into her arms.

Chapter Twenty-Five

The next morning Anna and Phillip pulled up to her parents' house. Anna phoned her dad from the truck, asking him to come outside so Phillip could talk to him privately and without the kids seeing. As soon as Phillip came to the point, Art pulled Phillip into a hug and slapped him companionably on his back. He came around to the other side of the truck and pulled the door open to give his daughter a hug. He wiped the moisture from his eyes.

"I'm so happy for you," Art said, as he hugged her tight. Ellen approached the truck and Anna showed her the ring. Immediately, Ellen's tears began to flow and she hugged her daughter fiercely. She then turned to Phillip and hugged him as well.

"I have one more surprise," Phillip said, a huge smile on his face. Anna's heart leaped to see his gorgeous smile. It hadn't shown itself very much. He pulled a small gift bag from under the driver's seat. "Let's go talk to the kids."

They all gathered in the front room. Phillip's face was a mix of nerves and excitement. Brody and Zoe came in and sat next to their grandparents.

"So, your mom and I have something very important to share with you," Phillip said.

"I knew it!" Brody said. "You're getting married."

Zoe sucked in a breath. "Are you guys really?"

"Before we talk about that," Phillip said. "I have something very important to ask Zoe."

Zoe's face lit up and she walked over to stand near Phillip. "Zoe, I love your mom very much. But I couldn't love her like I need to if I didn't love you and your brother too. Being a daddy is a very important responsibility, and so I want to make sure you know that I will do everything in my power to be a good daddy to you and your brother."

Phillip handed her the small gift bag. Zoe eagerly pulled the black velvet box out and then when she saw what was on the inside, she gasped. She pulled out a necklace. It was a small emerald that matched the color of her mother's, surrounded by tiny diamonds on a thin silver cord.

"Zoe, even though I can't be your real daddy, I want to try and be the next best thing. Would you let me take care of you as I plan on taking care of your mom?" Zoe blinked and looked at him. She threw herself into a hug with Phillip.

Phillip took the necklace from Zoe and latched it on the girl. "Now, that is only for special occasions. I want you to make sure you don't lose it so you can wear it on the day your mom and I get married. When we're done today, give that to your mom for safekeeping."7

Phillip stood up and walked over to Brody. They did their special hand sign, and Phillip pulled Brody into a side hug. Brody came over to Anna.

"Well, I guess if you're gonna marry someone, at least it's someone as cool as Phillip," he said and he bent over and gave his mother a hug. Fresh tears sprang to her eyes. She couldn't remember the last time she'd been so happy and it was all thanks to Phillip. She looked over and beamed at him. She was lost in the soft look he gave to her.

"What am I going to do with you?" Anna said, snuggled on the couch with Phillip that evening, her legs across his lap. She smoothed back his hair from his forehead.

"Well, I've got a few ideas but maybe it's not polite to say out loud," he said, tracing a finger down her cheek.

Anna slapped him on his chest. He grabbed her hand and kissed it.

"When are we getting married?" Phillip said.

"I was so surprised you asked, I haven't even thought about it," Anna said. "A summer wedding would be more practical. I don't have to work, so going on a honeymoon will be easier. Though a fall wedding sounds nice. It would make it easier for Marge and Hank to come. Either will give me some time to get something put together."

"Definitely could not forget Marge and Hank," Phillip said.

"And I don't want anything big," Anna said. "I think a few friends and family should be enough. Turn your back to me. You work so hard, and I know you're exhausted."

He did as she asked and she started to massage his shoulders. His muscles were tighter than bound cords. They sat in silence as she worked his shoulders. She pushed her thumbs up against the base of his skull and he groaned.

"That is amazing," he said. "Never ever stop."

"Even my amazing hands will give out eventually," Anna said.

"I just hope I can return all the amazing that you have given me," he said.

"I'm not worried about it, Phillip," she said. "You have been strong for me when I needed it most."

"But now we're not talking about part-time," he said. "We're talking about being there for you and the kids full-time. I just hope I don't disappoint you."

"Never," Anna said, kissing his ear.

"You don't know that," Phillip said.

"The only possible way you could disappoint me is if you stop trying," Anna said.

"There's this scenario that plays through my head sometimes," he said, almost as if he hadn't heard her. "We're having problems with the kids, and no matter what I do or say it's always the wrong thing. Then something bad happens to one of them and I can't forgive myself for not doing the thing that would have saved them."

"Phillip, you'll be fine, I promise," Anna said, gently pulling him back to lean against her. "What you described is what every parent thinks about. I thought the same things when the kids were born. Would they have some terrible disease and I didn't do enough to figure it out? Or what would happen if I dropped one of them while trying to push my wheelchair and they'd be damaged for life? I've seen how you are with the kids, and for a guy who's never had kids before, you do an amazing job."

"You have to say that," Phillip said.

"No, I don't have to say that because not every guy is as naturally nurturing as you," Anna said. "It wouldn't be a complete deal breaker if you weren't, we'd just have to work it out before we got married. But I am not worried about you as a dad at all. In fact, I think your worrying means you'll be a good parent."

"Anna, can I ask you something?" Phillip said.

"Sure," Anna said.

"Why do you love me?" Phillip said.

Anna smiled. "Well, I guess 'because you're a damn handsome sexy devil' is probably not the answer you're looking for, so I'll have to go with kind, enthusiastic, smart, hard-working, dedicated, and persevering. And can I tell you something? You make me so proud. People that work with you have nothing but awesome things to say about you. You are a natural at your job and it shows."

Phillip sat silent for a long moment. Anna wondered if he had fallen asleep. He turned around on his seat to look at her and put a hand to her face. "Thank you for having so much faith in me. I hope it isn't misplaced."

"Why would you say something like that?" Anna said. "You're being so odd tonight, Phillip."

He shook his head. "Nothing. It's being up half the night last night that's talking." He gave her a crooked smile.

Anna took his hand from her face and held it. "Talk to me. Tell me what's going on. I can try to help."

"Really, I'm fine," he said, leaning his head back against the couch.

"Phillip, I can be a lot of things, but insincere is not one of them," she said, making him look at her. "I'm telling you with as much honesty as I can, you have so many strengths that I admire and love you for. It's true whether you think so or not. And I know you're tired. You have so much pressure on you between work and us. I don't pretend to know what you go through day to day. But I know you, and you deserve all the positivity and encouragement that you give to other people."

Phillip looked away but held her hand in his lap. They sat like that for a long time.

"I better get going," he said, as he stood up from the couch. He bent over and kissed her briefly.

Anna took in a breath to say something, maybe to invite him to stay overnight but he was out the door before the thought had fully formed.

She let out a long breath. The conversation had taken a direction that had her concerned and confused. He'd indicated some doubts about his job in the past, but tonight felt different. Was it anxiety? Should she talk to his boss about it? She just wished she knew the right thing to do to help the man she loved.

Chapter Twenty-Six

Anna threw the keys on the kitchen counter. "Guys, make sure to bring everything in. I don't need the frozen stuff defrosting."

She looked through the mail. There was a letter from a real estate broker, but she threw it aside. She helped her kids put away the groceries when there was a knock at the door. Phillip walked in.

"Hi, Phillip!" Zoe said.

"Hi," Anna said, as he leaned over to give her a kiss.

He put a folder down on the kitchen table and helped the kids put away the rest of the groceries.

"What's this?" Anna said as she picked the folder off the table. It was from the same real estate brokerage that she had gotten the letter from.

"It's something to look at and think about," Phillip said.

"I know it's not something we talked about, but I don't want to sell the house," she said, putting the folder down.

"Why not?" Phillip said.

"Well, it's nearly paid off and this is the house the kids have grown up in," she said. "You don't think moving right now would cause undue stress on them?"

"I guess I see it differently," he said. "I see a house that you lived in with your first husband and it might be nice to start over fresh with a new house for our family to grow up in."

"Even if I wanted to sell, which I don't, now is not the right time to look for a house. And looking for a house with me is a pain. There are so many accommodations for my wheelchair that need to be present in a house. It makes looking for something new tedious. Building's not much better because anything that needs to be done to the blueprint is considered an upgrade, which they charge a premium for. All of that and planning a wedding? I'd be gray before we made it to the honeymoon."

"It's like you're trying to come up with reasons to not even consider it," he said.

"Have you been listening?" Anna said, glaring at Phillip. "I'm not 'trying.' I'm being realistic. There are too many reasons to keep it and not enough good ones to sell."

"Have you considered how I'd feel about living here?" Phillip said.

"No, because I didn't think it would be this big a deal," Anna said. "You've never said anything about being uncomfortable before."

"Of course I haven't, because I had my own place," he said. "But we're going to be making a family together and I'd prefer somewhere the ghost of Darren isn't present in every corner."

Anna clenched her fists. "I understand your point of view. I don't agree."

"And so that's that?" he said. "You've spoken and there's no further discussion?"

"I didn't say that," she said. "I just said I don't agree, which means we just have to think it out and talk about it later."

Phillip turned his back on the kitchen and folded his arms. Brody wandered back in.

"What are we talking about?" he said, oblivious to the argument.

"We're talking about living arrangements after Phillip and I get married."

"Oh, I thought we were living here," Brody said.

"I just suggested that we try living somewhere else in a new house," Phillip said.

"What new house?" Zoe said.

"Our new house," Phillip said.

"We get to live with Phillip?!" Zoe jumped up and down, just about coming out of her skin.

"Yes, but after the wedding," Anna said. "You guys really want to move out of this house?"

Brody shrugged. "It wouldn't be the worst thing that ever happened."

Zoe looked torn. "We wouldn't be able to stay here?"

"No, that's not what we said," Phillip said, squatting down to look her in the eye. "I just said that maybe we should look at finding a new house when we become a new family."

Zoe didn't seem convinced.

"I was just telling Phillip we don't have to move to a new house to have a family together. We could stay here and make this place work for our family," Anna said.

"Yeah, but wouldn't it be weird for Phillip to move into the house you and Dad bought?" Brody said.

Anna gave Phillip a look.

"I swear I had nothing to do with the opinions of anyone other than myself," Phillip said, raising his hands.

"Not that the children's opinions have much weight in the final decision," Anna said.

"But would mine have any weight?" Phillip said.

"Yes, but I'm not sure whether you understand how I'm feeling about this whole thing, and I'd rather not discuss it in front of the kids," Anna said. Phillip nodded.

She motioned him to follow her into her bedroom. He shut the door behind him.

"First of all, this is my house," Anna said. "What possessed you to even take the initiative and contact a brokerage without even consulting me about it?"

"I honestly didn't think it would be as big a deal as it apparently is," Phillip said. "I felt like it was an option we should explore together, and I didn't realize it would upset you."

"But do you understand why I'm upset?" Anna said.

Phillip ran his hand through his hair. "No."

"Really?" Anna said. "I'm upset because you didn't even talk to me about it. You just did it, and you did it for a piece of property that wasn't even yours."

He sighed.

"Then I apologize. When you put it like that, I can understand how you feel, and I was out of line," he said sitting on the bed. "That still doesn't change the fact that we need to discuss the idea of where to live when we get married."

"Would you honestly find it offensive to live here?" Anna said.

"That's putting it a little dramatically," Phillip said. "I just wish that we could start over fresh somewhere else. If we had no other options then I would just suck it up, and stay here. But we do have options we can look into."

Anna rubbed her face. "I don't know that I have the energy to go through the hassle. And it is a very big hassle."

"Would it be such a hassle if we did it together?" Phillip said.

"Yes," said Anna. "You know what I should do? I should make you go house hunting with me, just so you can get an idea of what I'm talking about. You give the realtor the basics—number of rooms, number of bathrooms, square footage, garage, yard size, and then make sure I can get in all the doors in the house, make sure a ramp can be built in the front or garage and in the backyard."

Phillip nodded at each point as if he was taking mental notes of all the items Anna had listed. "Next weekend then?"

"I suppose," Anna said.

"I'll make the arrangements since this is my idea," Phillip said.

"Just make sure the realtor understands we're just looking, and that I'm in a wheelchair," Anna said.

"Gotcha," Phillip said. He winked at her.

Brody and Phillip had just come back from their Saturday morning run when the realtor showed up.

"Hello, you must be Anna," the woman's voice dripped saccharine. "My name is Sheila Bruster. Phillip called me and told me all about your situation. I just wanted you to know I know exactly how you feel. I was laid up with a broken leg for about a month, and getting around in a wheelchair is such a nightmare."

As she talked, she looked around the house, eyes appraising it. "Such a cute home. I'm sure there would be no problem selling it. Now, I'd love if you could show me the bedrooms, then I'll just pop outside and inspect the yard."

"Um, excuse me, Sheila, was it?" Anna said. "I'm not looking to sell my house right now. Didn't Phillip say we were only looking at what's out there?"

"Oh, yes," she said, peeking out of the patio doors. "But I am totally confident I can find something you and Phillip will be so happy with you couldn't move out of here fast enough."

Phillip walked out of the master bedroom where he had showered after his run. He smiled until he saw the look on Anna's face.

"There he is," Sheila said. She looked him up and down. "I was just telling Anna that I'm confident that I can find you two something you'll just love."

"Uh, do you have some examples with you?" Phillip said, sitting down at the kitchen table. He moved a chair over so Anna could sit next to him. Sheila sat on the other side of Phillip almost elbow to elbow with him. She pulled out her portfolio and took out a few printed examples of properties for Anna and Phillip to look at. Reaching across Phillip, she laid them down on the table.

"Phillip said you wanted to stay in the area or close to downtown. This condo is in Sugarhouse. It's a three-bedroom, two-bath unit, eleven hundred square feet, and amenities including a workout room and keypad entry."

"Is there any green space?" Anna asked.

"There's a lovely park about a half mile down 900 East," Sheila said.

"No, I mean, is there any place for my kids to play there?" Anna said.

"Oh, well, there's an outdoor space on the roof but you have to rent that for throwing parties and things," Sheila said.

Anna frowned. "Not even a pool?"

"No. Okay, so I'm getting this isn't quite your first choice," Sheila said. "Let me show you this one."

She pushed the sheet towards Anna. Sheila's breast rubbed up against Phillip's arm as she did so. He stiffened and coughed.

"I'll be right back," he said, standing up. Sheila's disappointed look wasn't lost on Anna.

"This one is in North Salt Lake. It's a cute little rambler in an established neighborhood."

"This says it's only got two rooms on the main floor and that they built the master bedroom in the basement."

"Yes," Sheila said.

"Does the house have an elevator?"

Sheila giggled. "No."

Anna waited for Sheila to catch up. "So, if it doesn't, then how am I supposed to get to my master bedroom?"

"Oh," Sheila said. "Right. How about this one?"

She pushed another sheet at Anna. Phillip returned and sat down on the other side of Anna and pulled his chair as close to her as possible, putting his arm around her waist and twining his fingers with hers.

"Sheila, let me ask you a question," Anna said as she leaned back into Phillip's arm. "Did you take my wheelchair into consideration, besides the condo, when you printed out any of these? Phillip, you told her that I was wheelchair-bound right?"

"Yes, I definitely told her that," Phillip said.

Sheila looked at a loss. Anna rolled her eyes internally. "For me to even look at the house it's got to have a yard, at least fifteen hundred square feet on the top floor, a two- or three-car garage in a quiet neighborhood, standard-sized doors throughout—even closets and bathrooms, main living areas on top floor, laundry on top floor, large en-suite, and bonus points for previously-installed ramp access to front door or garage door and backyard."

Sheila's mouth worked to say something.

"Phillip, do you have any requests?"

"A basketball court would be nice," Phillip said. It took everything in Anna's power to not burst out laughing.

"So, yeah, I guess I have my work cut out for me," Sheila said. "Let's keep in touch and I'll do some more looking around. You guys make an adorable couple and I hope we can find something that works for everyone!"

She pushed a business card at them, gathered her stuff up and let herself out of the house.

Anna put her head in her hands. "Well, she was persistent, I'll give her that. If she is able to come back with a house that fits everything we asked for—including the basketball court—I will go look at it with you."

Phillip rubbed her back. "Fair enough. Hopefully, I won't have to hide behind you next time."

Chapter Twenty-Seven

Anna drove the van up to the middle school and waited. Her brain was a tempest of thoughts and feelings. Because of the realtor fiasco, she needed to talk to Phillip to resolve some things before they continued the wedding planning. She had texted Phillip that morning asking him to come over, if he hadn't planned on it already.

Brody got in the van and said, "Mom, Kyle is having a Beyond Duty get-together at his house. Can I go?"

"Brody, it's Thursday," she said, pulling out of his school. "It's still a school night. Can't you guys do this on Saturday?"

"This isn't like a birthday party or anything," Brody said. "It's just a bunch of us getting together."

Anna sighed. "Okay, you remember that your curfew is nine p.m.?"

Brody nodded, though he had started to put his earbuds in.

"How are you getting home?" Anna said.

"I'll have Kyle's dad bring me home," he said.

"Okay, but remember—this is a school night."

"Yeah, Mom, I got it. Sheesh. Can you drop me off?"

Normally, she'd fight him a little harder but she liked Kyle. He was a good kid, and his parents were good people. Brody needed good people in his life to keep him away from the little jerks that got him into trouble before. The little jerks that made it necessary for Brody to wait around until she could pick him up from school. But Brody going over to his friend's house meant one less kid for the night. One less set of small ears to listen in on her conversation with Phillip.

Anna pulled into the elementary and picked up Zoe. "Hi, Mom! Hi, Brody!" She reached over and gave her brother a hug.

"Sit down, Zoe," Brody said. "Mom can't go until you're buckled in."

She looked at her daughter through her rearview mirror. "So it looks like it's just us and Phillip tonight," she said to Zoe. Zoe clapped.

"Mom, can we have spaghetti and meatballs for dinner?" Zoe said. "That's Phillip's favorite."

"I'll think about it, sweetie. Let's get to the house first."

Phillip. Even the small mention of his name made her smile, and she looked at the beautiful ring he'd given her. She prayed he was in a good mood tonight. She stopped. When had she started thinking like that? Why should she have to worry about his mood all the time? She gritted her teeth. Ever since his little outburst the day they got engaged, he'd been a bit better, but his moods were still an issue. She never knew who would walk through that door anymore. Would it be good-mood Phillip, or grouchy-leave-me-alone Phillip or touchy-I-don't-want-to-yell-at-you Phillip, or affectionate-I'm-sweeping-you-off-to-the-bedroom Phillip? Maybe she'd been single too long. She didn't remember Darren being so hard to read.

She set the box that contained her school project items on the table. She started the sauce and meatballs, while she helped Zoe with her homework. A knock came at the door. "It's just me," Phillip said as he came in. "Oh, yes. Spaghetti and meatballs."

"It was a special request from Zoe for you. Would you help her finish her homework while I finish up dinner?" Anna said. Phillip came up behind her and wrapped his arms around her.

"Your wish is my command," he said, then kissing her softly on the mouth.

Good-mood-I-might-sweep-you-off-to-the-bedroom-later Phillip. Good, she thought.

Phillip sat down at the table as she prepped for dinner. He talked to Zoe while Anna drained the noodles. She turned around and noticed he'd been fingering her planner, which was open to her list of things to talk to Phillip about.

"Where's Brody?" Phillip asked.

"He went to play Beyond Duty at Kyle's house," she said, setting a plate down for him. "He's supposed to be back at nine."

Phillip nodded. "What's this?"

"I was hoping we could sit down tonight and talk about a few things. I've got to put together these project folders for my classes. I'll stuff folders while we talk about wedding and marriage stuff."

"Okay," he said. He put a forkful of noodles in his mouth. "You know I'll help you with the folders."

"I would love that," she said, kissing some sauce off the side of his mouth, then wiped the rest off with her thumb.

After dinner had been eaten and the table cleared, Zoe ran off to the front room to watch her princess show.

"Okay, let's see what we have here," Phillip said, pulling the planner towards him. "Wedding venue and honeymoon. Hmm, well, I couldn't care less where we get married as long as you show up. The honeymoon I think should be something neither of us has done or gone before so that we have something special we'll share."

"I've never been on a cruise, though honestly, I'm a little leery of doing big water like that. What if I get seasick? That would be terrible on our honeymoon," she said.

"True. I've never been to the Caribbean or Hawaii," Phillip said.

"I've been to Jamaica—a girl's weekend one of my friends' parents paid for," Anna said. "But I've never been to Hawaii either."

"Hawaii then?" Phillip said. "It'd be great to get you in a bathing suit again."

"I'll call a friend of mine who's a travel agent and see what she can find for us," Anna said.

"Make sure to have her include somewhere near Pearl Harbor," he said. "I'd love to visit."

"Okay, honeymoon—check. Wedding venue. There's this beautiful cathedral-like church near the capital. I wonder if they have any restrictions on who they marry or if they're even wheelchair accessible. Guess I could call and find out."

"What's next on your list?"

"The kids."

"Are you sure you want to talk about this now?" Phillip asked, glancing over where Zoe sat watching her show on TV.

"Yes," Anna said. "I think we've been pussyfooting around it long enough and I don't want it to stay a source of contention between us."

"Okay, may I make a suggestion?" he said. "Let's both make a list of expectations we have for the kids and then exchange the lists and compare notes."

"That sounds fair," Anna said, taking out a couple of loose papers from her planner. They both wrote down their thoughts and then exchanged the papers. "Ladies first," Phillip said.

"'Agree on rules that we will both enforce.' Doesn't that go without saying?" Anna asked.

"No, it doesn't," he said. "I don't feel validated when I'm dealing with the kids. I need to know you have my back when they do something to break the rules. But I also know you, love, and I need you to be confident that I will only discipline in the way we've agreed upon."

"It's like the one I wrote saying 'Agree on forms of discipline to be used.' I do need to know that we both agree on the way we discipline. I don't believe in aggressive physical confrontation or voices."

Phillip looked skeptical. "I'm willing to try that approach. Mostly because you're his mother and you know him best, but also because I'm not so sure it will work as well as you seem to think it will. Not saying I'm planning on beating the crap out of them, but sometimes your voice has to get a loud for it to get heard"

"And I disagree," she said, feeling a little annoyed. She'd half expected him to just agree with her so they could move on. Why was he being so stubborn about this? "Phillip, I do respect your opinion. I see in you the kind of man I want Brody to become for the most part. I just want to make sure that you model all the good things a man can be for him so he knows what it's like to be responsible, kind and strong at the same time."

Thank you for thinking of me so highly," he said. "But I'll be honest when it comes to the kids, it's all or nothing with you. I highly doubt I'll do anything right for you when it comes to them."

"That's not at all what I think," she said. "I welcome your opinions and ideas."

"But do you?" Phillip said. "Would you be willing to test a theory I have? Once in a while, you let me take the lead in discipline and then after the situation is resolved, we discuss it to see how it worked and how we both feel about it."

Anna bit her lip. "I guess that's fair."

Phillip chuckled. "I love you so much but I can see what's going on in that brain of yours."

Anna shot him a dirty look. "This isn't funny."

"I never said it was. I just know that when push comes to shove, you won't let me deal with the kids."

Anna pulled the school box up on the table. "Help me put these project folders together?"

"Sure," Phillip said, pulling it towards him and looking inside. "I know what you're doing. Deflecting our focus instead of really talking about this won't make the situation better."

"You've brought up things I hadn't thought about, and in fairness, I think I should be able to give it some thought."

"Good enough," he said, pulling the folders out and putting them on the table.

"You're still looking really tired," she said as she organized the papers.

"I am," he said, sighing. "Things have been stressful lately, but short of going on medication to help me sleep, there's not a whole lot I can do about it. If I can make it through the holidays everything should slow down enough for me to be able to relax. That and marrying you." He gave her a wan smile.

She smiled back at him. She wished so much that she could take some of the burdens from him, or at the very least allow him to sleep so that he could face his problems with a clear mind and rested body.

They chatted and she showed Phillip the order she wanted the papers in. They stuffed folders and discussed the wedding until it was time for Zoe to go to bed. Anna had just come back into the kitchen when Phillip asked "What time is it? It's 9:10. Wasn't Brody supposed to be home by nine?"

"Yes, I wonder where he's at," Anna said, looking at her phone. She hoped she had gotten a text from him but there was nothing.

In the next moment, the front door opened and Brody walked in, earbuds in his ears. Without looking up or acknowledging anyone, he took a sharp left to head to his room.

"Hey!" Phillip barked. Brody looked up, surprised. "Do you know what time it is?"

Brody looked at his phone again. "Nine something."

Anna gritted her teeth. Was Phillip really going to test this whole parenting thing now? Instead, Anna glared at Brody. "Right. Your curfew for school nights is nine."

"I forgot and then I had to wait for Kyle's dad to bring me home," Brody said, looking like he was going to continue on to his room. "Sorry."

"I don't think you are," Phillip said. "Do you think you can just wander in whenever you want, and there won't be consequences?"

"Phillip, I have this," Anna said.

"Why? So you can just let him off the hook?" Phillip demanded.

Anna felt heat rising up to her cheeks. She shot Phillip an angry glare. "Phillip, please. Brody, if you can't follow the rules then you'll lose the privilege to follow them. Do I make myself clear?"

"Yeah," Brody mumbled.

"What did you say?" Anna challenged.

"Yes, Mom," Brody said louder.

"The rule is you are in the house before nine. The next time you are late, you won't be able to go anywhere at all and your gaming privileges will be taken away."

Brody scowled but he nodded his head.

"It's time for bed," Anna said.

As soon as Brody was in his room, Anna rounded on Phillip. "What was that?"

"Nothing," he said, continuing to shove papers into folders. "I'm just going to sit here and do what you asked me to do."

Anna folded her arms. "Really?"

"I'm keeping my mouth shut as you asked me to," he said, looking up at her, anger blazing in his eyes.

"Don't pull that with me, Phillip," she said. "What was that?"

"My attempt to enforce rules you established and he knew quite well enough to have followed them."

"I'm pretty sure we've just talked about this. I don't appreciate being undermined in my own house."

"Undermined. Really? You? It happened exactly like I thought it would," he said. "I step in to help and you shut me out."

"This is the first time this school year that Brody missed curfew. He gets one chance. Next time, rest assured, he'll be suffering those consequences you seem to think I don't administer."

"I'll believe it when I see it," Phillip said.

"You won't have to see it because I believe in my son enough that the threat of punishment should be enough to keep him from doing it again," Anna said. "I don't know why we have to constantly run this circle. You are not their dad."

Phillip sat silent for a moment, his jaw flexing. "I know that. You don't have to constantly remind me." He got up from the table and headed towards the sitting room and paced. "What are we going to do when we get married? Is it always going to be like this?"

"Like what?"

"Me being constantly cut off at the knees when it comes to dealing with Zoe and Brody?" Phillip said. "I want what's best for them, the same as you. And if we're going to be family, we have to figure out a better way of doing things because it can't be like this after we're married."

"Phillip, I'm tired and I don't think we're going to get anywhere with this tonight, obviously," Anna said.

"Avoid discussing it with me if you want, but it's something we need to talk about and resolve," Phillip said. "I'm going to head out."

He walked over to her, kissed her on the head, and walked out the door. If Anna had been able to, she would have stomped her foot in frustration. Somehow, he always managed to turn the argument around on her. But she had been right. She gathered up the rest of the papers and folders. Phillip's paper fluttered to the ground. She picked it up and looked at it. The last line of his list was "Let me be their dad."

Anna rubbed her face with her hands. She was so tired of arguing with him. The arguments and the mood swings were getting old. She went to her room and transferred over to her bed. She looked at the ring on her finger. The brilliant green emerald sparkled in the lamplight. She had been so happy when he had given it to her. She had been ready to marry him the next day if he had asked her to. Now it was hard to be excited when they seemed to be under so much stress all the time.

She thought back to the summer and Ophelia's party and the anger and hurt blazing in Phillip's eyes. All over her sitting on her own cousin's lap. The scenario still made her mad. She thought of the story Garrett had told at the party. In her rush to be with Phillip, had she overlooked some warning signs? Is that what Garrett's mother had done, ignored red flags she saw in her horrible ex? Anna couldn't ignore what she was seeing though.

The problem is she didn't know what to do, or how to talk to Phillip about it. He'd been so defensive lately. She didn't know how to make things better as they slowly seemed to get worse. But if she didn't say anything what would happen then? She couldn't bear the idea that at some point their fighting would kill the love that had been between them, that he would look at her with blank, emotionless eyes as he walked out the door, never to come back, taking her heart with him.

A knock came at her bedroom door. Brody peeked his head in.

"What are you still doing up?" Anna asked.

"You make it kinda hard to sleep when you and Phillip argue like that," he said, coming all the way in.

Anna's heart sank. She hoped they hadn't been loud enough to wake the kids. "What's up?

Brody sat down on the end of her bed. "Why do you guys always have to argue like that?"

Anna sighed. "Phillip and I are just working some things out."

"That's not what it sounded like," Brody said.

"Honey, you and Zoe don't always see eye to eye. It's the same with Phillip and me. We don't always agree. And we're still learning to work out our differences."

"You guys aren't getting married anymore, are you?" Brody asked. The concern on Brody's face broke Anna's heart.

"We are," Anna said. "Things are going to be a little bumpy for a while while we learn about each other. But whatever happens, I want you to know that I only want what's best for all of us. And if that means not including Phillip in our family then I hope you understand it wasn't because we didn't love each other or you."

Brody's brows furrowed. "If you love each other, then you get married. You don't love each other and not get married. That's dumb."

Anna reached out to him and grabbed his hand. "You really want Phillip and me to get married, don't you?"

Brody pulled his hand out of her grip. "Doesn't matter what I want. You're going to do what you want. Like you always do, and then we won't see Phillip again." He got up off the bed. "I'm going to bed."

"Brody—" Anna said, but he had already shut her door.

She rubbed her temples. This day had spiraled out of control. And once again she came away feeling like the bad guy to the men in her life. She felt the exhaustion in her bones as she lay in her bed staring at the ceiling.

Sleep eluded her as she thought about how it had been between Phillip and her lately. As much as he accused her of deflecting, Phillip refused to acknowledge things were hard for him. He never wanted to talk about it; how could she help him if he wouldn't tell her what was wrong? And the fallout from their arguing was affecting her children. Brody had grown close to Phillip and it was no wonder he was quick to defend him.

Her stomach hurt. She rolled over on her side and clutched her middle. She needed some perspective. She wanted someone to tell her that she wasn't being overly sensitive or reactionary. She didn't want to break her engagement with Phillip, but she couldn't in good conscience let their arguing affect her family. She needed some validation that she was doing the right thing, no matter how much the thought of it made her feel sick.

Chapter Twenty-Eight

Anna parked her van in the usual spot in front of her parent's house. She thanked the Lord that, when she'd texted her mother earlier, a dinner invitation was quick to follow. She needed someone else to make dinner and someone else to entertain her kids and someone else to tell her what to do. The house smelled amazing as they entered through the garage.

"I hope lasagna is okay for dinner," Ellen said.

"It's perfect," Anna said. "Anything I didn't have to make is perfect."

"Oh, honey, you look tired," Ellen said.

Anna gave her a weak smile. "That's because I haven't been sleeping very well."

"Why? Is Phillip keeping you up at night?" her mom said with a little grin.

"Yes," Anna said. "Not in the way you think."

Ellen gave her a curious look. She was about to say something to Anna when Art walked in and wrapped his daughter in a hug.

"I'm glad you brought my grandmonsters over," Art said. "We don't get to see near enough of you lately."

"Well, here I am," Anna said. "Would it be all right if we talked after dinner, just us three?"

"Sure," Art said. "Is something wrong?"

"Yes, but I think I'd rather talk to you about it after dinner," she said as she wheeled herself to the kitchen.

Dinner was served but Anna found she couldn't eat more than a few bites and a glass of water. The sick feeling that'd started the night before hadn't entirely left her. The stress of everything was starting to get to her. It's why she loved her parents so much. They always seemed to know what to say to her to make things seem not as bad.

She listened to them interact with her kids and felt so blessed having them in her life. They were her rock. They supported her after Darren died, practically moving in to help out, and they never said no to time with their grandkids.

Art corralled the kids into their entertainment room, then joined Anna and Ellen in the sitting room. Anna looked out of their large picture window and saw hints of fall in the leaves of the trees and in the colors just starting to pop up on the mountains. She looked back at her parents and saw the concern and expectation on their faces. Anna burst into tears. Ellen immediately popped up and held her daughter as she cried.

"I don't know what to do anymore," Anna said. "I love Phillip so much, but he argues with me all the time. It's like he's trying to pick fights with me."

"Oh, my darling," Ellen said, smoothing her daughter's hair. "Does this have to do with his workload?"

"I thought so at first," Anna said. "I don't know anymore. But his moods are so mercurial. It's scary sometimes."

"He hasn't laid a hand on you, has he?" Art said.

"No. No, he hasn't," Anna said. "He just blows up over the littlest things. We've been arguing about the kids a lot. I never seem to do it right according to him. But they're not even his kids!"

"But they will be," Ellen said, "after you get married. He'll be promising to not only take care of you till death do you part but those kids as well. Now don't get me wrong. I'm not saying he's right, but you have to remember that marriage is a series of compromises. He has to give a little, but so do you; you have to meet far enough in the middle to satisfy you both."

"I remember that, Mom," Anna said.

"What I remember is that Darren was so laid back that he was perfectly happy to let you run the show," Ellen said. "But Phillip's a different type of man. It's not going to be easy when you both have been used to running your own shows for so long. You're going to have to learn the art of compromise for you both to be happy."

"It's more than two stubborn people trying to work something out, though," Anna said. "These rages, I'm not sure I can live with them. I'm not sure I want my kids to be subjected to them. There have been times when I really feel like I might have made a mistake, especially when he storms out of the house to go to his apartment. I'm just so tired of it."

"Have you asked him if he's having a problem somewhere in his life that he hasn't told you about?" Art said.

"Every time I ask him, he says he's fine," Anna said. "I can't stand that phrase, 'I'm fine.' He's not fine, but he won't tell me what's going on, or how he's feeling."

"We men are funny creatures, Anna," Art said. "Especially us military men. Feelings are difficult to express let alone admit to when things are hard. You can't expect him to sit down and spill his guts to you. He's trying to be strong for you, for his patients, for everyone else but himself. He may not even know how to express how he's feeling."

"Oh, he knows how to express emotions," Anna said. "There's anger, raging, and stomping around."

"But he also knows how to be affectionate and kind," Ellen said.

"Yeah, sometimes. Is that enough when we have to walk on eggshells all the time?"

"No, that's not fair to you or the kids," Art said.

Anna held her breath. She wasn't sure she wanted to say what she was thinking out loud. "Should I break my engagement with him?"

Art and Ellen looked at each other. "Is that what you want?" Art said.

"No," Anna said. "But I also don't know how much more of this I can put up with."

"You know your mom and I will support any decision you ultimately make," Art said. "And I certainly wouldn't want you to stay in a relationship that has become abusive. Maybe you guys should spend some time apart. Let him get his head cleared, let things ease up at work. Time alone may be what he needs to wake him up to what is really important to him."

"Thanks, Dad," Anna said. "Maybe that's a good idea, I don't know. Part of me feels that I would be abandoning him when he needs me."

"Yes, but you can't help him if he doesn't want help, or if he hasn't come to the realization he needs help," Art said.

Anna nodded. Art went over to his daughter and brought her into his arms. They sat like that for a long time. Anna hadn't known how much she needed that. "Love you, sugar. As much as we love Phillip, you have to do what's best for you and your children first."

On the drive home, Anna's mind was so conflicted. Like she had told her dad, she felt like a separation would just make Phillip feel abandoned. But if he was unwilling to recognize how his behavior affected all of them, then what choice did she have? Her engagement ring glinted in the glow of the freeway lights and the feeling of nausea threatened to overwhelm her. She didn't know what was right, or best. All she knew for sure was that she loved Phillip, and that was tearing her up inside.

Chapter Twenty-Nine

Anna looked out the front room window. Phillip still had not arrived and the late afternoon sunlight would not last much longer. Halloween was days away and this outing was supposed to be fun, not stressful or rushed. But as late as he was, the likelihood of everything being relaxed and calm was beginning to shrink.

"Does everyone have shoes on?" Anna said. "Does anyone need to go to the bathroom before we go?"

"No," both Brody and Zoe said at the same time.

"Okay, as soon as Phillip gets here, we'll head out to Lagoon," she said. "And I don't want you guys begging for stuff because we're just there to go on rides. Okay?"

Anna double checked her purse for the tickets. Still there, and kids not needing to use the bathroom.

Phillip knocked on the door and let himself in. "We ready?"

"Yes!" Zoe said, jumping up and down.

"Okay, let's load 'em up," he said, herding the kids towards the garage and the van.

Everyone was in and Anna was nearly down the driveway when Zoe piped up from the back.

"Mom!" she said. "I have to go to the bathroom."

"Really?" Anna said, looking back at her daughter. "You can't hold it?"

"No, I have to go really bad," she said.

"Fine, go in through the garage, and hurry," Anna said.

"Starting out fantastically," Phillip said, sighing.

"You didn't have to come," Anna said. Her patience with Phillip had grown thin lately. She didn't like this sarcastic side to him.

"I want to come," he said. "We don't seem to get enough time together lately." He reached over and squeezed her hand. He gave her what he probably thought was a reassuring smile but it looked fake to her.

"Okay, but I want to warn you, it will be crowded," Anna said.

"I'll be fine," he said, leaning his seat back. Anna gritted her teeth. Again with the fine answer. Now was not the time or place for them to have yet another conversation about how fine he really was, but she knew it had to happen. She just couldn't allow him to slide by with dismissive comments like that when they both knew very well he was not fine. They sat in silence instead.

"What is taking so long?" Phillip grumbled.

"I don't know," Anna said. The door to the garage was still open. "Brody, hop out and find out what's taking Zoe so long."

Brody rolled his eyes and yanked the handle to open the side door.

"Hey!" Phillip said. "Do what your mom asks and drop the attitude."

Brody slunk towards the house. Zoe came running out just as Brody got to the door and they were finally able to leave.

Anna didn't say anything. She didn't want to. The tension was already bad. She could only imagine what would happen if the park was crowded. Phillip would probably lose it. Maybe this had been a bad idea.

They drove mostly in silence as they made their way towards the amusement park. Frightmares was their annual Halloween festival and she thought it would be a nice diversion for them all. They found parking and got past the front gate. People dressed up as various monsters and ghouls ran around.

"So what do we want to do first?" Anna said, looking at the park map. "The straw maze looks fun, though I think Brody's too big."

"Good," he said, messing with his cell phone.

"And they have a few haunted houses, and then there are all the rides too," she said.

"Can we do the rides first?" Brody said.

Anna looked over at Phillip. He was scanning the area. He took Zoe's hand and started walking towards the middle of the park. "I agree with Brody. Let's go on a ride first," Phillip said.

"Can we go on the Rocket?" Brody said.

"Sure, let's do it," Anna said. Anna hated these kinds of rides but she wanted to make sure they had fun tonight. Anything to lift the mood.

The crowds weren't too bad. It was chillier than a normal evening, which was probably what kept people away. Brody couldn't hold still as they waited in line, he was so excited. Anna took Phillip's other hand. As she suspected, he was tense. She may as well have not taken his hand for all the grip he had. She decided not to protest. There had been so many arguments lately. When the district offered discount passes to Frightmares, she jumped on them. It was an activity she hoped everyone could enjoy. When she had told Phillip about it, his response had been lukewarm, which was better than declining outright. He was always tired and at the time, she was glad he was trying to include himself.

Sooner than she liked, it was their turn. She got in the seat and Phillip got in the seat next to her after he stowed her wheelchair.

"Ready?" he said. He'd actually managed a smile.

"No," she said.

"It's okay," he said, reaching out to her. "Just hold my hand."

She smiled at him. She loved it when he was sweet like this.

Suddenly the ride shot into the air. The force of gravity pushed the air out of her lungs and she was only able to start screaming as the ride free-fell back down. She closed her eyes. Anna did not want to see it anymore. When the ride stopped, she looked over at Phillip. He smiled at her, probably trying to not laugh at her. "I think you broke a finger or two," he said.

"I'm sorry," Anna said, managing a half-smile.

He shook his head. "It's okay," he said. "Now I know how much you hate these kinds of rides. Another thing to go on the list I call 'Anna's Loves and Hates.'"

Despite her racing heart, she managed to laugh.

Brody kept begging to go on the biggest rides, but Zoe, taking after her mom, did not like the Rocket and didn't want to go on any more of the big rides. Anna's stomach didn't either.

"I don't mean to be party poop but that last ride made me feel a little queasy," she said. "I think I'll sit out a few rides."

"How about this?" Phillip said. "I'll take Zoe over to the straw maze and you go with Brody. You can just relax while he goes on the ride, and then Zoe can run around in the maze as much as she likes."

"That sounds like an excellent idea," Anna said. "Let's go, young man."

Anna waved as Phillip and Zoe walked away, holding hands. She had to smile. The sight was so sweet.

"Mom, are we going?" Brody said. "Can we go over to the Cannibal?"

"As long as I don't have to go on it with you, you can ride whatever you want," Anna said. She smirked when they got to the line, and the people dropping out of the tower screamed at the top of their lungs.

"This is going to be awesome!" Brody said as he ran up the ramp.

Anna looked around. A vendor nearby was selling snacks and soda. She paid for a Sprite and sipped it while she searched for wedding dresses on her phone. She grimaced. What wasn't ballroom style had enormous trains, trailing sleeves or extra-long lengths—everything that would get caught in the wheels. It occurred to her that she might have to get something custom made, but that thought conjured the image of huge dollar signs. She switched over to headware. She was sure she didn't want a veil. When she and Darren got married her veil had blown all over the place, whipping into her face at the most annoying moments—like when Darren would try to kiss her. She was looking at bridal hats and fascinators when she got a text from Phillip.

Do you have Zoe with you?

No, why? Isn't she with you?

She got away from me in the straw maze and when I got around to the exit she wasn't there, and the park staff doesn't remember seeing her.

Anna's heart went up into her throat.

As soon as Brody gets off this ride, I'll be there

Brody strolled off the ride. "Mom, that was so amazing! Can I go on it again?"

"Your sister is missing. We need to get over to the straw maze," Anna said.

"What?!" Brody said as they hurried as fast as her chair would let them. "I thought she was with Phillip?"

"She was, and now they can't find her," Anna said, the need to get to the maze keeping her from throwing up the entire contents of her stomach.

When Brody and Anna got there, they found Phillip holding a very upset and crying Zoe to him.

"Oh, baby!" Anna said and went up to her daughter, who immediately clung to her mother.

Anna looked up at Phillip. He looked green.

"When she got out of the maze instead of coming towards where I was, she went in the opposite direction and circled around to the entrance. I was still at the exit. The employees brought her to me when they found her." By this time, sweat had broken out on his brow, and he was panting. He got up and walked away behind a nearby building. When he didn't come back after a minute or two, Anna turned to Brody. "Sit here and watch your sister. I don't want you to move from this spot until I come back." Brody nodded, and Zoe snuggled into her brother as she wiped away the last of her tears.

Anna went over to where Phillip had disappeared to. She rounded the corner and found him sitting against the building, his hands over his head and his head between his knees. His ragged breaths shook his whole body. She engaged the brakes on her wheelchair and got down on the ground next to him. She put her hand on his arm. It was sweaty and he was trembling.

"I can't believe I let that happen," he said, his repressed sobs making his voice uneven. "She could have been kidnapped or hurt and it would have been on my watch." His breaths were full-blown pants now, just on the verge of hyperventilating.

"But she wasn't," Anna told him, using the softest voice she could manage and still be heard. "And she was found safe and sound."

"No thanks to me!" he said loudly. His sobs took over. She left her hand on his arm. She wanted him to know she was right next to him, but she didn't want to be too intrusive. It was so hard to tell what was needed at a moment like this. She just knew she couldn't leave him. After a while, his tremors lessened and the sobs stopped. He just breathed in and out. He turned to Anna and took her in his arms and held her tightly. She ran her fingers through his damp hair, waiting until the tremors stopped all the way. She kissed the side of his face and wiped as many tears as she could with him still holding her close. He eventually relaxed enough that he let go of her and she put her forehead to his.

"Ready to get out of here?" Anna asked. He nodded and gave her a brief kiss before standing up and then reaching down and picking her up and putting her back in her wheelchair. Before they left, she pulled his face down and wiped away the rest of his tears.

"I love you," she said. He closed his eyes. "I want you to know that I don't blame you. It's happened to every parent since the beginning of time. And it's scary as hell. Next time, Zoe will make sure she looks out for one of us before she wanders off."

She took his hand and they went back to where her children, bless them, had stayed right where she had told them to. Brody had let Zoe play on his phone. Brody perked up when he saw them coming back and the relief on his face was apparent.

"I think we've had enough excitement for one night. What do you guys think?" Anna asked.

"Yeah, let's just go home," Brody said, still watching Phillip.

"I don't want to be here anymore," Zoe said.

"Okay, let's get out of here," Anna said. Phillip was still very pale as they got back into the van and he didn't say a word the whole way home. When they got back to the house, he said, "I think I'm going back to the apartment tonight."

Before he got in his truck, he knelt down next to Anna's chair. He pulled her into a tight hug. "Thank you for being there for me."

"You're welcome," she said, resting her head on the top of his head. "I'll always be there for you. No matter how hard it gets. I'm here."

He nodded and stood back up. He took her chin in his hand and kissed her softly.

Anna watched him as he got into his truck and drove away. The troubled sadness in his eyes scared her. More than once she wished there was something she could do to take it away for him. Part of the problem was he wasn't letting her in enough to so she could.

Phillip paced back and forth. Halloween was the next day and Anna wanted to make some cookies. He'd offered to help but he couldn't hold still. Anna looked up from the mixing bowl and watched him for a minute. He hadn't been doing well. Ever since Frightmares he had seemed like a caged animal, not knowing what to do with himself. He sat down at the breakfast bar, his knee bouncing up and down. He watched her as she worked. She used the rolling pin to flatten the cookie dough. She picked up her Halloween cookie cutters and offered the pumpkin one to Phillip. He shook his head. She sighed and started cutting the cookies out herself. After she loaded the first batch into the oven, she rolled near to where Phillip sat. She put her hand over his, looking up into his tired face.

"You look exhausted," she said. "Want to go take a nap?"

He didn't answer her. "Phillip?"

He pulled his hand away. "I don't need you mothering me to death. If I wanted a nanny, I would have hired one."

"Excuse me?"

"Anna, I don't want to fight."

"You have a funny way of showing it," she said. "But you sure as hell are not going to talk to me like that."

"All day long, I get told how I'm not doing enough and I'm not doing it well enough," he said, almost shouting. "I come here because I thought it would be the one place where I could find some peace. But even here, all you do is get after me."

"What are you talking about?" Anna said. "You're being monumentally unfair right now."

"Is there anything I do that's good enough for you?" he said. "I'm doing my best. I try to live up to your expectations of me but nothing I do satisfies you. I handle the kids wrong, I don't spend enough time with you, I work too much, I don't sleep enough, and on and on and on."

"I don't know where all this is coming from, but you better settle down right now or you can leave," Anna said. "First of all, the only expectation I have for you is to show up on our wedding day. But if you're having doubts about that then you better tell me right now, because I'd rather not waste my time with planning."

"You would want me to say that, wouldn't you?"

"No, I wouldn't," she said. "But I am getting ready to say I won't participate in this conversation anymore."

"Yes, run away from the conversation," he said. "Avoid telling me how you really feel. Avoid taking responsibility."

"You are unbelievable!" she said. "What do you want me to say, Phillip? That everything that's gone bad lately is my fault? Seriously?"

"Well, if the shoe fits."

"Get out," Anna fumed.

"What?"

"You heard me. Get. Out. Now," she said. "And don't come back until you can keep a civil tongue in your head. All we do is argue and I'm tired of it."

"Fine," he said. He got up, ripped the front door open, and slammed it behind him.

Anna put her face in her hands and sobbed. Her heart ached and her mind whirled. Exhaustion and nausea exacerbated her confusion. Why couldn't she say or do something to fix this? She'd tried already and nothing had worked. She wrapped the rest of the cookie dough up and put it away, then pulled the baked ones out of the oven and left them on the sheet. Baking cookies had lost its appeal and all she wanted to do was curl up into a ball and sleep.

Once she was in bed, she couldn't hold back the tears. She reached for her cell phone on impulse and stared at it. He'd been so unfair. Did he really feel that she was such a nag? That hurt her heart. If she was, she didn't mean to be. And his freaking out about the nap? She had only meant to help him get the rest he obviously needed. She threw her phone on her nightstand and put her hands on her face. There was nothing to say, and no way she could think of to fix it.

Chapter Thirty

Brody sat near the front door waiting. It was already after ten a.m. and Phillip still hadn't shown up.

"I honestly don't think he's coming this morning, Brody," Anna said.

"He always comes," he said. "Probably slept in or something."

Anna shook her head. After earlier in the week, he was probably still sulking in his apartment. It's not like she really wanted him to come over now. She hadn't forgiven him for the way he acted. She went into Zoe's room.

"Honey, I told you to clean your room today," Anna said.

"But Mom, Jessica at school wants me to come to her birthday party today," she said. "You said I could go."

"I'm not taking you anywhere until this room is clean. Is that clear?" Anna said, harsher than she meant to.

Zoe's lip trembled a little but she nodded her head and started cleaning. Anna went out of Zoe's room and rubbed the sides of her forehead with her fingers. Now she was losing her cool. She put her purse on the kitchen table to be ready to take Zoe then heard Brody yell, "Mom, he's here."

Anna's heart sank. She wasn't in the mood for round two—or was it round thirty—of World War III.

"Brody, go sit down somewhere so I can talk to him," she said. Brody moved from the doorway. She went to the door and blocked the entrance. Phillip was just getting out of his truck. He turned to look at her, tucking his hands in his pockets.

"What are you doing here, Phillip?" Anna demanded, arms folded.

"I need to talk to you," he said.

"I'm not interested in being your punching bag today," she said.

"Can we please talk about this?" he asked, running his hand through his hair. "I'll be on my best behavior."

"Well, I'm sitting here," she said. "Talk."

"I'm sorry for everything," he said. "I'm sorry about my behavior lately. I love you and I want to be with you for the rest of our lives. That hasn't changed. I want to take care of you and the kids."

"What about you?" she said. "How can you take care of us when you won't take care of yourself?"

"I don't know what more you want from me, Anna. I made a commitment to you and the kids. I'm trying to fulfill that commitment before anything else," he said, pacing.

"How are you fulfilling this commitment of yours, when all you ever do is stress out, freak out or run out?" Anna asked. "Every minute we're together lately, we have to make sure you're not upset at whatever. This isn't just about me. It's about my kids too. They don't deserve to be yelled at by the person that tells them he supposedly loves them. It's too confusing.

"You need to get some help. You need to do it for yourself more than you do it for me or the kids. Phillip, my love for you hasn't changed, but I am unwilling to let you bully me and the kids when you're upset over whatever it is that day you're upset about. If you're not willing to fix that, then you might as well get back in your truck and go home."

"Tell me what you want me to do and I'll do it," he said, practically yelling.

"I just told you what I want you to do! I want you to admit you need help with your stress, with whatever has been eating at you for the last few months, and take care of you. If you won't let me help you, then I want you to go to your boss at work and tell him you need help. Then take the help. You've been under so much pressure lately. Get some help for you and then we'll talk," Anna said, sighing and running her hands down her face. "Ever since we got engaged, I almost don't recognize you as the man I fell in love with."

"Please, I'll do better," he said.

"Good. I'm glad. But getting help first is non-negotiable, Phillip," she said. "Do that and then we can talk again."

He hung his head, not saying anything. She wanted so badly to reach out and have him come to her but she resisted. She didn't want to give him the impression that he was in any small degree forgiven.

He looked up at her, his beautiful brown eyes were troubled. "I guess I better get going then."

All Anna could do was nod her head and let him leave. A sense of unease gnawed at her. Usually, when Phillip wanted something badly, he wouldn't go down without a fight. The fight was gone and he drove away looking defeated.

Anna loaded the washer with clothes. She picked up a pile and noticed that Phillip had left one of his tank tops. She brought it to her face. She scrunched her nose. It was definitely Phillip's scent, just a very potent post-running scent. She sighed. He hadn't called or texted all weekend. It was now Tuesday afternoon and she was starting to get worried. If he'd asked for help, like she hoped, she figured he needed a cooling-off period. She was tempted to call him but if he was doing the bear-in-his-cave thing, then he needed some space.

All of it bothered her. There was something she was missing about this whole situation with Phillip. She could feel it. She got on her phone and typed in the words "panic attack," "temper," "insomnia," "mood swings." The search results were frustrating. Most of them were about menopause, and he certainly wasn't suffering from that. She was near the bottom of the page when she saw an advertisement about vets and PTSD. Before she could click on it, though, her cell phone rang.

"Hi, is this Anna?"

"It is," she said.

"Anna, this is Alice," the voice on the line said.

"Oh, hi, Alice. How are you?"

"I'm fine. But I was wondering if you had heard from Phil this week."

Anna's blood iced over. "No. This week? He's been working through some stuff and I sent him home this weekend. Why, what's going on?"

"Well, Phil left for lunch on Friday afternoon, then never came back," Alice said. "He hasn't called and I was just hoping you had heard from him."

"He didn't come into work on Monday?" Anna said.

"No, dear," Alice said. "I'm a little worried about him. He's been so busy lately. And then what happened to one of his patients."

"Oh, really? What happened?"

"Um, oh, I thought he might have mentioned something to you," Alice said uncomfortably. "One of his patients killed himself on Friday."

Anna felt the air rush out of her lungs as if she'd been punched. "No," Anna said, her voice trembling. "He didn't say anything to me about it." Anna swallowed back the lump in her throat.

"Well, have him check in when you hear from him, will you?" Alice asked.

"I will," Anna said, her whole body slowly going numb.

Over the next hour, Anna sent a flurry of text messages and phone calls to Phillip's phone with no response. She got in her van and rushed over to Phillip's apartment. The truck was gone. She went up to the door and knocked at first, but then resorted to banging when there was no answer.

"He's been gone since Saturday," a man walking down the stairs said.

"Saturday?" Anna blinked incredulously.

"Yeah, grabbed a bunch of stuff and drove off in his truck. Asked me if I would keep an eye on his apartment while he was gone," he said.

"Thanks," she said, shaken. "Did he say where he was going?"

"Nope," he said.

"Okay, thanks anyway," she said.

Anna got back in her van and put her forehead against the steering wheel, nausea roiling in her stomach. He left without saying anything to her. Since Saturday. A deep pit of fear and worry only made the nausea she was feeling more acute and she hurried to open the driver's side door and dry heave. Where had he gone? She hurried to text Brody. She needed to get to her parents' house. She didn't know what to do. She couldn't fall apart in front of her kids alone. She managed to hold herself together during the trip back to her house and then to her parents'. One look at her face and even Brody had enough sense to keep his questions to himself.

She pulled up to her parents' house and pushed her way into the garage entrance. She didn't wait for her kids to get out of the van or even to knock on the door.

"Mom?!" she said.

"Honey, oh, my gosh, what's wrong?" her mother rushed over to her and held her. As soon as her mother came into view, Anna finally lost it.

Hiccupping, Anna managed to get out, "I can't find Phillip."

Her mom took her into the sitting room, then got her a cold cloth to put on her neck and some tissues.

"Tell me what's going on," Ellen said.

Anna recounted the last week-and-a-half's worth of fights. "And then Alice told me his patient killed himself over the weekend. Phillip didn't call or text or anything. I've been trying to get a hold of him but his phone is off. Mom, I basically told him to get away from me. He needed me and I let him down, again!" Fresh sobs took over her voice for a while. Ellen held her daughter as she cried.

When Anna had calmed down a little, Ellen asked, "Do you know where he might have gone? Is there any place he likes to go to unwind?"

"No," Anna said. "He usually goes running around my neighborhood. It's his stress relief. He showed up Saturday but then left right after. Mom, I don't know what to do."

"Have you filed a missing person's report?" Ellen asked.

"No, I didn't even think to," Anna said. "I didn't even realize he was missing until a little over an hour ago."

"That's probably something we should do first," Ellen said. "We'll start with that."

Anna nodded. It was a good idea and she didn't know what else to do. *Please, Phillip, don't have done anything stupid,* Anna thought. *I need you.*

Anna lay in bed. She was pretty sure there were no more tears to cry and her heart felt hollow. It was Thursday and nothing. Phillip had disappeared and she had no idea if she would ever see him again. She looked down at her hand and her ring. The emerald reminded her of Ireland, her heritage, and the Utah mountains in the summer. Phillip knew her so well that he hadn't even had to ask her what she wanted before he had chosen it, and it was perfect. He always took care of her, even if she didn't know herself what she wanted. But did she do the same for him? No. Like a spoiled, selfish little brat, she'd kicked him to the curb when things got hard, and left him to fend for himself. The look in his eyes haunted her—hopeless, sad, and confused. And now he was gone. Her worst nightmare had come true. There was a good chance he'd never come back, and she had brought it all on herself.

For a while, she had wracked her brain trying to think of ways she could've handled things differently. But eventually, she concluded that she had done the only thing she could. Living in fear of his outbursts was not acceptable, and he had refused to get help. The logical part of her brain knew that, just as her dad had said, you can't help someone who doesn't want help. But her heart insisted that if she had just come up with the right words he needed, like a spell, they would have made him realize what was wrong but that everything would be okay. Then his hurts would go away and they would be able to start their life together in happiness.

Her phone buzzed. She hurried to look at it. It wasn't a phone number she recognized. She answered, hands trembling. "Hello?"

"Anna?" The female voice sounded familiar.

"Marge?" Anna asked.

"Oh, honey, I'm so glad I got a hold of you," Marge said.

"How did you get my number?" Anna asked, willing her to say it was from Phillip.

"I checked our old reservation records and called your dad."

Anna breathed a sigh of relief. "Oh, Marge, please tell me you've seen Phillip."

"He's here," she said. "I think you need to come as soon as you can."

A hard lump came up into her throat. "Is he . . . ?"

"He's with us for now," she said. "He goes back and forth between Sweetwater and his house. But he needs you. Can you come?"

"Yes!" Anna said, "I'll get there as soon as I can. Is he okay?"

"No, he's not," Marge said, her voice wavering.

"Thank you for calling me, Marge. I've been sick with worry," Anna said.

"Just hurry, then I'm sure he'll be all right," Marge said.

The next hour was a flurry of plans and arrangements. Anna raced around her room gathering clothes. Every time she turned around bile would come up into her throat and she did her best to keep it down. She was in her bathroom when a light clicked on in her head. When was it that she last menstruated? She couldn't remember.

She pulled her bathroom drawers open and started digging around. Right in the very back and at the bottom, she found a test. It was easily a decade old but she figured if it looked even a little like it was positive, she could just buy a newer one. She prepped the test and waited. And waited. The clock ticked so slowly. At the same time, she was afraid to look. Two minutes went by and she picked up the test and looked. There were two bright pink lines.

Chapter Thirty-One

Anna's van zoomed down the I-80 freeway as fast as she could without risking a ticket. The trip had been miserable. It seemed like right as she needed to get to California as quickly as possible, her morning sickness had kicked in in the worst way. For the first few hours, she had to pull over every thirty miles or so to be sick. She pulled into a gas station in Elko to get gas and rushed into the store. She cried with relief when she found old-fashioned lemon drops, pretty much the only thing that had ever helped her sickness that didn't require a prescription. She bought a couple of bags and rushed out to her van again.

The lemon drops allowed her to travel a little longer than before, but with all the delays, she felt she was crawling along. No matter how fast she wished she could go, the speed limit and her own body betrayed her. She didn't reach Reno until early the next morning. She made herself stop and take a nap. Her eyes had been closing on their own and she wouldn't be helping anyone if she fell asleep at the wheel.

Sleep, however, brought her no peace. She dreamed of getting to Sweetwater and finding Marge and Hank loading Phillip into an ambulance, with accusatory looks on their faces. The sound of the slam of the ambulance doors on Phillip, pale and lifeless, startled her awake, heart pounding. She swallowed back tears and got the van started again. It was just a dream, a terrible one, but it wasn't real. It was already close to noon when she got back on the road, and despite the small amount of rest she got, she felt worse than before. Even the lemon drops seemed to have stopped helping and her tongue was raw.

Along the highway, memories of the trip that brought her and Phillip together dominated her thoughts. The sense of deja vu wasn't wasted on her. She found she remembered so many of the landmarks as she drove by them. Finally, a little after sunset she started to see signs advertising Sweetwater Lodge. She pulled the hand control just a little more, praying that no sheriffs were around to pull her over. She had to get there. She was so close. Finally, she pulled into the parking lot at Sweetwater. As she got her wheelchair out of the van, the world swam a little. She put her head down for a moment but she pushed herself to get out and get to the office.

She banged on the door. The light at the back switched on and she saw Hank coming for the door.

"Hank," she half-yelled into the door jamb. "It's me, Anna."

"Anna!" he cried, fumbling to get the door open.

"Is he okay? Have you seen him?" Anna said, holding her head.

"Yes, hon. Come in," he said, pulling her into the office. "You look pale."

"I have to see him, Hank," she said, as tears ran down her face. She felt on the verge of hysteria. Suddenly the world spun in a sickening spiral and a high-pitch squeal sounded in her ears. The last thing she saw was Hank catching her before she could fall out of her wheelchair.

When she awoke, it was still dark out but the changing colors of the sky told her it was nearly dawn. She was in a strange room and a small window framed the lightening sky for her. On the nightstand near her was a glass of water. She sat up carefully, grabbed it, and tried not to guzzle it. She could kick herself. Not one time in all the visits to gas stations had she grabbed a bottle of water. She took a deep breath before finishing the glass off. She still felt woozy but not dizzy. She was getting in her wheelchair when Marge rushed into the room.

"Oh, honey," she said, trying to help Anna get back in her chair. "Are you sure you should be getting up?"

"I don't know," Anna said, leaning on her knees. "What happened?"

"You passed right out into Hank's arms," Marge said, feeling Anna's forehead. "How are you feeling now?"

"Weird," she said. She didn't want to tell Marge yet about the baby. She wanted Phillip to be the first one to know. She hadn't even told her own parents.

"I'll bet you need some food in your belly," she said, shuffling back out of the room with her curlers and house robe. Anna followed her out into the living area behind the office. It was simple. The furniture and appliances looked old but well taken care of.

Marge tried to offer Anna a cup of coffee but the smell wasn't sitting well. Anna accepted Marge's offer of oatmeal, though. She added a dash of brown sugar and found herself perking up as she ate. Marge sat down across the table from Anna, worry lines deeply furrowed in her face.

"What happened?" Marge said. "He just showed up on Sunday morning. He looked like he hadn't slept in days and was going on about Scott and someone named James. We could barely understand him he was crying so hard. Hank forced him to sleep here that first night but as soon as he woke up he was gone to his house. He's been going back and forth and he looks worse every time we see him."

"Did he say anything about me?" Anna said.

Marge shook her head. "He's not saying much anymore. He just sort of comes over offers to help Hank and when there's nothing for him to do, he goes back to his house."

Anna closed her eyes. "I have to see him. I need to talk to him." The tears started to leak out of her eyes.

"Oh, honey," Marge reached over and grabbed Anna's hand. "I'll give you directions on how to get to his house. Maybe you can snap him out of whatever's going on with him. He's hurting. We don't know any way to help him, so maybe you can."

"I hope so," Anna said. "I love him so much, Marge, and he's been so hard to deal with. I need to fix this somehow."

Marge pulled a notepad and a pen out of a drawer and drew a map for Anna. "It's not too far away, but the roads can easily be missed. If you get lost just come back here and Hank and I can go with you."

Anna took the little map, then went around the table and hugged Marge.

"Don't hesitate to call if you need help with him," Marge said. "We've done all we can think of for that poor boy, so we're hoping you're the miracle he needs."

By the time Anna got out to her van, the sun was just starting to peek over the horizon. Her hands were shaking as she looked down at the map. She prayed that she could find Phillip's house on her own. She wanted to see him alone. She was determined to make him see that a solution was possible for him, for them—and for their baby. She pulled out of the campground, steeling herself for what she would find. She prayed Phillip was still there.

The wheels of her van crunched on the loose gravel driveway of Phillip's family home. The house was modest; more along the line of a nice prefab than a cabin or trailer home. Phillip's truck was parked along the side of the house. Anna breathed a sigh of small relief. He was here.

Her heart pounded in her chest and for the first time since she'd hit the road, she wondered if she was doing the right thing. He had been so upset and nothing she had said or did seemed to make any difference. But there was more than one reason now to at least try to talk to him. She sent up a small prayer that he was safe. His despondent, hopeless eyes, her last image of him, still frightened her.

Bracing herself against the worst of her fears, she opened the side door of the van to get her wheelchair out. As she was positioning herself in her wheelchair, Phillip came around the far side of the house. He stopped mid-stride, staring at her. His face was pale. His beard had started to grow back. He looked gaunt, like he hadn't slept or eaten in days. Tears sprang to her eyes to see him like this.

"Hi," she said, lifting her hand a little.

"How did you find me?" he asked, not moving.

"Marge," she said. "She called me."

He nodded. "Figures."

"She cares about you," Anna said. She pushed her wheelchair but the loose gravel was like quicksand to her tires. She barely got an inch. It was going to take much more effort to get off the driveway than she had anticipated. "Just like I care about and love you. I've been worried sick."

He continued to stare impassively at her. "Well, thank you for your concern. I'm fine."

Anna pushed her fists into her eyes and tried not to scream.

"You are not fine," Anna said finally, emphasizing the word fine with a growl. "I wish you would stop saying that."

"What do you want me to say?"

"I want you to tell me what's really going on! I want you to trust me enough to tell me when you're hurting or upset or angry. I'm supposed to be your safe place, Phillip."

She tried to push her wheelchair again to get to him, but it took almost a Herculean effort to get just a few feet. She needed to touch him, hug him, anything to take away that haunted look in his eyes.

"You deserve better than me," he said, looking down. "All I ever do is disappoint you."

"You know that's not true," she said, her breath coming in and out raggedly.

"Did you know that James killed himself last Friday?"

"It was James?" Anna gasped, feeling once again like she was going to be sick. Poor Amanda. "I had heard some—"

"His wife called to thank me," his voice cracked. "To thank me for all the help I had given him. For being his friend." His words shuddered. "To thank me. It's like Scott all over again. But worse. I knew what to do. I didn't see it. I should have seen it. He was too calm the last time we talked. Feeling better too quickly."

"Phillip, it's not your fault," Anna said. "You can only know what he tells you. Maybe he didn't want you to see that part of himself."

"I was the professional!" he yelled. "I should have seen it."

She struggled to get her wheelchair another foot forward. "You're a good counselor, but you're also human. You couldn't have known what he didn't want you to see. Maybe he didn't want you to see him as a bad person or a failure."

He looked at her for a long moment. He shook his head.

"Please, Phillip, come home with me."

"Just go home, Anna. You're right. I am a failure. How am I supposed to be able to take care of you and the kids? I can barely take care of myself, remember? A guy died on my watch. A guy who'd reached out to me for help. And I let him down. I'm pathetic--first Scott, then Zoe, now James," he said. His body seemed to curl in on itself, and for a long moment he was silent. Anna struggled once again to move forward but between the lack of sleep, the nausea, and the little she'd eaten she just didn't have the strength to go any further. Her heart hurt seeing him like this and be able to do nothing about it.

"You and Zoe can keep the jewelry. I won't be able to do anything with it. Just do yourself a favor—get back in your van and get as far away from me as you can. You guys are better off without me. In fact, I'll make it easy for you. We're not getting married anymore. I'm not the man for you."

His words felt like a physical attack and she covered her face with her hands against its violence. Sobs erupted from so deep within her that she could hardly breathe. They hit against her chest so hard she held her arms across it to keep from falling apart. She wasn't sure what was worse—the morning she got the call from the hospital about Darren, or this moment, with Phillip telling her he didn't want her anymore. No matter how she tried to get the sobs under control, they kept coming. Her heart was splintering, cracking with each deep inhalation of breath. She shook so hard she felt like she was coming apart. She bent over her knees, nausea overwhelming her.

Anna lay there across her knees until she heard the crunch of gravel coming towards her and warm hands began to rub her back. The tears kept coming, though she wished they would stop so she could talk. But all the worry, the stress, the anger, the fear and, yes, the love wouldn't allow it and it was like a dam had burst. She started to dry heave. Phillip's strong arms picked her up and, sitting in her wheelchair, placed her on his lap. She clung to him, trembling and crying, not able to get close enough to him. They sat like that for a long time, Anna crying and Phillip just holding her.

Her sobs subsided after a while. She tucked her face against his neck, taking deep breaths to calm herself. She breathed him in, felt his warmth against her face and around her waist. She needed him so much more than even she had suspected. And just like he had said when he proposed to her, the thought of leaving him here made everything in her life seem wrong. Her mind whirled with what to say to him and how to say it. He needed to know.

"Don't tell me to go away without you, please," she whispered, her voice raw. "I need you. I love you so much."

His chest started to heave in and out, and she placed a hand on his face and made him look at her. "I love you. I love you no matter what. I need to be by your side. I want to be a family. My kids want you in their lives." She hesitated. Could she say it? "Our baby needs you."

His eyes widened and for the first time, he really saw her. "What?"

She nodded, and took his hand and placed it on her stomach. "I found out yesterday."

"Are you sure?" he asked.

She nodded. "Pretty much like the first two times, but I also took a test."

He then took her face in his hands and kissed her, deep and lingering, making heat shoot through her. His kiss made her heart flip around in her chest and she relished being able to be close to him in this moment. He pulled away and looked into her eyes.

"Really? For sure?"

"Yes," she said. He hugged her, laughing and crying at the same time. She hugged him back, but fear gripped her gut. She had to tell him a truth she knew he did not want to hear—not just for him but for all the things that she planned on building with him.

"Phillip, would you let me say something, and please don't react or stop me before I'm done?"

He looked suspicious but nodded his head.

"We can't keep doing this," she said, taking a deep breath. "It's a hard thing to learn after being on your own for so long, but you have to learn to trust me with everything. We marry because together our burdens are lighter. But I can't help you if I don't know there's a problem. I need to know you're in it for the long haul. And you can't do that if you refuse to see the problems you've been trying to avoid. I can't live in fear that one day you'll just up and disappear again and not come back. I've already lived that nightmare once. I know we've kind of put the cart before the horse now, but your child deserves to have a father he can count on to be around. So do Zoe and Brody. And, quite frankly, so do I."

"So, what do you want me to do about it?"

"You already know what I want you to do—I want you to get some help," she said, making him look at her when he tried to look away. "You spend all day long telling people that, but somehow you don't think it applies to you. It applies to anyone, but particularly you. Not because it makes you weak, but because you've seen and experienced things as a soldier that no human should ever have to. How can that not affect you? And you try so hard to be strong for everyone except yourself. Right now, I'm trying to be strong for you, for once. As I should have been. And I'm sorry I didn't insist sooner, for your sake. I took for granted that we were going to be happy and ride off into the sunset. I thought you'd just get over it, or we'd get through the rough patches and everything would be perfect. I should have known that you'd put aside your own needs to try to meet everyone else's. I'm asking . . . no, honestly, I'm begging you to come home with me, get some sleep, and talk to your boss and ask him to get you the help you need. I'll be right by your side every step of the way, but only if you want me to and you're serious about it. Otherwise, when I get back in that van, I'll have to leave you here and hope you don't do something both of us would regret. And it will rip my heart out."

He examined her face for a long time. She could see the doubt and confusion in his face. His jaw flexed, but then the tears leaked from the sides of his eyes. She reached up and wiped them away. He closed his eyes at her touch and he shivered. She put her head to his forehead and wrapped her arms around his neck.

"Every step of the way, Phillip," she said. "No matter what it takes, and as long as you're trying to get the help you need."

"Anna, I never know what to say," he said quietly. "Sometimes I want to say what's going on in my head, but I don't want to scare you or subject you to the demons there. I keep thinking if I can be strong, I'll just power through the really bad times. But when James died, I couldn't do it anymore. I couldn't let you see the kind of person I really am. I wanted to talk to you last week but then I realized I'd pushed you too far. Expected too much. You can't marry me, Anna. I'm too broken. It wouldn't be fair to you or the kids."

"No, Phillip," Anna said. "I can't just abandon you when you need my help the most. We'll work it out together. I know exactly what kind of man you are. You can't fake that kind of compassion and dedication. You may be broken but that doesn't mean you're worthless. You're worth it to me. I want to help you. I want you to want help. We can do this."

"I can't believe I'm going to be a dad," he said, rubbing his hand on her stomach. "I'm so confused, Anna. I want you and me and Zoe and Brody and this baby to be a family. I want this baby with you. I just don't know if I can be the kind of man and father you need me to be."

She kissed his cheeks. "You were already doing it. Zoe and Brody love you so much. And they depend on you. And we've talked about this before—they don't expect you to be perfect. I don't expect you to be perfect all the time. I just want you there, with me. We'll work out the rest."

He leaned his face into her cheek.

"Please? Come home with me," she said.

"I love you so much. I don't know what I did to deserve you. If you still want me the way I am, I'll come home," he said before he kissed her softly.

Chapter Thirty-Two

The soft ruffles of chiffon on Anna's sleeve rustled in the early spring breeze. She absently rubbed her belly. She'd been having a few contractions but it only served to remind her that there was a little bundle of love within, made from the love between her and Phillip. Normally, she would have hated the idea of being a pregnant bride but it was either that or take an infant on a honeymoon. The choice was pretty easy for her.

She looked around the grounds of the church. The tulips and hyacinths were in full bloom, and they perfumed the air. Before she could turn around, a pair of arms grabbed her from behind and encircled her shoulders.

"I'm so happy for you!" Ophelia said, hugging her tightly. "And I'm so happy you didn't make me a bridesmaid!"

Anna smiled and patted her sister's arms. "Do I know my sister, or what?" she said, chuckling. Once Ophelia let her go, Anna turned around and saw that Justin, in a smart blue-gray suit, had followed Ophelia up the church steps. "I'm so glad you could make it, Justin. Phillip will be so glad to see you."

"I'm glad Ophelia decided to invite me," he said, smiling. "You look beautiful, by the way."

"If you can call two hundred pounds of beached whale beautiful," Anna said.

"Not two hundred," Ophelia said. "One hundred and seventy, max."

"I have a surprise for you," Ophelia said. She pulled her phone out of her purse. She turned the screen so that Anna could see. It was the wedding cake Ophelia had made for Anna. It was exactly as Anna had hoped for. But then she noticed the top of the cake. Sitting among the sugared roses was a little statue. It was made of wood and depicted two figures embracing. The Sweetwater legend statue.

"How-?"

"Marge sent it to Phillip," Ophelia said. "And he gave it to me especially for today."

"Oh, Phee," Anna said, hugging her sister. "I absolutely love it."

"I couldn't wait until the reception," Ophelia said.978-1-7355425-8-4

Art came up to his two daughters. He shook Justin's hand.

"Daddy!" Ophelia turned to her dad and gave him a hug. Then she went around to his back and straightened his slightly snug Army dress uniform and sharpened his shoulders. "There. Doesn't Anna look pretty, Dad?"

"She does," he said with pride in his eyes. "It's almost time. Are you ready?"

"Only for about two years," she said.

"You two go on inside," he said to Ophelia and Justin. When they were out of earshot, Art said, "So what's the status on that?"

Anna shrugged. "She keeps him around. If that's good or bad, I'm not sure. But it looks like he's determined to stay, so we'll see."

Art reached down and hugged his daughter. "You look just as radiant as you did when you married Darren."

"Thanks, Dad," she said, hugging him back.

"Grandpa!" Zoe came running out wearing a mint green dress—adorned with the delicate emerald pendant, straw hat, and white cotton gloves—the very picture of spring. Her long auburn curls blew about in the breeze. "The marriage guy says it's time."

"Okay, okay," he said. "Hold your britches on. We're on our way."

The little church Phillip and Anna had chosen was old but graceful, and almost entirely not wheelchair accessible except for a small door on the side of the building. When they got inside, she could see Brody in his tux playing on his phone. He'd actually styled his hair. Phillip had probably made him do it. They made their way around the pews to the back where Zoe and Ellen were waiting. She scanned the audience and found Hank and Marge sitting not too far away. Marge turned to Anna and smiled. Anna mouthed "Thank you" to her. The older woman nodded her head in understanding. Anna blinked away tears and turned to her dad.

"Okay, Dad, ready?"

Art signaled to the pianist and guitarist. The strains of Vivaldi's Guitar Concerto filled the nave. Anna saw Phillip step up to the officiant and her heart filled to bursting. He still had shadows under his eyes, but a radiant smile on his face. He wore his blue dress uniform and his beret, and she couldn't imagine anything sexier when he winked at her.

Ellen and Zoe walked down the aisle and then Anna and Art followed. Her eyes were only for Phillip. Her only thought was how close they had come to not having this day at all. She loved this man with all her heart.

She had taken him home with her from Sweetwater that day, and then the hard work of getting on the path to healthy had begun.

As promised, Phillip went to his boss and got himself counseling. Knowing what was wrong was almost as powerful as acknowledging that it was there in the first place, and she watched him come in from the rain as he worked through his combat-related PTSD and depression. He'd also insisted on couple's therapy before they got married. Anna had appreciated that as well. He wasn't the only one who needed to learn to communicate better and it brought them closer together, as much as him moving in with her and the kids did, and watching together as her belly steadily grew larger with their child

Anna, in turn, tried as best she could to fulfill her promise to him. She had sat outside his therapist's office during his sessions when she could, and had sat in on them when he requested it. Sometimes it was hard. He would tell awful stories of things he'd experienced on the other side of the world, things that would leave him shaking, crying and exhausted. Some days he wouldn't tell her anything at all and she just had to trust that he was working through it with his therapist. He'd often wake suddenly in the middle of the night and she would quietly hold him as he forced his heart to calm down.

He was worth the heartache and sleeplessness, though. On his best days, he was an amazing man to his own clients, to her children, and to her. And she knew that one day soon he'd make an amazing father to his own child. She knew because the thing that made him the happiest in life was taking care of someone—something he'd been denied with the deaths of his best friends and parents.

Anna handed Zoe her bouquet as her maid of honor, and Art joined Anna's and Phillip's hands before stepping away. She looked briefly over at Brody. She hadn't seen her son happier or prouder than when Phillip had asked him to be his best man. Right now, his smile seemed wider than his face as he stood behind Phillip.

Anna looked up at her almost-husband. It was overwhelming how those brown eyes of his could reach down to her soul and capture it. She lost herself in them when they first met and now, they were the only things she wanted to look at as they said their vows.

He slid the diamond wedding band on her finger. Her hand trembled a little as she put his band on him and that was it. He was hers. She started to cry in earnest. She couldn't imagine being any happier. He picked her up out of her chair and kissed her softly in front of everyone they loved. She laughed as the tears rolled down her face. Placing her back in her chair, he rubbed her tummy.

"I love you, Mrs. Laughlin," he said looking into her eyes. "I'll never get tired of saying it."

"I'll never get tired of hearing it, my husband," she said, putting a hand to his face. "Thank you for being my happily ever after."

Acknowledgements

I'd like to take a second to thank my editor, Lia, without which Sweetwater would not be half as good. And to my readers on Wattpad who gave me the confidence to take the step forward and finish something I started—for once.

A Note from the Author

If you have enjoyed reading Sweetwater, please consider leaving a review! It doesn't matter where—**Amazon, Goodreads, Bookbub** or your own social media.

Reviews are like gold to an indie author and I appreciate them so very much!

Scan the QR code to sign up for my monthly newsletter! Get the latest book information, sneak peeks, and exclusive content for subscribers only!

About the Author

Whitney Sivill blames her mom for her obsession with romance. Mom raised her on a steady diet of musicals, Disney movies, and Gone with the Wind. When Whitney is not writing, she can be found binge watching BBC costume dramas, cheesy holiday romance movies, and reading other indie romance author's books.

Whitney lives with her family in a little grey house in the middle of Utah's West Desert. She enjoys writing stories that reflect issues that affect her, such as motherhood, disability and the bonds of love that connect people.

Author Website